ow large the room was. When she
ard her voice bounce back like an
a large cavernous space, but there
ewhere.

e, her hands ticd behind her back
with rough heavy, twine, her ankles tied together with
the same binding. She lay on her right side.

If I can turn on my back and pull up my knees, maybe
I can scoot backwards to the wall. With a heave, she
rolled onto her back. Every part of her body ached. No
time to think about pain. Think of the rats. Think of
water. Think of your family.

Oh God, if I don't die here, Nate will surely kill me
for getting into this fix. Why didn't I listen to him?

————————————————— ★ —————————————————

HELEN MACIE OSTERMAN

The ACCIDENTAL Sleuth

WORLDWIDE®

TORONTO • NEW YORK • LONDON
AMSTERDAM • PARIS • SYDNEY • HAMBURG
STOCKHOLM • ATHENS • TOKYO • MILAN
MADRID • WARSAW • BUDAPEST • AUCKLAND

To John

THE ACCIDENTAL SLEUTH

A Worldwide Mystery/February 2010

First published by Five Star.

ISBN-13: 978-0-373-26701-9

Printed in U.S.A.

Acknowledgments

First and foremost I must thank my writing muse for opening the door to the world of ideas and introducing me to Emma Winberry. This charming lady has been with me for a long time and, hopefully, will remain for many years to come.

Thanks to my writing group, The Southland Scribes, for their valuable critique and support: Jane Andringa, Linda Cochran, Sherry Scarpaci, Nancy Conley, Ralph Horner, George Kulles, Ryan O'Reilly, Lydia Ponczak, Joan Poninski, Sandi Tatara. Special thanks to Michael Black for his expertise on police procedure and to my exuberant editor, Julie Hyzy.

Thank you, Sylvia and Ed Kuta. This engaging couple was kind enough to share their experiences as movie extras.

Thanks to cinematographer P. Scott Sakamoto for infomation on the care of motion picture equipment during inclement weather.

And a special thanks to John Morton for his patience in reading and rereading this manuscript, and for suggesting the last line.

ONE

Emma Winberry looked around, frantically searching for a familiar face. Her clothes were in tatters. Two greasy men gripped her arms, pulling her up to a platform.

"What's the charge, Citizen?" shouted a shabby fellow wearing a dirty white wig and a long filthy magistrate's robe. "Fraternizing with the aristocracy." One of the men pointed at Emma and spat.

"Guilty! Off with her head!"

The gavel banged, sounding her doom as they dragged her away.

"Wait," she shouted. "This is the wrong century. I belong in the twenty-first, not the eighteenth." She looked up in terror at the guillotine blade dripping with the blood of the previous victim.

"Nate, help me. Nate!"

"EMMA, EMMA, wake up. You're having another nightmare."

Emma woke with a start, looking wildly around. "Oh Nate." She clutched at him, gripping his arms.

"Easy, easy, it's all right. You're safe." He pulled her trembling body close, rubbing her back and murmuring words of comfort.

"I was going to the guillotine," she said, crawling further into his arms.

"This is the third night this week you've had these dreams," he said, with a worried look. "Is something bothering you?"

"Nothing I'm aware of. I wish I knew what they mean."

"Lie down and try to go back to sleep."

"No, the dream might continue. I'll have a little warm milk and stay up a while. You go back to sleep." She kissed him tenderly, slipped out of bed, padded into the kitchen and looked around. It was so modern. It had taken some getting used to after her old-fashioned kitchen in Brookfield, but she soon found the conveniences a real plus. The butcher block island in the center of the room was her favorite. She did some serious baking there.

While the milk warmed in the microwave, Emma thought about her dreams. They all posed a danger to her. Usually when she had disturbing dreams they were about others and meant something unpleasant was going to happen.

Okay, Guardian Angel, now what? I told you before I don't want this "gift," this "sixth sense." I resign.

The ping of the microwave made her jump. She took the cup of milk and walked into the atrium. She felt at peace in this room, surrounded by her beloved plants. The floor-to-ceiling Thermopane windows let in the light, but kept out the elements.

Emma took a deep breath, looked past the roof garden, past Michigan Avenue and out at Lake Michigan. The full moon reflected on the unusually placid water, only tiny wavelets marring the surface.

As she sipped the milk, she took deep abdominal breaths until she felt calm. Perhaps it was the book she had been reading the past few nights, a mystery involving some pretty gruesome crimes.

She shook her head and took a deep breath, then slowly let it out. She was about to get involved in something unpleasant again, whether she liked it or not.

A FEW DAYS LATER, as she sipped a cup of steaming coffee and chewed on a piece of whole-wheat toast, Emma scanned the morning paper.

"Nate, look at this notice in the Arts Section. An independent movie company is shooting a film in downtown Chicago. It says here that they're looking for extras." She looked up, surprised by the scowl on his face. Furrows formed between his owl-like eyes; his usually sensuous mouth pursed in disapproval.

"What about it?" he asked.

"Well," she said, suddenly unsure, "it might be fun. Remember when we met that couple who were extras in a number of famous movies? They talked about the stars and their experiences. It sounded great."

"My dear, in case you've forgotten, we're already extras in the opera. Do we need more?"

She fidgeted in her chair. "The season at the Midwest Opera doesn't start until January and it's only August now. It says here they'll be filming this fall." She mustered her best pleading look, knowing he was a pushover for her long-lashed gray eyes.

"Sparrow," Nate said, calling her by his pet name and taking both her hands in his, "aren't you happy here? We've been in this condo together four months now. Are you getting restless? Are you sorry you gave up your house in Brookfield?"

"Oh Nate, no!" Emma stood to cradle his head in her arms, tenderly kissing the shiny bald spot. "I don't regret my decision for one minute. That old house with all the stairs and the big yard is like a distant memory already. I didn't realize what a burden it was until I left it. I love living here with you, this place, the excitement of the city."

She looked around the spacious rooms, the soft watercolors on the walls and her beloved poster of the opera *Turanot,* one of her prized possessions. Nate's lovely upright piano hugged one wall. The huge windows, unobstructed by curtains or draperies, offered a panoramic view of Lake Michigan and the city, as well as the giant Ferris wheel at Navy Pier in constant slow motion. She gazed at him, her eyes shining with love. "I love you, Nate Sandler. I'm so thankful you came into my life."

He smiled, held her close and nestled his face between her tiny breasts, inhaling the scent of her body.

"Good. Now that we've determined that we're both happy together, why do you feel the need for this added responsibility?"

"I just thought it might be fun. Case closed. Forget about it. It was just a suggestion."

Later, as she cleared away the breakfast dishes, she noticed him scanning the article.

Nate cleared his throat. "We might look into it."

"Look into what?" Emma asked with feigned innocence.

Nate frowned, but she knew she hadn't fooled him. "It says here to send a recent picture to a P.O. Box in Chicago. They want all the stats on the back: name, address, phone number, age, height, weight, color of eyes and hair. Do you really want to give out all that information to total strangers?"

"Well, it's not like they're asking for our Social Security numbers or our bank accounts, or anything like that."

"Humph. They probably won't want a couple of oldsters like us anyway." He looked at her with a mischievous grin on his face.

Emma put her hands on her slim hips and pursed her lips. "I take offense at that remark. We're young seniors and we look pretty good, if you ask me."

He laughed and pulled her back down on his lap, kissing her nose, her earlobes and her lips. "And very sexy young seniors I might add. Go ahead, if you want to. Those pictures from the Fourth of July picnic are pretty good. Send some of them."

"I might just do that," she said, sliding off his lap and heading for the kitchen. She had a vague feeling that such a venture might lead to an interesting experience.

Emma had learned from childhood that her hunches and premonitions were usually right. And her Guardian Angel helped her through almost every scrape she got herself into. Occasionally, though, her Angel seemed to enjoy taking time off.

She watched Nate walk into the large atrium facing the roof

garden. This room and the bedroom were the only ones with window coverings—Roman Shades of soft microsuede that could be lowered to keep out the sun.

"Someone's out there examining your tomato plants," he said.

"Oh?" Emma's huge potted plants were her pride and joy. She hurried to the atrium and out the door to the roof. A three-foot-high brick wall separated the two sides of the roof, but a gate in the center allowed access. Emma saw no need to lock it. That might seem unfriendly. "Hello," she called.

A middle-aged woman looked up, a startled expression on her face. "I'm sorry to intrude." She smiled and extended her hand. "I'm Laura Evans. My husband and I are buying the condo next door. I hope you don't mind my looking at your plants."

"Not at all. Emma Winberry," she said, taking the woman's hand. It felt cold and she noticed a slight tremor.

The woman's nervousness seemed to keep her talking. "We'll be moving in a few days. I understand we'll share the roof garden with you."

Emma was about to respond when Laura continued.

"Your plants are certainly beautiful," she said. "I know nothing about growing things." She looked from one pot to another. "We've always lived in apartments and condos. My family never had a yard. I missed all that." The woman looked off into the distance with an expression that might have been regret. She turned to Emma and smiled. "Perhaps you can teach me?"

"I'd be happy to. You can grow wonderful things in your atrium year round, too. I'm looking forward to growing vegetables and, maybe even a fig tree. There's nothing like fresh figs right from the branch."

Emma noticed Nate watching them from the atrium doorway. "Nate, come and meet our new neighbor."

He smiled a greeting that lit up his face as he extended his hand. "Nate Sandler."

"This is Laura Evans, dear," Emma said. Did the woman wonder about their different surnames? She didn't seem to respond, but she did appear uncomfortable.

"I have to go now, but I'm sure we'll see each other again soon." She turned and walked abruptly away.

Nate and Emma looked at each other, puzzled by the quick end to the conversation. They went inside and closed the door against the August heat that threatened to rise into the nineties.

"She seemed pretty distant," Nate said. "Maybe she's not the friendly type."

"No, there's something else. I felt it, something deep and disturbing." She frowned and looked out at the placid lake.

"There you go again with your premonitions."

"I can't help it and you know it. But, if it will make you happy, I promise to mind my own business and not get involved with anyone's problems." She pursed her lips and gave her head a vigorous nod.

"Oh, ho. That'll be the day. This I want to see."

Emma walked into the study and sighed. I mustn't get involved with that woman's problems. As Nate reminded me, it's none of my business. I just want to lead a nice quiet life.

She felt a gentle nudge, and knew better.

TWO

On Monday morning Emma went through the stack of photos from the picnic. She felt a warm feeling of contentment as she looked at her children: Stephen and Pat with little Susan, who had just turned three trying to hold her squirming five-month-old brother, David; Sylvia and James with their boys, James, Jr., two and Frankie, ten months. They were a handful. And there were Martin and Bertie, still acting like newlyweds.

"These should do." She chose two pictures, one of her and one of Nate, then printed all the demographic information on the back. She smiled as she put down her weight, a ten pound gain in the last two years. Now, at least, she had some semblance of a figure; a little rounding of the hips, a fullness in the thighs, and breasts that did more than apologize.

Emma remembered her embarrassing purchases of padded bras and panties when she first became a supernumerary for the Midwest Opera Company. She had disposed of those long ago.

She had been content before then, busy with her family and her garden. But something was missing. Since she became involved with the opera and Nate came into her life, she had blossomed. Her life was full of love and excitement. So then, why did she feel she needed more? She thought for a moment. Did she want to do this? Yes. She put the photos in an envelope, addressed and stamped it.

A strange feeling came over her; she felt a shiver up her spine as she recalled her dreams. For a moment she was tempted to throw the letter away and forget the whole thing. *Okay, Guardian Angel, what's this all about? Is it a warning? Please don't let me get embroiled in anything dangerous.*

We'll probably just be part of a crowd scene. What can happen?

But the feeling remained.

Later that morning Nate came in from his daily walk along the lakeshore. Emma usually went with him, but decided today was too warm to walk in the sun.

"Your face is as red as a beet," she scolded. "And what happened to your hat?"

He shook his head, went to the sink and splashed cold water on his face and neck. "I should have listened to you. It's hot as blazes out there and the wind blew my hat into the lake."

"You never listen to me," she said, placing a cold cloth on the top of his head.

"On the contrary, my dear, I listen to you all too often. Now stop fussing and give me some of that lemonade you made yesterday."

As she handed him the frosty glass, she asked, "Did you mail the letter?"

"Yes, just as you instructed."

Emma tried to put it out of her mind, but couldn't shake the uneasy feeling.

LADEN DOWN WITH PACKAGES, Emma pushed her way through the front door, almost tripped on the carpeting, and struggled toward the elevator.

"Hello there," a soft voice called.

She peeked over her parcels to see her new neighbor, Laura Evans, accompanied by a teenaged girl.

"Oh hello, Laura. I'm so loaded down I didn't see you. I couldn't help taking advantage of all those end-of-season sales."

Emma laughed. "Went a little overboard."

The woman gave her a weak smile and nodded. "I want to introduce you to my—niece, Teresa Adams. She'll be staying with us for a few weeks. Her parents are—away."

Laura seemed uncomfortable with the introduction.

Emma turned to the girl and tried to control her initial reaction. "Hello, Teresa," Emma said. The teenager was painfully thin; her skin seemed excessively dry with an unhealthy yellowish hue. Her hair was three shades of pink and blue, and her face was pierced in places Emma had never seen pierced before.

Teresa gave a slight wave of her hand but avoided eye contact.

"There are lots of things to see in Chicago," Emma said. "Like rock and roll concerts in the park. You might enjoy them."

The girl frowned, looked down at the ground, and shrugged.

Laura hesitated a bit too long. "My husband and I don't care for that sort of thing. Come on, Teresa, let's go." She gave Emma a condescending smile and hurried the girl out the door.

Emma frowned. *Something isn't right there. I feel it.*

By the time she reached the front door of the condo, the packages were slipping out of her arms. "Nate," she called, knocking with her knee. "Nate, let me in."

He opened the door, shook his head, and grabbed the bundles. "For a person who doesn't like to shop, you apparently did all right."

"The prices were so good I couldn't pass them up." With a deep sigh, she plopped herself into a chair.

Nate handed her a large glass of water. "Drink, you're probably dehydrated."

"Thanks."

"You're making faces," he said. "What are you thinking about?"

"I met Laura Evans downstairs with a teenaged girl she introduced as her niece. She said the girl would be staying with them for a few weeks, but didn't seem pleased."

"What about it?"

"She hesitated before she said the word 'niece,' and seemed evasive about the girl's parents being away." Emma pursed her lips and frowned.

"Don't go reading anything into it, my dear. It doesn't sound strange to me."

"Have you ever seen the husband?"

"No, now that you mention it."

"The girl looked ill. She was pale as a ghost and terribly thin and she was wearing a heavy sweater." Emma shot Nate a pointed look. "This is August. The temperature is eighty-five degrees out there." Continuing, she gestured around her own face. "There are all kinds of rings hanging from her nose and eyebrows and cheeks. And her hair is three different shades of pink and blue." With a shake of her head, Emma sighed. "Not only that, she avoided eye contact and didn't say a word."

"Young people don't usually have a lot to say to older folks. Mind your own business, Emma Winberry."

"Humph! Something is seriously wrong with that girl."

"HI GLADYS," Emma said, holding the phone in one hand and a glass of iced tea in the other. "How's your weather on Long Island?"

"Sweltering! I'm not leaving the condo today, not even to go to the pool," she answered in her throaty voice. "And how are you adjusting to life in the city?"

"Oh, just fine. There are so many things to do, one never has time to get bored. Our weather is hot but the breezes off the lake make it tolerable."

"So what is it?"

"What do you mean?"

"Emma Winberry, I've known you since we were kids. You didn't call to talk about the weather."

"True." Emma sighed and hesitated for just a moment. "I'm concerned about the folks who recently moved in next door. There are two units here on the sixth floor and we share the roof garden. There's a low wall between the properties, but there is access through a gate."

"Sounds chummy. So, what's the problem? Have they been raiding your tomato plants?" Gladys laughed.

"Very funny. There's no problem per se; it's just that something isn't right. I know it."

"There you go again with your premonitions."

"You've known me long enough to agree that I'm right most of the time," Emma said defensively.

"True. You were right when you got involved with those opera singers. They were in trouble."

"Absolutely. I believe I was instrumental in preventing a serious mishap."

"Okay, okay. Now tell me about these people next door."

"The woman, Laura Evans, has made a few attempts to be friendly, but they were lukewarm, if you know what I mean." Emma took a swallow of tea and sucked the lemon slice out of the glass.

"Are you eating something?" Gladys asked.

"I'm sucking on a lemon. You know I always think better when I have something in my mouth."

"Why do I ask? What else about your neighbors?"

"They've been here a couple of weeks and neither Nate nor I have seen the husband. And yesterday Laura introduced me to her niece who's going to stay for a while. The girl looks anorexic and she has weird hair and multiple piercings on her face and ears. God only knows what the rest of her body looks like." Emma felt better venting to Gladys.

"So, you think this girl needs help and you're the one to do it?" "I didn't say that." "You implied it. I know you'll get involved, you can't help it.Keep me posted. You do have a tendency to get embroiled in some rather interesting situations."

"There's something else," Emma said, hesitating for just a moment. "I'm having terrible dreams again, three times this week."

"Oh, oh. Who's in trouble this time?"

"I think I am," Emma whispered.

"Why do you say that?"

"The danger is always directed at me. In the last dream I was going to the guillotine." Emma felt a chill run up her spine as she recalled the image.

"I've never heard you talk like this before," Gladys said, a note of concern in her voice. "You be careful, you hear me?"

"I will. Don't worry. It's probably just my overactive imagination. Give my love to Cornell and the girls."

"Keep in touch, Emma."

"I will."

Guardian Angèl, why does this feeling persist, no matter how I try to explain it away? I hope you're on the job. I think I'm going to need you.

THREE

I HATE THIS PLACE! It's too fancy for me. Why did my parents send me here? I'm fat and ugly and they don't want me. Uncle and Laura don't want me, either. I heard them arguing. All married people do is argue. I hate them.

They're whispering again, probably about me. Uncle's telling Laura not to get too friendly with the neighbors, not to tell them about any of his business. What is his business, anyway? As if I care.

If I can find out where they keep money around here, maybe I'll take some. Get on a bus or a train and just go away.

There must be money if they can afford a place like this. I'll snoop around the next time they go out.

FOUR

EMMA BUSIED HERSELF preparing for her children's first visit to the condo. "What are we going to do with all these little ones running around?" She went from room to room picking up a vase here, a photo there, and putting them out of reach.

When Nate walked into the living room, Emma saw the surprised look on his face as he studied the change in the room. The top of the piano sported all the articles usually kept on the end tables, including the TV remote.

"Are you getting ready for a siege?" he asked, scratching his head.

"Well you know how small children are. They want to touch everything." She picked up a decorative paperweight and added it to the already overloaded piano.

"We already decided to keep everyone out on the roof garden. It's a gorgeous day. They'll be so busy watching the boats on the lake, they won't want to come inside."

"Oh Nate, do you think it's safe out there?"

"Emma," he grabbed her hands. "The brick wall around the perimeter of the roof is three feet tall with a wrought-iron railing of three feet above that. Unless any of the children suffers from gigantism, believe me, they'll be safe."

"I know, I know. They can't squeeze through the railings, can they?" She looked outside, biting down on her lip, mentally trying to calculate the distance between the rails.

"That possibility was factored into the design before the wall was built. Trust me, it's safe."

"All right. Will you put those toys out there, please?"

Emma had purchased floor games, huge bottles of bubbles, and battery-operated cars at the end-of-summer sale. Now Nate patiently took the items from the closet and arranged them outside. He set up extra card tables and chairs for the adults.

Nate saw Teresa inch her way out of the condo next door. He watched her without being obvious about it as he prepared the grill. They kept it out of the way in a corner of the roof surrounded by potted plants which gave him a perfect vantage point to keep an eye on the young girl. He turned his attention away to ensure that the grill's flames lit, and when he looked up she was gone.

An hour later the house resonated with adult chatter and children's shouts. "This place is lovely," Pat said. "Stephen, when our children are grown, I want something just like this. Look at that view."

"Dream on, Pat," Stephen said. "Since Susan is only three, you're going to have a long wait."

"Daddy, I wanna go outside. See the boats." Susan grabbed his hand and led him toward the door.

Sylvia and James followed them out watching James Jr. running wildly around. His brother, Frankie, still unsteady on his feet, clung to his father's hand, tugging, trying to follow the others.

Martin and Bertie, Emma's youngest son and his wife, arrived soon after and put their stamp of approval on the new abode.

The next hour sped by in a flurry of activity. The women took charge of the children; the men congregated at the grill drinking beer and watching over the steaks, burgers and hot dogs.

Bertie joined Emma in the kitchen. Together they tossed a salad and put the condiments and buns on a tray. "Who is that wraith next door?" Bertie asked. "She's trying to hide, but I saw her watching the children."

"Isn't she sad?" Emma said. "She looks anorexic; her color

is awful. She's staying with her aunt and uncle who own the condo, but they don't show much interest in her."

"What a shame," Bertie said. "From the colors of her hair and the number of visible piercings, I'd say she has a real self-esteem problem."

"Do you see many girls like that at the mental health clinic?" Emma asked.

"Quite a few. They usually come from disruptive homes, and from families with a history of violence and abuse. Is that her story?"

"I don't know. I don't know anything about her, really."

"I can tell you that the anorexic girls I've seen seem to think that self-starvation is a way of drawing attention away from a family problem. The person feels that if everyone is concerned about her, the problem will go away." Bertie shook her head. "Unfortunately, it doesn't work. That girl needs to be loved."

"Oh dear," Emma said spilling lemonade on the floor. "Look what I did." She grabbed a roll of paper towels and began wiping it up.

Bertie knelt down beside her. "If I know you, you'll find a way to help that girl better than any psychiatrist."

Emma stopped cleaning long enough to give her daughter-in-law a hug. "I'm so glad you married Martin. There's such a change in him. He's actually grown up."

"He's a good guy, just needed some direction. Men think they do all the decision making, but we know better." She winked at Emma as they got up off the floor, then Bertie picked up the tray and walked outside.

When everyone finished eating and the very last hot dog disappeared, Emma brought out a Bundt cake dripping with lemon icing.

"Cake," the children shouted.

As Emma cut thick slices of the soft confection, small hands reached out, dropping crumbs to the ground. Emma took a piece to the gate separating the two properties. "Teresa," she called, knowing the girl was within earshot. "Do you want a piece of cake?"

Teresa walked hesitantly toward Emma. She seemed about to speak, but was interrupted when Susan ran up.

"Why is your hair pink and blue?" the child asked, a look of wonder on her face.

Teresa pulled back.

"Isn't it pretty, Susan?" Emma asked.

The child smiled, nodded and hurried off. "Mama, I want pink hair," she shouted running up to Pat.

Teresa's hand came up self-consciously. She fingered her hair as she watched the child run away. With a pained expression on her face, she reached out, took the plate of cake and slowly walked into the house.

LATER EMMA AND NATE sat quietly in the atrium relaxing after the taxing day.

"Everything went well," Nate said.

"Yes it did. But it sure is tiring having them all around." She looked at Nate. "Bertie noticed Teresa. She sees a lot of kids like her at the clinic. She said they usually come from disruptive homes. It's so sad."

"I agree," Nate said, "but there's nothing you can do about it, my dear." He took her hand. "So don't get involved."

Emma gave him an ingratiating smile, sighed and closed her eyes.

I will try to mind my own business, this time. But she knew better.

FIVE

FOR THE NEXT few days temperatures soared into the ninety-degree mark, keeping Emma and Nate confined either to the air-conditioned condo or the BMW. Twice a day Emma faithfully watered her plants on the roof garden; they, in turn, rewarded her with succulent tomatoes, colorful nasturtiums to spice up the salad bowl and an abundance of herbs.

"Emma," Nate called. "Come here, please."

Her arms laden with ripe tomatoes and herbs, she walked inside and looked questioningly at Nate. He appeared to be on hold as he cradled the phone in his neck.

"This is that movie company. Do you still want to be an extra?"

Emma nodded enthusiastically.

"Yes, I'm still here," Nate said turning back to the phone. "What's that address again?" He scribbled on a notepad. "All right. We'll be there."

After he hung up, he looked at Emma and laughed. "You look like Mother Harvest with all that stuff in your arms. Go put those things in the kitchen."

"Well, what did they say? Where are we supposed to go?"

Nate followed her, picking up bits of parsley and nasturtium blossoms from the floor.

"On Monday morning we're to report to this trailer in Grant Park just off of Balbo. The scene they're shooting is a wedding in front of Buckingham Fountain. We'll get our instructions and sign the contract then."

"We have to sign a contract?" Emma put down the tomatoes she was carrying.

"Certainly. There are rules to follow and they're obliged to pay us for an eight-hour day."

"I didn't think this would take eight hours," Emma said, making faces.

Nate shook his head. "My dear, they do have to rehearse and the first filming isn't necessarily the one they use. Remember how many times we rehearsed some of those scenes in the opera?"

"Hmm. I suppose. I just thought we'd be part of a crowd walking down the street or something like that."

"You still want to do it?"

She frowned and thought for a minute. Something was nagging at her, but she didn't know what. "Sure, let's do it, just this once."

THE RELENTLESS HEAT WAVE continued through the weekend. Emma and Nate moved some of the plants on the roof garden into the shade. Only the tomatoes seemed to thrive in the hot sun.

On Sunday morning Emma went out early to water. She saw Teresa standing next door watching her. The girl wore a long-sleeved shirt buttoned up to the neck.

Something's definitely wrong with that girl, Emma thought as she waved. "Hi, Teresa."

The girl lifted a hand and gave a tentative wave. That seemed to be all the socialization she was capable of. Emma bent to her task, pinching spent nasturtium blossoms from the plants. She was surprised when a shadow fell across her field of vision. She looked up to see Teresa standing there. For a moment Emma saw herself as a young girl, thin and wan and self-conscious, trying to cover her stick-like arms and legs. She remembered the teasing and cruel taunts of the other children. Her heart went out to this unhappy-looking girl.

"Those are pretty," Teresa said.

"They're called nasturtiums. The nicest part about them is that you can enjoy their colors and their flavor. In a salad, the leaves and flowers taste spicy, like a radish." She picked off a leaf and put it in her mouth, then handed one to the girl.

Teresa hesitated for a moment then reached out a skeletal hand. Emma noticed the nails bitten down to the quick, blood encrusted on the tips.

Teresa took a minuscule bite, then another.

"Isn't it good?" Emma asked.

She nodded and held her hand out for another.

The girl looked like she was starving. "How about trying one of these tomatoes?" Emma asked. "They're so sweet." She walked to the tomato plants and chose a ripe, firm fruit. "Here, Teresa." She handed it to the girl.

"My name's not Teresa," she said in a belligerent tone.

"Oh, I must have misunderstood what your aunt said. What is your name?"

"Tracie, with an i-e, and she's not my aunt." She took the tomato and bit into it, juice dripping down her chin. Slowly she took tiny bites until it was gone.

"She's not your aunt?" Emma asked, handing her a paper towel from a roll she kept nearby.

"No, she's not. She only thinks she is." The girl blotted her cracked lips, careful not to dislodge the ring hanging from the lower one. Emma noted the stud in the tip of her tongue and shuddered. Tracie turned and walked away without further comment. Emma stood for a long time watching and wondering about her.

THE HEAT WAVE PERSISTED into Monday, breaking records as the temperature inched toward the one-hundred mark.

"Why don't we take an Alaskan vacation?" Nate asked as he scanned the morning paper.

"What time are we supposed to be at Grant Park?" Emma asked, having serious doubts about this movie-extra endeavor.

"Between nine and one."

"I'm wearing sandals and the lightest weight slacks I own," she said.

"I hadn't planned on wearing a three-piece suit if that's what you're insinuating. Let's be there about nine. It should be the coolest part of the day."

"What's the weather forecast?" Emma asked. "How much longer is this intolerable heat supposed to last?" She looked anxiously at her outdoor plants.

"Says here there's a front coming with storms on Wednesday or Thursday. That should either break the heat wave or make it more humid. Take your pick."

"Well, I'm sure they'll wait until then to shoot this movie," Emma said, a hopeful look on her face.

"Don't bet on it. I think these people are on a tight schedule with budget constraints. I never heard of this company. It'll probably be a B-minus movie."

"Hmm." At this point Emma wanted to forget the entire venture, but something wouldn't let her. She supposed it was her stubborn nature.

THEY LEFT THE CONDO at eight forty-five. Heat waves undulated before their eyes. Emma wore lightweight slacks, a gauzy blouse, a large straw hat and sunglasses. Nate wore shorts and T-shirt, sandals and a cap on his head. His look dared Emma to criticize.

They caught a bus on Michigan Avenue and arrived at their destination a few minutes after nine. A line of about ten people waited outside the locked trailer. Some grumbled. Others kept looking at their watches.

"This does not bode well," Nate whispered.

Just then a taxi stopped in front of the trailer, and a man and woman jumped out.

"Sorry, folks," the man said. "Traffic." He opened the door and let the first four people in.

Emma heard the window air-conditioner start up. At least it would be cool inside.

A half hour later Emma could feel Nate's irritation. She knew he was just about ready to leave, when the door opened and they were ushered in. They sat at a desk covered with file folders and papers. A woman began her spiel, reciting as though she had said it a hundred times.

"We plan only two days of shooting at this location. The scene is a wedding taking place in front of Buckingham Fountain. After the ceremony there will be a dinner reception at tables set up in the park, followed by a DJ. You folks will be the guests.

"During the ceremony you'll sit on the chairs provided and just look happy. For the reception, you'll be seated at the tables that will be set up in Grant Park where waiters will serve you. Just act natural and talk in a low tone."

"That's all?" Emma asked.

"That's it."

It sounded easy enough.

"We'll shoot the ceremony tomorrow night and the reception on Wednesday. Might have to go into Thursday, but I hope not.

"That would mean extra expense."

Emma remembered the storm prediction for Wednesday.

"Are you both agreeable to this?"

Nate sighed and looked at Emma.

"Yes," she said with a nod.

"Here's a standard contract. We agree to pay you each fifty dollars for eight hours. If we go over, you'll get more. You agree not to talk to the stars and to follow explicit instructions. If anyone gets hurt on the set, our insurance covers the cost of treatment. Fill in the information at the top and sign on the bottom. After your part in the film is finished, we'll mail your checks to your address."

She handed a contract to each of them. They filled in the information and signed where indicated.

"What do we wear?" Nate asked.

"Something appropriate for a wedding. You, Mr. Sandler, should wear a dark suit with a light-colored shirt and a dark tie.

"You, Ms. Winberry, wear a dark-colored dress, no stripes or flowers and definitely no plaids. They don't photograph well."

"Do I wear a hat?" Emma asked.

"If you wish, but something simple. Now if you have no other questions, be at Buckingham Fountain at eight o'clock tomorrow night. The cameras start rolling as soon as the lights go on around the fountain."

Emma and Nate nodded and left the trailer.

SIX

"EMMA, THAT WRAITH from next door is stealing one of your tomatoes," Nate said, an indignant tone in his voice.

"I told her to help herself whenever she wanted one," Emma said, glancing out the window. "The poor thing looks starved to me."

"There isn't much to her," Nate agreed. "She told you that Laura Evans wasn't her aunt?"

"That was a peculiar thing to say. 'She only thinks she is' were her exact words." Emma frowned as she continued to fold laundry.

"Someone's confused," Nate said, "but it's none of our business. Do you hear me, Sparrow?" He lifted her chin in his hand and looked into her eyes. "None of our business."

Emma merely smiled and went back to her laundry.

That evening they dressed with special care. Emma was excited at the thought of being in an actual movie, even if it wasn't destined to be a blockbuster.

"I think I'll wear my new hat," she said, taking a small, navy-blue straw hat out of a box. It had a perky bow in the back and would set off her midnight-blue dress perfectly.

"My, you do look fetching, my dear," Nate remarked as he deftly tied a Windsor knot in his muted silk tie. "It's too hot to wear this thing," he grumbled loosening it a little.

They caught a cab on Michigan Avenue and arrived at Buckingham Fountain a little before eight. Other extras stood around chatting. A few minutes later a limo pulled up and deposited the principal characters. The bride fussed with her dress complaining that the train was too long. Emma looked closely at her, but didn't recognize the actor. She was pretty but not glamorous. The plain-looking leading man was not familiar, either. I guess Nate is right about this being a low-budget film, she thought.

"Attention please, everyone," the director called. "We'll run through this scene a couple of times before we begin filming. You extras, come over here, please."

Emma and Nate walked to the side of the fountain with the others.

"That's good. Right there. Bridal party, here in front. Minister, there."

At that moment the lights went on around the fountain, wrapping the spouting water in soft pastel colors.

"Perfect," the director said.

The actors went through the scene twice with a few minor corrections.

"It sure is muggy," Nate whispered. "I can feel the sweat running down my back."

Emma nodded. She was just as uncomfortable.

"Okay, everyone, let's get the cameras rolling." Bright lights went on around the group adding to the heat. "Everybody ready? Quiet. Rolling. Action."

The cameras started as the scene began. When the bride was about to repeat her vows the camera zoomed in on her radiant face gazing at her groom. "Yuck," she said and began coughing violently.

"Cut, cut!" shouted the director. "What the hell is wrong?"

"I swallowed a bug."

Someone rushed over with a glass of water. Then the makeup artist ran in to touch up the faces of the principals.

"Why couldn't you shoot this scene in a church?" the bride complained. "An air-conditioned one."

By now Emma's new shoes had rubbed a blister on her heel. She regretted not wearing an older pair.

"Again, from the beginning," the director said.

Groans from the actors.

"Everyone ready? Quiet. Rolling. Action."

The cameras started again as the actors said their lines. Emma thought they sounded flat, as though they were simply reading from the script. No wonder she'd never heard of these actors before. She certainly didn't intend to see this movie.

The director stopped a few times; each time it was because he claimed something was "not quite right" in the scene, but to Emma's mind it was always something very small. By the time the director was satisfied, it was past midnight.

"Thank you, everyone," he said wearily. "Tomorrow night we'll shoot the reception scene in Grant Park. I promise you some good food. Be here at eight o'clock, and you must wear the same clothes. After all, it's supposed to be a continuation of the wedding." His weak laugh brought no response from the actors and extras.

Emma limped behind Nate, her dress wilted, her foot burning with each step. He hailed a cab on Michigan Avenue and they rode home in silence.

When they entered the air-conditioned condo, they both breathed a sigh of relief. "Do you really want to go back there tomorrow?" he asked, pulling off his tie and unbuttoning his damp shirt.

Emma sat on the bed peeling off her pantyhose and noting the bloodstain on the right heel. "Ouch!" She limped into the bathroom, showered, then put antibiotic ointment on the offending blister and covered it with an adhesive bandage.

After Nate showered, he sat on the bed beside Emma. She lay still, her left hand over her eyes. He picked up her right hand and kissed the fingertips. "You didn't answer my question."

"I don't know. We've signed a contract, made a commitment. I think we should honor it."

He sighed as he lay down beside her. "The cleaners down the street should be able to do something with our clothes. I'll take them down first thing in the morning."

She snuggled up beside him; his arm snaked around her pulling her close.

"You are a dear, Nate, and I love you."

"I know, but I don't think I want to do this sort of thing again."

THE NEXT MORNING the humidity inched up towards ninety percent. When Emma walked out on the roof garden, watering can in hand, she gasped. It felt like stepping into a sauna. A bank of clouds lay to the west, unmoving. The weatherman predicted a storm guaranteed to break the heat wave. Emma prayed it would come before evening.

"I wonder if they'll cancel the filming tonight," she said, walking back into the atrium as Nate came in the front door.

"I certainly hope so. The cleaner said our clothes will be ready about four this afternoon." He picked up the newspaper and settled into a lounge chair, leaned back and raised the footrest.

Emma busied herself watering the plants in the atrium. She looked out at the shimmering heat and saw Tracie stretched out on a lawn chair, baking in the sun. Gone were the long sleeves and sweaters. She was bareheaded in a scant swimsuit that barely covered the little bit of femininity she had.

"That girl is going to suffer heatstroke," Emma said, shaking her head.

"Huh?" Nate looked up.

"Tracie. She's lying in the sun, cooking. She must have a death wish."

"There are adults in charge," Nate said. "It's not your responsibility. By the way, how's your blister?"

"Better, but I'll wear my black sandals tonight. No one will notice."

Nate grunted and turned back to the newspaper.

Emma went into the atrium and sat in a chair in the corner supposedly examining the leaves of a red and yellow croton. Her head jerked up at the sound of voices. Laura stood outside the door, hands on hips, shouting at Tracie. Emma couldn't make out the words, but their gestures and raised voices told her it wasn't a pleasant conversation. Tracie waved her stick-like arms in the air, shaking her head vehemently. A moment later a tall well-built man walked out. He spoke a few words to both women. Laura went into the house and Tracie followed.

"Nate," Emma said excitedly. "I think I finally saw the husband."

"What are you talking about?" He put down the paper and took off his reading glasses.

"Laura and Tracie were arguing, probably about the danger of sitting in the hot sun. Then a man came out, said a few words, and they all went inside."

"So?"

"So, he must be Laura's husband."

"That's fine, but I really don't care, and neither should you."

Emma frowned and went into the kitchen, mumbling, "I shouldn't care but I do. Oh why am I always minding other people's business?"

By early evening the cloud cover slowly inched its way over the city. Nate had called the number the movie company gave them and got a recorded message saying the shoot was still scheduled for eight o'clock.

They dressed in silence. Emma thought it advisable not to engage Nate in conversation. She knew he didn't want to go, and talking about it would only aggravate him.

At seven-thirty they climbed into a taxi and joined the other extras in Grant Park. Tables were arranged under the trees. Champagne bottles containing ginger ale sat in ice buckets, their sides sweating.

The tables were tastefully set with white plates edged in gold, matching cutlery beside each. Gold-colored rings held up the white napkins standing like tiny pyramids. Flutes and water glasses, also edged in gold, graced the settings. A floral arrangement of carnations and ferns sat in the center of each table.

A slight breeze drifted over the crowd of guests. Emma gave a grateful sigh and then smiled as Nate and the other extras murmured their pleasure.

"Everyone, take your places," called the director. "We want to shoot this scene with the first take. A storm is on the way and we're just ahead of it."

The extras sat in their designated seats while the bridal party walked up to the head table.

"All right, extras, when the food is served, please eat as you normally would; pretend to engage in table conversation, but keep your voices down."

As the bright lights went on, Emma heard a low rumble of thunder in the distance. Oh, oh, she thought. She and Nate exchanged glances.

"Ready. Quiet. Rolling. Action."

The scene began: a toast to the bride and groom; a short speech by the best man; and dinner was served.

The wilted lettuce salad looked pitiful on the plate. "Do we have to eat this?" Nate asked.

"Pretend," Emma said, smiling.

Next came plates of overcooked prime rib, half of it fat, mushy asparagus, and dried out mashed potatoes. Emma heard groans from the extras next to her. She nodded in commiseration.

Suddenly an argument broke out at the bridal table. The cameras kept rolling, as Emma, Nate, and all the other extras' attention shot to the scene. The director hadn't told them about this part, so their collective reaction was spontaneous and real. Maybe the director knew what he was doing after all, Emma thought. The bride threw a glass of champagne in the groom's face just as distant lightning streaked across the sky. A clap of thunder shook the ground. Almost as though choreographed, the camera crew opened huge umbrellas to protect the equipment.

A fine rain began falling across the scene. It threw everyone, from the actors to the director, into turmoil. A sudden gust of wind blew Emma's new hat away.

"Cut," called the director. The filming lights went out and, as lightning streaked closer, the storm broke with a vengeance, soaking everyone and everything. "That was great," he shouted above the rising wind. "We'll keep the storm scene. It fit perfectly. That's all. Thanks to all you extras. Your checks will be mailed to you, and send me your cleaning bills. I'll see that you're reimbursed."

The bride swore openly, dragging her gown through the puddling water; the leading man looked daggers at the director. The cinematographer and his crew quickly covered all the equipment and ran it into waiting vans.

Nate led a bedraggled Emma toward the taxis standing at the curb. Neither one spoke as they rode home.

Nate slammed the door as they entered the condo. "This suit is ruined, and you lost your new hat. For this we get a hundred bucks each?"

He turned to Emma, his face a mask of anger and frustration. "I don't know about you, but I will never do this again," he said as he stalked into the bathroom.

Emma slumped into a kitchen chair, dripping water over the floor. She had expected it to be fun. Instead it was a total disaster. Now Nate was angry, his suit ruined, her new hat gone. She put her head down on the table and stayed that way for a long time.

SEVEN

EMMA WOKE ENCIRCLED in Nate's arms. She snuggled close and kissed his chin.

"I'm sorry, Sparrow. I shouldn't have taken my frustration out on you," he said.

"It's okay. It was my idea, and not a very smart one."

"No more?"

"No more."

"Good. Now I'll fix us a nice big breakfast. As I recall, we didn't have much dinner last night." He smiled and caressed her cheek.

After feasting on bacon, eggs and toast, Nate took their clothes down to the cleaners again.

"Maybe they can do something with this suit," he mumbled as he walked out the door.

The phone rang moments later. Emma looked at the caller ID and smiled.

"Hi, Gladys, you're the only person I want to talk to this morning."

"Oh, oh, what happened?"

"Well," Emma began her long narrative. "Swallowed a bug…terrible food…pouring rain…" As awful as the night was, Emma found that by the time she finished talking about it, she was laughing so hard she couldn't speak.

"I get the picture," Gladys said. "I presume that's the end of your movie career."

"Absolutely! Now what's going on in your life?"

"Cornell and I are coming to Chicago. He has to see someone about a rather large project he and his partner are taking on, and I decided to come with him."

"That's wonderful," Emma said. "It's been too long since we've been together. You can stay with us."

"Thanks, but we have accommodations at the Drake, all expenses paid." Gladys sighed. "It'll be like a second honeymoon."

Emma knew that her friends had a vigorous sex life and she felt herself blush at the images that sprang to mind.

"But I am eager to see your new place," Gladys said.

"Yes, yes. Now that this heat wave is over we can do lots of things. When are you coming? How long are you staying?"

Nate walked in hearing the last questions, looked at her and frowned.

"We'll be there next Friday and stay a full week," Gladys answered.

"Wonderful. Nate will be so glad to meet you at last."

"Me too. I'll call you before we leave. Bye."

"Who?" Nate asked, giving her a suspicious glance.

"Gladys and Cornell are coming to Chicago on business, staying at the Drake. You'll finally get to meet them."

"Oh." He relaxed. "I'll enjoy that."

"What did the cleaner say?"

"He'll try, but he doesn't hold out much hope for the suit. Maybe the movie company will spring for a new one." Nate shrugged, then gave Emma a hug. "I've always said life with you would never be dull."

THE FOLLOWING MORNING Emma sat on the roof garden drinking coffee and daydreaming. Her plants had survived the brutal heat wave and now seemed to revel in the reprieve. The temperature and humidity had dropped to normal for late August.

Emma smiled at the Tom Thumb tomato plant, the tiny fruit

peeking through the leaves. She sat back in her lounge chair and felt like pinching herself. Was this a dream? Would she wake and find herself back in that old house in Brookfield?

It seemed like another lifetime. She remembered last Christmas, with her family around her, when Nate gave her the key to the condo and asked her to "come live with me and be my love." She sighed. So romantic.

"Good morning."

Emma turned to see her neighbor, Laura Evans, standing at the gate.

"Good morning, Laura. I was just savoring the lovely breeze off the lake. Join me for a cup of coffee, won't you?"

The woman hesitated, then walked over and sat ramrod straight in a deck chair.

"I'll be right back," Emma said. She returned with a tray, carrying a coffeepot, sugar and cream, another cup, and a plate of cookies.

"You didn't have to go to all that trouble," Laura said.

"No trouble. It'll give us a chance to get acquainted." Emma poured a cup for Laura then refilled her own. "Try these cookies. It's a new recipe I clipped out of the newspaper. Raspberry filling."

Laura took a swallow of coffee, bit into a cookie and nodded her approval.

"So, how do you like living here?" Emma asked.

"It's okay, but it'll take some getting used to."

"I feel liberated," Emma said. "I gave up a big house with a yard; it got to be too much for me. It just needed too many repairs. A young couple bought it. He's a carpenter and claimed he could fix it up all by himself."

She remembered the day she signed the papers and handed over the keys. She had felt both sad and relieved. She looked at Laura and said, "That was four months ago and I haven't regretted it for one single minute. Where did you move from?"

"Kansas City."

"Do you have family there?"

"No, no family."

Getting answers out of this woman was like pulling up the root of a dandelion. Emma didn't want to appear too nosey, but she felt an underlying tension, something Laura wanted to say, but couldn't.

"Nate and I are both retired," Emma said. "What does your husband do for a living?"

"He's in business." Her voice was flat, her expression vacant.

Hmm, Emma thought, if she wants to talk, she's not very forthcoming. Maybe I'll prod, just a little.

"Tell me a little about Teresa, or Tracie, as she calls herself," Emma said trying to sound casual.

Laura shook her head. "I don't know why she insists on using that name. I refuse to call her anything other than Teresa." She let out a deep sigh. "Bringing her here was a big mistake." She clutched the cookie so hard it crumbled in her hand. She didn't seem to notice that she had raspberry filling on her fingers until Emma handed her a napkin.

"I'm sorry. I'm just so upset." This was the first time the woman showed any emotion at all.

"If you want to talk about it, I'm a good listener." Emma sat forward in her chair. "Take a deep breath and let it out slowly. Good. Now another. Okay?"

Laura hesitated a moment then began. "Teresa is my husband's niece, an only child, spoiled rotten. Her parents gave her everything, toys, games, video equipment, her own computer, then a car, which she totaled the first week." The woman looked out over the placid lake, a pained expression on her face.

"It sounds like they gave her all the material things," Emma said, "but did they give her love?"

"Huh. I don't think they know the meaning of the word.

Teresa's mother is morbidly obese; it runs in her family. Her father is an alcoholic." Laura made a face that expressed exactly what she thought of her husband's family. "All they do is argue. Teresa hates the way her mother looks, not that I can blame her. She starves herself to stay thin, keeps claiming she's fat. She was hospitalized last year with severe anorexia, almost died."

Emma was shocked by the woman's lack of empathy when she said that Tracie almost died. The poor girl. If anyone needed love it was that child.

Laura continued. "The psychiatrist told them it was her way of getting back at them, but did they listen? They sent her to us." Her mouth formed a moue of distaste. "And she has all those horrid piercings on her face. She even does some of them herself." Laura shuddered. "Yesterday she shoved some awful things in her earlobes that look like logs. I don't know what to do with her. She won't even talk to me. My husband is always too busy. What do they all expect of me?" The woman put her head in her hands for a moment, but quickly regained control, sat up straight, and replaced the mask of distance on her face.

"I'm sorry to burden you with this. Please excuse me."

"Not at all," Emma said. "Everyone has problems and needs to sound off once in a while."

She smiled, but Laura didn't respond. The woman merely stood up, turned and walked back to her condo.

Well, Emma thought, those two certainly won't give the girl what she needs.

EIGHT

I LOCKED THE bathroom door so Laura doesn't see me. Here's the razor, brand new and very sharp. Nice and shiny. I like the way it looks, the way it feels in my hand. When I slice it across my arm it hurts, but it's a nice hurt. The blood is starting to drip in the sink, slow at first, now faster. It's such a pretty dark red color.

I want to do it again, to watch the skin separate, the drops of blood come out. I can do it or not. It's my choice, my body. There, I cut again, deeper this time, more blood. Ahhh... Two slashes, one right next to the other. Let the blood run down faster and faster. It feels sticky and warm dripping down my arm. So nice.

That's enough—for now. I'll wrap a bandage around it and clean up the sink so Laura won't see it.

Ha! But I'll leave the razor there, full of blood. They'll freak out. Let them wonder. Maybe then they'll care. Maybe...

NINE

LATER NATE AND EMMA took their daily walk along Lake Michigan. The temperature was rising, but the prediction was for the low eighties with negligible humidity.

"Laura came over for coffee earlier when you went out for bagels," Emma said.

"And?"

"She told me that Tracie was in the hospital last year and almost died. The girl had been starving herself."

"I don't doubt that. She looks like she just came out of a concentration camp. So what's she doing here?"

"It sounds like she comes from a dysfunctional family, mother obese, father an alcoholic. They didn't know what to do with her, so they sent her to Laura and her husband."

"You know, all you seem to hear about these days is dysfunctional families. It's the term of this generation. I would like to know exactly what a functional family is."

They walked on in silence for a while watching the gulls screeching at one another over tidbits of food lying in the sand.

"There's something seriously wrong there," Emma said.

"Where?"

"Next door. I could feel it. Laura wanted to say more, but something held her back."

Nate stopped walking and took both of Emma's hands in his. "Do you have to get involved in other people's problems all the time?"

"I can't help it. You know I've had these feelings and

premonitions all my life. I did tell my Guardian Angel I wanted to resign, many times, but it didn't work. I seem to be stuck with this sixth sense for the rest of my life. I try to ignore it, really I do." She looked at him with such frustration that he began to laugh.

"Okay, I knew about this from the beginning and I won't try to change you, my dear. When you decide what you can do for the girl, let me know and I'll help, if I can."

EMMA KEPT LOOKING at the arrivals board at O'Hare Airport. "Their plane should be landing soon," she said excitedly.

Nate sat calmly at the baggage claim area, but Emma couldn't sit still. She paced and kept looking at the board. When it noted that the flight had arrived, her heart began to race. She hadn't seen Gladys in over a year. This would be a wonderful reunion.

"There they are." She ran up to Gladys and threw her arms around her. They laughed and cried, acting like schoolgirls.

Nate looked at the tall, slightly overweight, balding man with smile wrinkles around his eyes and extended his hand. "Nate Sandler."

"Cornell Foster," the other man said. "It's nice to meet the man in person I've only known through e-mail." He pointed to the women. "They'll be like that for a while. I've seen this before. Let's get the luggage."

The men walked to the carousel that was squeaking its way around, bags beginning to tumble out of the opening.

"Where's Nate?" Gladys asked. "And Cornell?"

"Over there, claiming the baggage," Emma said. "We were so busy welcoming each other, we totally forgot about them. We'd better go and help."

"Nate, this is Gladys," Emma said, grabbing a case on wheels.

Nate's eyes widened as this Valkyrie enveloped him in her arms.

"You have to be a wonderful man," Gladys said. "Emma

looks marvelous. You're the most fantastic thing that's ever happened to her."

Nate was speechless. "I try my best," he said after a while, glancing at Cornell who was suppressing a smile.

The women talked nonstop on the long walk to the parking garage.

They loaded the luggage into the trunk, then Nate skillfully maneuvered the BMW out of the airport maze.

"So what brings you to Chicago?" he asked Cornell.

"My partner and I are doing pretty well as a small publishing house, as you already know. Now we have an opportunity to merge with a Chicago publisher and expand our line."

Nate nodded. "I'm impressed. That sounds like quite an endeavor."

"I'm here to talk to this man and work out all the particulars. You can do just so much by phone and e-mail. In my experience face-to-face contact gives you the opportunity to get the measure of the man."

"I agree with that," Nate said.

A peal of laughter from the backseat.

Cornell shook his head. "They're probably reliving their childhood."

"It's good to have old friends," Nate said. "Interesting that women seem to forge friendships that can last a lifetime. Most men don't do that."

"True," Cornell agreed. "Maybe that's one of the reasons women live longer."

That evening Emma and Nate entertained their guests at the condo. They broiled steaks and skewered vegetables. The women busied themselves tossing a salad and setting the table while the men tended the grill.

"This is a great view," Cornell said, looking out over the placid lake reflecting only a few clouds. Sailboats dotted the surface.

"It was worth every penny I paid for it," Nate said. "And Emma loves it here. Getting out of that big old house was a wise move for her."

Cornell nodded. "Gladys and I aren't sorry we sold our home for a condo. Much easier."

"Much," Nate agreed.

"And," Cornell hesitated for a moment, "your kids have no objection to the two of you living together out of wedlock?"

"None at all," Nate said. "Young people today don't live with the constraints of our generation. They were all for it, both Emma's and mine."

Cornell slapped Nate on the back. "You're my kind of man. Say, maybe you'd like to come with me tomorrow to meet the Chicago publisher. As one of my authors, I thought you might be interested, maybe get some ideas for another book. *Opera for Beginners,* that you and Emma wrote, is a good seller. We're on our third printing. Are you still writing articles for that investment journal?"

"Yes," Nate answered. "It keeps me occupied and out of trouble." He made a face and thought for a moment, then relaxed. "Maybe I will come with you tomorrow. Might learn a few things." He speared a steak from the grill. "Hand me that platter, please."

The men walked into the kitchen carrying the platter of steaks and vegetables.

"Here we are, girls, feasting time," Nate said with a flourish.

"Smells heavenly," Gladys said.

Emma put the salad on the table and poured chilled dark red Merlot. They toasted friendships, old and new and then started in on the meal.

After dinner, the women finished stacking the dishwasher, then went onto the roof garden, leaving the men to watch the evening news.

"Wow," Gladys said. "These plants are gorgeous. What kind of fertilizer do you use?"

"Nothing out of the ordinary. I give them plenty of water with strict instructions to do their best. They rarely disappoint me." She smiled at the healthy specimens then picked a spent leaf from a tomato plant.

Gladys settled her generous frame in a comfortable lounge chair, took a deep breath and a sigh and turned her gaze across the roof. "Emma, is that the girl you were telling me about?"

Emma looked over to see Tracie peeking out at them. She waved and called to the girl. "Come and meet my friend from New York."

Tracie inched her way over, eyes glued to the ground. She hesitantly picked a nasturtium leaf and began chewing on it.

"Tracie Adams, this is my dearest friend, Gladys Foster," Emma said, taking the girl's hand. Emma's eyes rested on the bandage around her stick-like arm, but she said nothing.

Tracie looked up for a minute then quickly looked down at her sandals.

"What a nice name," Gladys said. "You know, Emma used to be almost as thin as you are when we were kids, and I was always fat. What a pair we made." She threw her head back and laughed.

"The other kids made fun of both of us, but we learned to ignore them. We accepted each other just as we were, and, if the others didn't like it, too bad."

Tracie looked as if she were going to cry. She pulled away and clenched her fists, staring at Gladys.

"I used to tell fortunes a long time ago," Gladys said, giving Emma an expression that said don't contradict me. "Would you like me to tell yours?"

The girl shrugged and inched closer to Gladys, looking at her through squinting eyes.

"Here, sit down on this stool and give me your hand.

Hmmm…" Gladys busily looked at the thin hand, the dry leathery skin, the peeling nails bitten to the quick. Then she gently turned it over and studied the palm.

"You have an interesting lifeline." She nodded and traced a crease on Tracie's hand. "I see adventure, travel, an exciting life…"

Tracie's eyes widened, but, before Gladys could say another word, Mr. Evans barged out of the condo next door.

"Teresa," he called. "Don't you remember that we're going out and you're not even dressed yet? Come in here, now."

With a terrified look, Tracie pulled her hand back, jumped up and ran to her scowling uncle.

"What a rude man," Gladys said when Tracie was out of earshot.

Just then a dark cloud slid across the full moon; Emma shivered though the night was warm.

"What's wrong with you?" Gladys asked, turning toward her friend.

"There's something evil about that man. I can feel it."

"One of your premonitions?" Gladys asked.

"I hope not."

LATER THAT NIGHT Emma lay awake staring at the ceiling.

"That was an enjoyable evening," Nate said, climbing in beside her. "Gladys certainly does talk in superlatives," he said, chuckling.

"She's always been that way."

"Okay, what's bothering you? I can tell by the way you're lying there, straight and stiff."

She turned toward him and gave him a concerned look.

"When Gladys and I were on the roof garden, Tracie came over. Gladys seemed to have a real rapport with the girl, but before she could say much Mr. Evans stormed out shouting for Tracie to come in. He didn't acknowledge either one of us. He's a very rude man."

"Some people are antisocial," Nate said, pulling her close.

"No, that's not it. I sense something more, something wrong."

"Go to sleep, Sparrow, and stop looking for problems that don't exist."

But it was a long time before Emma was able to sleep. When she finally did, disconnected confusing dreams invaded her slumber.

THE REST OF THE WEEK went by in a blur highlighted by a picnic in Millennium Park where Emma, Nate and their guests walked under the Cloud Gate, the forty-foot stainless steel bean-shaped sculpture that reflected the passers-by. They looked up and laughed at their distorted mirror images. One evening they attended an outdoor concert in the state-of-the-art music pavilion under a star-studded, cloudless sky.

The men spent three days with the Chicago publisher discussing business while the women roamed the stores on Michigan Avenue.

In a boutique at Water Tower Place Emma stopped at a display of nightshirts, some for dog lovers, cat lovers, and gardeners. One in particular caught her eye. Playful kittens romped down the front of a bright pink shirt; it came with a pair of matching bed socks. She picked it up and looked closer.

"I didn't know you were a cat lover," Gladys remarked.

"I'm not but I have a feeling Tracie might like this."

"Does she like cats?"

"Something tells me she does, and you know I'm usually right." She picked up the shirt and socks and walked to the register. "Her hands are always so cold. I expect her feet are, too."

Gladys sighed, put her arm around Emma's shoulder. "Okay, Mother Teresa, always helping the poor and downtrodden."

Emma gave her a skeptical look, paid for her purchase, and they left the store.

That evening Emma and Nate drove their guests to the airport. The women hugged and kissed and Nate and Emma promised to visit New York soon.

THE FOLLOWING MORNING as Emma watered her plants on the roof, she saw Tracie sneaking out of the condo next door.

"Hi," she whispered, creeping up to Emma.

"Tracie, how nice to see you. Did you hurt your arm?" Emma looked at the two diagonal scabs on the inside of her left forearm.

Tracie quickly put her arm behind her back. "I scratched it on a nail."

Emma didn't believe her but decided not to pursue the matter. "Wait here a minute," she said. "I have something for you."

Before she came out the door, she looked at the girl biting into a Tom Thumb tomato and reaching for another. Emma shook her head. She smiled as she walked out and handed Tracie a package.

The girl gave her a suspicious look.

"I saw it in a shop yesterday and thought you might like it. Go on, open it."

Tracie slowly opened the parcel. Her eyes lit up when she saw the kittens. "Oh!" She clutched the nightshirt to her flat chest. "How did you know I love kittens?"

"Well, you just seem like a kitten person to me," Emma answered, delighted to see the girl smile.

"I'll wear it every night. Thank you, Mrs.…. What should I call you?" she asked.

"My name is Emma Winberry."

The girl thought for a moment then gave Emma a rare smile. "I'll call you Mrs. Win."

The look on Tracie's face touched Emma's heart. With a healthy diet and a proper hairdo, that girl could be very pretty.

A FEW DAYS LATER Emma sat at the kitchen table, skimming the morning paper.

"More coffee?" Nate asked, pot in hand.

"A little. Did you see this article about the body found in an alley on Halsted Street?"

"No, I haven't read that section yet. Anything unusual about it?"

"It says here the man's name was Samuel Porter, an inventor. He claimed to have come up with some type of engine design that would revolutionize the auto industry."

"I do remember reading about that. I think he was involved in government contracts some years ago." Nate leaned over Emma's shoulder and scanned the article.

"He sustained a blow to the head, it says here," Emma read, "but nothing was stolen except for two rings, one with a large diamond and the other, a class ring. An expensive watch and money in his wallet hadn't been touched. What do you make of that?" She looked up at him.

Nate shrugged. "Who knows? Maybe the thief didn't have time to take anything else. The question is, what was he doing in that area? It's not safe to walk around there." Nate drained his cup and walked to the counter for a refill.

"The police have no leads at this time and are asking anyone with any information to contact them." Emma closed the page, put her hand across her mouth and thought.

"What's going through that active mind of yours?"

"I think there's more to this than just a mugging."

"And what makes you think that?"

"Just a feeling, that's all." She gave him a fetching smile and blew him a kiss across the table.

TEN

"EMMA!" NATE CALLED. "Emma!" There was a note of fear in his voice. Something was wrong.

"What's the matter?" She ran in from the roof garden, watering can in hand.

Nate sat in a chair, his face ashen, his hands trembling. "My brother's in the hospital—heart attack."

"Oh my God!" She put the watering can down and knelt beside him, almost afraid to ask the next question. "How bad is it?"

"They're not sure. He's in Intensive Care. At least he's alive." He spoke the last words in barely a whisper.

"Oh Nate." Emma wrapped her arms around him and held him tight.

"I'll get the next flight out," he said.

"Of course. I'll go with you."

He hesitated for a minute. "No, it's best that I go alone. Besides, you don't want to miss Sylvia's birthday party."

"Oh," her voice dropped. "I almost forgot."

Emma paced as Nate fired up the computer and began checking the flights to Naples, Florida.

She went into the bedroom and pulled suitcases out of the closet, then opened drawers and stacked piles of underwear and socks on the bed. She put out shorts, slacks, T-shirts and button-down shirts until the entire bed was covered.

"What are you doing?" Nate asked, walking into the room.

"Packing."

"Emma, I won't need every item of clothing I own. I'll do my own packing—please."

"All right. I just wanted to help." She swallowed hard. *What a fool I am. Of course he can take care of himself, and so can I.* But the lump was still there.

He took her in his arms and kissed her. "I won't be gone long. Why don't you make us a cup of tea, hmm? I'll put what I want in this small case and if I need anything else, I'll buy it there."

She hurried into the kitchen and lit the burner under the teapot, sniffling. *I must be getting soft in my old age. Guardian Angel, please help us through this. If it is serious, Nate will need my support. I need to be strong for him.*

When Nate came into the kitchen dressed in tan slacks and a muted striped shirt, Emma was just putting the tea on the table beside a plate of cookies.

"I have a flight out of O'Hare at two this afternoon," he said, spooning a generous amount of sugar into his cup.

"How will you get to the airport?" she asked. "Do you want me to drive you?" She tried to visualize herself behind the wheel of Nate's expensive BMW. Not a chance.

"Thanks, but I've called the limo service. They'll pick me up here shortly."

"My, you've taken care of everything in a matter of minutes," Emma said. *I wish I could be that efficient,* she thought.

He looked at her, his eyes filled with love. "Emma, I don't ever want to come home to an empty house again. Do you understand that?"

She looked up at him and smiled. "I know, I'll be here, waiting. You'll call and let me know how your brother is?"

"Of course."

"Do you have Sylvia's number?"

"I have everyone's number. Now give me a kiss, and say a prayer."

Just then the buzzer sounded. Nate pushed the intercom and told the driver he would be right down.

AFTER NATE LEFT, the house seemed so much larger and so—empty. She walked from room to room looking for something to do. She watered and trimmed the plants, cleaned the house. She certainly didn't want to bake anything. Had no idea when he would be back.

She didn't want to go out because he might call. Fool, she thought. It'll take at least a half hour, maybe more, to get to the airport, then a three-hour flight. She couldn't expect to hear from him until evening.

With mixed feelings and a sun hat on her head, Emma left the house. A walk along the lakeshore might be just what she needed to pick up her spirits.

The fair weather brought walkers, joggers, cyclists, and nannies with children out on this early afternoon. Emma found her pace and walked steadily. When she reached Lincoln Park, she decided to sit on a bench for a short rest.

She closed her eyes, took a deep breath and relaxed. Her gut told her that Nate's brother would be all right. In the background she heard the sounds of the Lincoln Park Zoo, animal grunts, children squealing, earthy smells drifting toward her on the breeze.

After a short time, Emma felt someone staring at her. She opened her eyes to see Tracie holding something under her shirt.

"Tracie, what are you doing here?" she asked in surprise.

"I saw you go out and wanted to go along," the girl said.

"Why didn't you call to me?"

Tracie shrugged and made a face.

Young people, Emma thought, I certainly don't understand this generation.

"And what have you got there?" she asked.

"Nothing," the girl said, a little too quickly. "Just something I found. See you later." She turned and ran.

She's a strange one, Emma thought. No telling what she has. Besides, it's none of my business, I promised Nate. She stretched and started for home.

The still house unnerved her. She needed to hear the sound of a friendly voice. She called Sylvia to tell her what had happened. The two commiserated for a while then Emma hung up with a promise to keep her posted.

THAT EVENING Emma waited anxiously for Nate's call. She tried to read, but couldn't concentrate; started watching a made-for-TV movie, but quickly lost interest. Finally she found a nature program. At least she didn't have to follow a plot.

It was ten o'clock before the phone rang. Her hand shook as she grabbed it. "Hello."

"Hi, Sparrow. Relax. I can hear the anxiety in your voice."

"How is he?"

"Stable. Fortunately they were able to start treatment right away, before there was any damage. They gave him some of those new 'clot-busting' drugs. Then they did an angiogram and put in one of those, whatever you call them, those things to keep the vessel open. He's one of the lucky ones."

Emma realized she had been holding her breath. She let it out slowly, feeling the tension release.

"That's good news. Do you know how long he'll be in the hospital?"

"They want to run a few more tests tomorrow. Then, if everything looks okay, he'll go home on Friday."

"That quick," Emma said, surprised.

"They don't keep people in hospitals any longer than absolutely necessary these days. It keeps costs down, and folks do better in their own homes anyway."

Emma hesitated to ask him when he would be home; she missed him already.

Almost as though he'd read her mind, he added, "Sparrow, if you don't mind, I want to stay here for a few days to make sure he's following orders. He can be a stubborn old coot. Besides, my sister-in-law needs the moral support."

Emma hadn't met Nate's family yet. They had been too busy with the move. He'd told her his sister-in-law was a delightful woman, but that his brother could be intimidating.

"Of course. Stay as long as you need to."

"Are you all right?" he asked, a hesitant tone in his voice.

"I'm fine. No problems."

"I'll probably be home sometime midweek," he said. "Miss you, my love."

"I miss you, too," she said, a little too quickly.

"I'll keep you posted. And, keep out of trouble."

"I will. Love you."

"Love you, too."

When she hung up the phone, Emma sat for a long time staring out at the lake. She realized that her hands were shaking.

Get a hold of yourself, Emma Winberry. He'll only be gone a few days and you're acting like a child, she silently scolded herself. She realized how much he had become part of her life; she didn't want to face even one day without him.

ELEVEN

EMMA SLEPT FITFULLY that night—disturbing dreams filled with premonitions of danger. She woke feeling real fear—her heart pounding, breaths coming in short gasps, her body bathed in sweat.

When she looked at the clock it was only five-thirty. "I'm not even going to try to go back to sleep. Might as well get up." The sound of her own voice gave her a little comfort. She didn't feel quite so alone.

She dragged herself out of bed, took a warm shower, dressed in shorts and T-shirt, then downed two cups of coffee.

It was Friday. The following day was Sylvia's birthday party, but Emma was no longer even looking forward to it. Nonsense, she told herself. As soon as I see my children and grandkids, I'll feel better. But she knew that coming back to the empty house would make her miss Nate all the more.

With a deep sigh, she slipped on a pair of sandals and went downstairs for the morning paper. With the paper under her arm, a third cup of coffee and a raisin bran muffin in hand she went out onto the roof garden.

She took a bite of the muffin as she scanned the news. Nothing new—the same worldwide problems that had existed for millennia.

On the third page she noticed a follow-up article on the murder of the inventor, Samuel Porter. The police were tracking down a few leads. That means they haven't got a clue, Emma thought. The family was offering a ten-thousand-dollar reward for information leading to the killer. I'll bet the police love that. Dead end calls will flood the lines.

From the corner of her eye she saw Tracie inching toward the gate, cuddling something furry in her arms.

"Good morning, Tracie. Come over and show me what you have there."

The girl opened the latch, but hesitated a moment before approaching Emma. She smiled as she revealed a tiny tiger-striped kitten, with huge inquisitive green eyes, mewling softly.

"What an adorable kitten," Emma said reaching out and stroking the soft fur. "Where did you get it?"

"I found it, near Lincoln Park."

So that was what she was hiding, Emma thought.

"Laura said I can keep it as long as it stays in my room," Tracie said.

"What about your uncle?"

"He's out of town. He doesn't like animals, but if I keep it in my room, he won't mind. That's what Laura said." But the girl looked worried.

She sounds as if she's trying to convince herself, Emma thought, breaking off half of the muffin. She pushed it toward the girl. Tracie took a small bite on a corner and gave the kitten a few crumbs.

"What's its name?" Emma asked.

"Hope," she whispered.

Emma looked at Tracie's thin spiked hair in its rainbow of colors. She took in the various rings hanging from the girl's gaunt face and from her ears, as well as the new thick logs she had pushed through the lobes. Emma shuddered. Hope—it sounded like a strange name for an animal—but Emma knew it came from Tracie's own need for something positive in her life.

"Thanks for the muffin," the girl said and hurried back home.

How I wish I could help her, Emma thought. But what can I do besides be here for her?

Emma looked at the clock. It was still early. She thought for a moment then picked up the phone, checked the number in her book, and punched it in.

"Hallo."

"Maria, is that you?"

"Emma." Her old friend's delight carried over the wires. "I miss you, Emma."

"I miss you, too. I was wondering if we could go out to lunch today."

"You come over here. I make you a good Italian lunch, linguini with clam sauce and anchovies. I know how much you like that."

Maria's warmth dispelled the loneliness that Emma felt.

"And Nate, he come, too?" Maria asked.

"No, he's in Florida. His brother had a heart attack."

"*Madonna mia,* is it bad?"

Emma could see Maria making the sign of the cross as she always did in a crisis. "He's recovering nicely."

"But you lonesome, huh?" Maria laughed. "I know you. What time you be here?"

"Yes, you do know me, too well. How about around noon?"

"Good, good. Now I get busy."

"Bye, Maria."

Emma smiled remembering all the years they had shared as neighbors and friends; their children growing up in that friendly Brookfield neighborhood, supporting each other when problems arose. They had understood the pain when each of them was widowed within a few years. The bond remained strong even though they no longer lived side by side. After Maria had both her knees replaced, she sold her house and moved in with her daughter, Carmela.

Eagerly Emma boarded a bus to take her to the north side of the city. When she got off the bus, she looked around and spotted a tiny florist shop on the corner. As she walked in, the tinkling bell summoned a thin, friendly looking woman to the front.

"What can I do for you this lovely day?" she asked.

"I'm visiting a friend and want to take her some flowers."

The woman nodded, opened the refrigerated compartment and took out a lovely assortment of carnations. "These hold up best in this heat," she said.

"They are a pretty shade of pink, and so fresh," Emma remarked.

"Just came in this morning."

"I'll take them."

The two-block walk gave Emma an opportunity to study the neighborhood. Traditional Chicago bungalows lined the street. Each house sported a row of flowers in front, some more colorful than others. An evergreen tree grew at the corner of each lot as if an architect had laid out the plan for foliage when the houses were built.

She spotted Maria waving from the doorway. Emma hurried her step and was soon in the embrace of the round motherly woman.

"Emma, Emma, beautiful flowers." She accepted the bouquet graciously and led her friend into the house. The familiar smells of garlic and spices gave Emma a twinge of homesickness for their former lifestyle.

She looked around the living room. "Maria, isn't this the furniture from your old house?"

"*Si.*"

"You took off the plastic covers."

"Eh, my daughter don't want plastic. Says it's too hot to sit on. So now the couch is dirty already. She say, 'Don't worry, Ma. We clean it.'" Maria shrugged in her familiar way.

"I'm so glad to see you," Emma said.

"Come in the kitchen. Carmela wants to say hello."

Emma walked through the formal dining room into a thoroughly modern kitchen with oak cabinets lining the walls. The stove and refrigerator were state-of-the art. A microwave oven was built into the wall with more dials than Emma cared to master.

"Carmela, I haven't seen you in years."

The woman gave Emma a warm welcoming smile. She was a younger version of her mother, but stylishly dressed, her hair short and curled around her face.

"So," she said, "you finally put on a little weight, huh? Love is good for you." She let out an earthy laugh.

Emma felt herself blush. "I have to admit, I'm very happy with Nate."

"There's nothing like the love of a good man," she continued. "Ma has been flirting with the old man next door. Huh, Ma?" She gave Maria a nudge in the ribs with her elbow.

"Eh, he's pretty nice. We talk, that's all." Maria frowned and turned her back to the two, busying herself with the clam sauce.

"I'm going shopping," Carmela said. "You need anything?"

"No, no, go."

"You two have a good visit. Bye."

"That Carmela, she's so pushy," Maria said. "She thinks I should throw myself at that *vecchio* next door. He's just somebody to talk to, about the old days."

But Emma saw the light in her friend's eye and was happy for her.

As they enjoyed their lunch, they caught up with each other's lives. Over coffee and *biscotti,* they heard the front door open.

"I'm home," a voice called out.

"Connie, come and see who's here," Maria said.

A svelte young woman walked into the kitchen swaying her hips and smiling.

"Mrs. Winberry, hi," she squealed.

"Connie, you've grown into a lovely woman," Emma said, remembering Maria's granddaughter as a skinny girl with scraggly hair. Now her body was a soft round of voluptuous curves. Her luxurious locks were pulled back in an elaborate twist.

"Connie works in a beauty shop," Maria said proudly.

"Salon, Gram, not shop. We serve a wealthy clientele and offer the latest hairdos and facials." She pointed her chin in a snobbish pose and pushed out her ample breasts.

"Very impressive," Emma said unable to take her eyes off this elegant creature.

"You wanna eat?" Maria asked.

"Not now, Gram. Got a date." She waved and bounded down the stairs to the lower level.

"Carmela and her husband had the basement made into kind of an apartment for the girls," Maria said. "When Gina got married, Connie got it all to herself."

Emma stayed the rest of the afternoon, then regretfully took her leave with promises by both women to see each other soon.

TWELVE

THE FOLLOWING DAY, Saturday, was sunny and hot with thunderstorms predicted for the evening. Emma boarded a bus on Michigan Avenue that would take her close to Sylvia and James's townhouse. From there she only had a three-block walk. Stephen had offered to pick her up, but she felt she needed the exercise. Besides, she didn't feel like talking about all the things that nagged at her.

As she sped past the tall buildings lining the street, people entered and exited the bus with regularity, some chatting, others carrying briefcases and looking businesslike. Where were they all going? Emma suddenly felt very much alone.

Guardian Angel, what's wrong with me? Why do I feel this way? Nate's brother is out of danger and he'll soon be home. I'm on my way to a pleasant day with my family. So why am I disturbed?

The dream she had the previous night bode more danger— for her. She was again locked in a prison cell awaiting judgment. What did it all mean?

Past experience told her that something unpleasant was about to happen to someone. Was it Tracie? Or could it be me this time? *Guardian Angel, protect me, please, and don't let me do anything foolish.*

"GRANDMA," JAMES JR. CRIED, running up to Emma and clasping his arms around her legs.

"Let go of Grandma, James," his father said, laughing.

"Before you knock her down."

"I swear," Emma said, "the child has almost doubled in size since I last saw him."

"He's going through a growth spurt," Sylvia said, "and completely wearing me out."

Frankie peeked out from behind his mother, babbling and tottering on short, stubby legs. "And this one wants to do everything his brother does."

"Hi, Frankie," Emma said as the child shied away from her. She noticed the fresh bruise on his forehead. "What happened here?"

Sylvia shook her head. "He was trying to catch James and ran into the wall." She gave a deep sigh, picked up her younger son and preceded Emma out onto the enclosed patio of the townhouse. The space was just large enough to accommodate a table and four chairs with room on the side for the children to play. Toys had been stacked in the corner to make room for the family. Folding chairs and tray tables crowded into the area.

Emma greeted her sons, Stephen and Martin, and their wives, Pat and Bertie. Stephen's daughter Susan ran up to her with a hug and a kiss. Her younger brother David sat in a bouncy chair, bobbing up and down and clapping his hands.

"My, my," Emma said. "Am I a lucky Grandma, surrounded by healthy, loving children." Suddenly a picture of Tracie came into her mind. What kind of child had she been? From what Laura had said, Tracie didn't come from a family like this one. The thought made Emma sad.

"Mom," Sylvia called, "can you come into the kitchen and give me a hand, please?"

The caterers had just arrived depositing pans of chicken, roast beef, potatoes, vegetables, and salad. Bertie came in to help, too, while Pat took charge of the children. The men were lost in talk of sports and politics.

"We've outgrown this place long ago," Sylvia said as they laid out the food and plastic utensils on the countertops.

"It is a little tight," Bertie said. "Are you looking for something bigger?"

"As a matter of fact, we are."

Emma raised her eyebrows. This was the first she'd heard about an impending move.

"James contacted a Realtor last week. We both agreed we need a house with a yard for the boys."

"What area are you thinking of?" Emma asked.

"We want to stay in the city so James can be close to work. There are some great bungalows a little bit north of here in the East Rogers Park area. We can sell this place in a heartbeat."

"Sounds like a good plan to me," Emma said.

Bertie looked at the two women with a wry smile. "Martin and I will be glad to baby-sit while you look at houses."

"That would be a big help," Sylvia agreed.

"It'll give us some practice," Bertie said, picking up a bowl of salad. A flush spread across her cheeks.

"Are you trying to tell us something, Bertie?" Emma asked, giving her daughter-in-law a surprised look.

"I'm two months pregnant."

Sylvia hugged her sister-in-law while Emma contemplated the wonder of another grandchild. How my family is growing. I hope I can remember all their birthdays, she thought.

After everyone had eaten their fill and gushed over the mother-to-be, they sang "Happy Birthday" to Sylvia and ate whipped cream cake. Sylvia opened her gifts as thunder rolled in the distance.

"It's almost like a Wagnerian opera heralding the doom of the gods," James said, laughing.

A chill ran through Emma. It sounded like a warning, but she shook it off and joined the women with the cleanup. She didn't object when Stephen insisted on driving her home.

Emma was exhausted when she closed the door behind her. Strange how this place had become a welcoming home in just a few short months.

The light on the answering machine winked at her. She depressed the button feeling a catch in her throat at the sound of Nate's voice.

"Hi, Sparrow. Guess you're still at the party. Everything is going well here. As I anticipated, my brother is being a total pain in the ass about following orders. I'll call you later."

Emma fidgeted and paced until Nate's call came.

"Hi, Sparrow. How was the party?"

His voice sounded tired and strained.

"It was fine, but everyone missed you. They all send their regards to your family." She wanted to add, "I can't stand being apart," but thought better of it.

He hesitated for a moment. "I may have to stay 'til the end of next week."

"Oh Nate, why?"

"There are some money matters to straighten out. My brother bought some risky stocks. I want to go over his portfolio and convince him to transfer the money into more conservative investments.

"And I would like to see my son and the grandkids while I'm down here."

"Of course."

"How about joining me? We could have a holiday."

"That sounds wonderful." Emma's heart beat a little faster at the thought.

"I'll check on flights," Nate said. "If you come down on Thursday, we can stay through the weekend. Okay?"

"Yes!"

Emma gave a sigh of relief as she hung up the phone. In five more days they would be together. How would she keep herself occupied for those five days?

THIRTEEN

UNCLE CAME HOME last night. He got mad when he saw Hope—said he didn't like animals, didn't want any around the house. For once Laura took my side. Told him I'd keep the kitten in my room and he'd never see it. He said okay, but... I know he's mean. Wouldn't hesitate to throw Hope out the door. I'll keep her close to me, always.

They're talking again. Come on, Hope. Let's get right up close to the door. Maybe I'll hear something to help us get out of here. It's all about business and money. Sounds like Uncle owes somebody a lot of money.

Shit! I probably won't find any around the house. Haven't had a chance to look yet.

Now they're arguing about me. Laura's telling him about the razor and how freaked out she was. He says he doesn't care what I do to myself as long as I stay out of his way.

Now they're fighting about something else. Can't hear, but Uncle sounds real mad. A slap! Don't know who got hit, but I'd better be careful or I'll be next. We've got to get out of here, real soon.

FOURTEEN

SUNDAY DRAGGED. Emma went to the movies but didn't enjoy the film. It was depressing, about a love affair between two unlikely people. She walked out before the end. On the way home she stopped at a bookstore and looked through the new arrivals, but nothing grabbed her. Finally she picked up a couple of new mysteries.

Why is it, she wondered, that for ten years after her husband died she had adjusted to being alone and didn't mind it? Now Nate had only been gone a few days and she was so lonely, couldn't wait for him to get back.

Of course, when she lived in Brookfield, she worked two days a week in a bookstore and spent a lot of time with Maria. Their visit the previous day brought back the old days and made Emma miss her that much more. But Maria seemed content living with her daughter.

That evening she saw Tracie out on the roof playing with her kitten. Emma waved her over.

"So how is everything going with Hope?"

"Pretty good," Tracie answered as she walked slowly through the gate and reached for a nasturtium blossom. "My uncle came home last night," she whispered, biting into the spicy flower.

"And?"

"At first he was mad, but then he said as long as Hope stays in my room, I can keep her."

"You can do that, can't you?"

"Sure, I can do anything I want to."

Emma looked closely at the girl. If it were possible, she seemed even thinner.

"Tracie, what kind of work does your uncle do?"

The girl shrugged. "He's in some kind of business. Don't know what. He's gone a lot." She looked down with only a slight side to side movement of her head. "I'm glad he's not around more."

"Why do you say that?"

"Because they're always arguing about something. Married people never seem to be happy." She kicked a pebble on the roof and the kitten scampered after it.

"That's not true," Emma said. "Don't judge all marriages by your parents or your aunt and uncle."

A pained expression crossed the girl's face. "I'm never gonna get married. Never."

Emma shook her head and frowned. The girl certainly had poor role models. "I want to ask you to do me a favor. I'm going away on Thursday, but I'll be back on Sunday. Will you water these plants on the roof and pick the ripe tomatoes?"

"Sure. And can I let Hope run around here?"

"Of course. I'll pay you for the job," Emma said, looking into the girl's eyes. For a moment they brightened, then took on their usual faraway look.

"You don't have to. You been nice to me. I'll take good care of them. Come on, Hope, we have to go back now."

Emma agonized over how to help this girl. She decided to make a batch of muffins in the morning and give them to her.

The next day Emma puttered around the kitchen rear-ranging things on the granite countertops. She had to admit, they were easy to keep clean. Then she turned to her butcher-block island and began some serious baking. After making two batches of muffins and freezing some, Emma decided to read one of the new mysteries. She opened the book, read a few pages, then put it down. It just wasn't grabbing her attention.

She was just about to go out for a walk when the phone rang.

"Hello."

"Mrs. Winberry?"

"Yes."

"This is George Watkins from Consolidated Film Company. You were an extra in a movie we shot in Chicago a couple of weeks ago."

Emma hesitated. "Yes, but I'm not interested in doing it again."

"Well, we're in kind of a bind. We need someone for one night only. The person scheduled for the role is ill and we have to shoot tomorrow night."

"Why are you calling me in particular?"

"Because we need someone about your size to play a street person. We plan to film it in one take. You would only have to be here for about two hours max. And we'll pay you for the entire day."

Emma considered it. It would give her something to do. And, more importantly, keep her out of trouble. She heaved a resigned sigh.

"All right."

"Great. Come down to the trailer—same place as before— this afternoon to sign the contract. They'll tell you where the shoot will take place and give you the clothes to wear. And thanks again, Mrs. Winberry."

When Emma hung up she had her doubts about this venture. She had promised Nate that they would never do it again. But this didn't involve him. He didn't even have to know, and it was only for two hours. What could possibly happen?

FIFTEEN

TUESDAY NIGHT EMMA found herself dressed in an old, dirty and torn sweat suit, with a cap pulled down over her ears. The makeup artist added some washable stain to her hands and face.

"Ouch!" she said pulling back as the makeup artist smeared the stain on her face. "I got some of that stuff in my eye. Hold on a minute. I'd better take out my contact lenses."

Emma quickly removed her lenses and put them in the container she always carried in her purse. She would lock it in the director's trailer.

When the woman held a mirror before her face, Emma hardly recognized herself. Of course, in some of the costumes and makeup for the opera, the result was the same, although a little more dignified.

Emma made her way to the trailer with some difficulty. Everything looked blurred. After depositing her purse, she followed an aide to the location.

The shoot took place in a shabby South Side area slated for urban renewal. Just a block away were signs of gentrification: old buildings boarded up; new facades on others; empty lots where some had already been torn down.

"Mrs. Winberry," the director instructed. "All you have to do is sit in that cardboard box covered with that old blanket. Huddle up in a corner, like you're cold."

Emma grimaced at the torn, dirty piece of cotton that passed for a blanket. At least it wasn't wool. Already she was soaked with sweat on this hot, muggy night.

"Are there any rats in this alley?" she asked, looking around at bags of garbage trailing out of a Dumpster.

"No, we checked the entire area. And all these garbage bags are filled with paper. There's nothing for you to worry about.

"The actors playing the police officers will search the alley, shine a flashlight into the box and walk away. They're supposed to be looking for a bearded man. Just grimace at the light and pull back. That's all."

That won't be difficult, Emma thought. No problem. I'll be out of here and back home in no time.

With a slight feeling of trepidation, she crawled into the box and pushed herself as far back as she could. It was a tight fit, but she made it. I shouldn't be doing this, she thought. Nate will be upset with me, but I really don't have to tell him. *Guardian Angel, are you here?*

While the principals were getting last-minute instructions from the director, Emma heard sounds coming from outside. First the muffled breaking of glass, then something scratching at the back of the box. Damn, there were rats here. She was about to crawl out, when the back of the box ripped away. Rough hands grabbed her. She was so startled, she couldn't cry out. A hand clamped over her mouth and a deep voice said, "Don't say a word or you're dead."

The smell of alcohol and rank sweat assailed her nostrils as strong arms dragged her out of the back of the box and through a broken window. Ragged spikes of glass cut through the sweat suit and gouged her arms and legs.

"Ugh," she groaned.

Someone wrapped a rag around her eyes. She tried to open her mouth, to bite the hand that held her in a stranglehold, but couldn't. She heard a ripping sound, then felt rough tape plastered across her mouth.

Oh God, she thought, they're going to kill me and I don't

even know why. Will my family ever find my body? *Guardian Angel, where are you?*

"Okay, Minnie," Deep Voice said, tying her hands behind her back with a rough fibrous binding. "We want what you took from that stiff in the alley."

Emma shook her head vigorously. How could she tell them they had the wrong person?

Deep Voice slapped her across the face so hard her ears rang. Stars bounced before her eyelids. Tears seeped out from under the blindfold.

"Don't ever say no to me, ever."

"Whath's all the commotion in the alley?" a piping voice asked.

"I dunno. Let's get out'a here." He lifted her and threw her across his shoulders like a sack of potatoes and quickly walked away from the sounds.

They're looking for me, Emma thought. She heard someone call her name. If only she could cry out, but she was trussed up like a hog going to slaughter.

Emma heard two sets of footsteps, the one carrying her and one other. The only way I'll ever be able to identify these two is by their voices. Despite the terror she felt, she realized she had to listen carefully to these two.

Is that you, Guardian Angel? Where have you been?
Listen.

"Thith way," the piping voice said.

He has a high-pitched lisp, I must remember that.

"Come on," Deep Voice said. "Into the truck."

Oh no, they're taking me away. Emma winced as she felt herself thrown on the floor of a vehicle. Doors slammed, the engine missed, then caught, and the truck rumbled away.

SIXTEEN

SYLVIA HAD SPENT the last hour cajoling her sick children. They had coughed and moaned until the cold medication finally took hold. When the phone rang, she winced. Quietly closing the kids' bedroom door, she called out to her husband.

"James, will you please answer that before it wakes the boys?"

He spoke in a low tone, which was good. The last thing she needed was to have the two little ones woken up by Daddy's conversation. Wandering into the kitchen, she paused to watch her husband as he talked. The look on his face was unreadable. And it dawned on her that he wasn't just speaking softly for the kids' sake. Something was wrong.

When he ended the call, he came to her. "Sylvia." James sounded distraught.

"What is it?"

"Sit down." He took his wife's hands in his as he guided her toward the sofa. When she sat, he blew out a breath, then lowered himself next to her. "I don't know a good way to tell you this. Your mother is…missing."

"Missing? What do you mean? How can she be missing?" Sylvia couldn't comprehend her husband's words.

"That was the movie company. Remember when she and Nate were extras in that film?"

"Yes, but they weren't going to do that anymore."

"Well, apparently Emma decided to give it another try.

She was supposed to be a street person in just one take, but she disappeared."

"I don't understand." Sylvia sat there, totally bewildered. Her husband's words didn't register on her brain.

"I'm going down there," James said. "Where's Nate?"

"In Florida, with his sick brother."

"Do you have the number?"

"No," she whispered dropping her head in her hands as the reality of the situation began to take hold.

James put his arms around her. "It's probably just a mistake. You know your mom sometimes gets things a little mixed up. I'll call you on my cell phone as soon as I know the details."

WHEN JAMES ARRIVED at the spot where the movie was being filmed, he saw two police cars and yellow tape cordoning off an area in the alley.

"Sorry sir, you can't go in there," an officer said, blocking his way.

"I'm James Greene, from the Midwest Opera. Mrs. Winberry's son-in-law. We received a call from the director. Who's in charge here?" His executive tone produced immediate results.

"Right this way, sir."

James spotted the one he presumed to be the director. The man stood shifting his weight from one foot to the other and wringing his hands. He spoke to an imposing man taking notes. James walked up to the two and introduced himself.

"I'm George Watkins, the director of Consolidated Films," the harried one blurted out. "And this is Detective Spaulding."

The detective frowned at the director and took over the inquiry. "Mr. Greene, were you aware that Mrs. Winberry had agreed to act as an extra in this film?"

James shook his head. "No, she didn't say anything about it."

Mr. Watkins broke in. "I called Mrs. Winberry yesterday and asked if she'd fill in for the woman who was scheduled to appear. She had a personal emergency."

"She never told us," James said, exhaling the breath he had been holding.

"It was just supposed to be for a couple of hours," Mr. Watkins continued. "Oh God, nothing like this has ever happened before."

"Just what did happen?" James asked becoming annoyed with the man.

Detective Spaulding held up his hand to quiet Watkins who was sputtering and pacing back and forth.

"Mrs. Winberry was in that cardboard box over there." He pointed to the box being carefully examined by his team. "Apparently someone cut through the back of the box and pulled her through a broken window of that abandoned building right beside the alley. We found blood droplets on the floor inside."

James winced at the thought of helpless Emma hurt and abducted for no apparent reason.

The detective turned to Watkins. "Are any of Mrs. Winberry's personal effects around?"

The man looked at the detective with a vacant expression. "Uh, I think her handbag is in the trailer, over there."

"I'll need that. There just might be some clue as to why this happened." He turned his attention back to James. "Do you know why anyone would want to harm Mrs. Winberry?"

He shook his head. "Absolutely not. She's a quiet woman, not involved in anything that would precipitate something like this."

"We'll find her, Mr. Greene," the detective assured him. "Please go with this officer and give him all the information we might need."

James nodded and walked away with the officer. He felt a spasm twist his gut. What would he tell Sylvia?

SEVENTEEN

As EMMA BOUNCED around on the floor of the truck, she became aware of a stinging sensation on her arms and legs. *Those thugs pulled me through that broken window. I wonder if there's glass in these cuts? What else will they do to me before this is over?*

After a short ride, she felt herself being dragged from the vehicle. A gentle refreshing rain on her face gave her a moment's relief. She took a deep breath before the thug slung her over his shoulder again.

They entered a building reeking of stale air, urine and other odors that Emma didn't want to identify. As the man dropped her on the floor, Emma's head knocked against the concrete. A wave of dizziness and nausea washed over her. Dots danced before her bound eyes. For a moment she wavered between reality and oblivion.

"Be careful, or ththe won't be able to tell uth nothin'," Squeaky said.

"Okay, Minnie," said Deep Voice. "No more stallin'. Where is it?" He grabbed the end of the tape and ripped it away—white hot pain seared her face as the tape came off—taking bits of skin with it.

"Ouch!" Emma yelled, shaken to full consciousness. She spoke as fast as she could, trying to make them understand. "You've made a mistake. My name is Emma Winberry. I'm an extra for the movie that's being filmed in that alley. I don't know anyone named Minnie."

One of the men grabbed her legs, then pinched and pulled on them. "Ththe'th right. Ththe'th got two legs. Ththe ain't Minnie."

"That's what I told you," Emma said.

"Christ! We grabbed the wrong dame," Deep Voice shouted.

"The bawth won't like that," Squeaky lisped.

"Don't you think I know? Okay, Genius, who told you Minnie would be in that alley?"

"Danny the Dago thaid that'th her alley."

"Sure, like she owns it," the other one said with scorn. "That's what I get for listening to you. We'll just have to find Minnie."

"And what do we do with thith one?"

"Please, just let me go," Emma pleaded.

"Can't do that, lady."

"We ain't gonna kill 'er, are we?"

"Shut up and lemme think."

Emma could hear the man pacing and cursing under his breath. She bit down on her tongue gently to increase the flow of saliva in her mouth, then ran her tongue over her bleeding lips. Ouch, that hurt. *Guardian Angel, protect me.*

"We could toth her in the river," Squeaky suggested.

"Any more bright ideas? We ain't dumpin' nobody in the river. Let's just leave her here. The way she's tied up, she ain't goin' nowhere. By the time somebody finds her…" He left the sentence unfinished, but Emma got the message.

"Thorry, lady," Squeaky said. "You wath just in the wrong place at the wrong time."

EIGHTEEN

NATE PICKED UP the phone and punched in the numbers as if the instrument were his enemy. It rang, over and over, until the answering machine kicked in and he heard his own voice asking the caller to leave a message.

"Emma, where are you? I've called three times and you're not there. Call me."

Maybe she spent the night at Sylvia's, he thought, looking through his pockets for his phone book. Where is that thing? He noticed his hands trembling as he found the book and checked the number.

Sylvia answered on the first ring. "Hello?" Her voice sounded tired and strained.

"It's Nate. Is your mother there?"

"Oh Nate. I wanted to call you, but didn't have your number. Something terrible…" She began to cry so hard she couldn't continue.

"Sylvia," Nate called out. "What is it? What's wrong?"

A pause, then James's voice came over the line. "Nate, I…" His voice sounded ready to crack, too. "I have bad news. Emma's missing."

"What are you talking about? How can she be missing?" He listened in disbelief as James told him the incredible story. Nate's hands shook so he almost dropped the phone. His legs grew weak; his head spun.

"So far, the police haven't found her," James said, his voice almost a whisper.

"I'll be home on the next flight."

After Nate hung up, he sat with his head in his hands trying to make sense of it all. It wasn't possible. This couldn't be happening, not to them. Emma, my little Sparrow, why did I leave you alone in the city?

"Nate, what's the matter?" His sister-in-law, Rachel, hurried to him and put her hands on his trembling shoulders.

He looked up at her anxious face. "Emma's in trouble. I have to go home."

"Is it serious?"

"I don't know. They can't find her."

"What do you mean?" Rachel asked, clenching her fists.

"She was playing a part in a movie…didn't tell me…disappeared from the set…"

"Oh my God!"

"Don't tell Sal. It would only worry him. Just tell him there are some problems with the condo that I must take care of. I'll call you as soon as I can. And, Rachel, say a prayer."

She nodded as he picked up the phone and called the airlines.

NATE WAITED IN the terminal for the flight to Chicago. It was delayed due to violent thunderstorms over the entire Midwest. He felt as if he were in a dream world. Any moment he would wake and find out that none of this was really happening.

He went over and over all the things James had said, but nothing made sense. Emma had been just as turned off by their experience as extras as he had. What made her change her mind? Who had taken his little Sparrow? What had they done with her? He went up to the desk and asked, again, if there was any departure time scheduled.

"Sir," the distraught girl said, "I told you before, we don't know any more than you do. As soon as we get the notice, we'll announce it."

"Thanks. Sorry to bother you." He turned away feeling like

a broken old man. He walked to a bar in the terminal and ordered a double scotch, neat. A ballgame played on the television set. Patrons laughed and cheered when their team made a home run.

How can people be carefree and happy when my Emma is missing? He visualized her, frightened, maybe in pain, maybe…No! That picture he blotted out of his mind.

"Flight 259 to Chicago O'Hare is now ready to board."

Nate downed the scotch and ran to the gate.

BY THE TIME the plane landed and he was able to get a cab, it was five-thirty. A steady fall of rain and poor visibility further hampered the rush-hour crush of traffic. Nate wanted to urge the driver on, but there was nowhere to go. The lines of cars inched along like snails on a lettuce leaf.

Nate took out his cell phone and tried Sylvia's number. No signal. Damn thing was out of juice again. It's old and useless, he thought, just like me. Out of frustration he threw the phone on the floor, swearing.

"You okay, mister?" the driver asked.

"No," he said, trying to control his voice.

"Yeah, the traffic, the rain. It's a real bitch," the driver said.

"Yes it is." Nate didn't say any more, unable to face the possibilities.

It was almost seven by the time the cab reached the condo. Nate handed the driver twice the fare and ran into the building.

He opened the door and held his breath—hoping. "Emma?" No answer, only the lonely feel of an empty house. The blinking light on the answering machine caught his attention. Four messages. He depressed the button and heard his own voice. The first three messages were from him, but the fourth was from a Detective Spaulding.

"Mr. Sandler, we were given your name as Mrs. Winberry's partner. Please call me at…"

With trembling fingers, Nate punched in the numbers.
"Spaulding here."

"This is Nate Sandler. Has Emma Winberry been found?"

"Not yet, sir, but we do have some evidence."

"What kind of evidence?" By now Nate was half hysterical and he knew it was reflected in his voice.

"We know that she was removed from the abandoned building. A thorough search turned up some drops of blood and a scrap of fabric from the clothing she was wearing at the time.

"We found two sets of footprints in the dust on the floor and tire marks from a vehicle that pulled away from the back of the building. By the imprint, it appears to be a small truck or van."

"I thought the movie company was supposed to check out the area for safety," Nate said, his voice rising in frustration.

"They did, sir. The building was thoroughly inspected, but there was a trapdoor in the alley leading into the basement. A Dumpster obstructed it from sight. This is where we found the tire tracks."

"So what next?"

"We're looking for any vehicle in the area that we can match to the tire casts and questioning anyone who might have seen anything.

"We have Mrs. Winberry's purse, but didn't find anything inside to give us any clues, only a copy of the contract and a case with a pair of contact lenses."

"Why would she take out her contacts?" Nate stammered. "She can't see a thing without them."

"I can't answer that," the detective said. "And, after questioning her son-in-law, I don't think this was a planned kidnapping with Mrs. Winberry as the target. But, please have someone at the phone at all times, just in case you get a ransom call."

"Can I offer a reward?" Nate asked.

"Not yet. We haven't disclosed Mrs. Winberry's name to the press. All they know at this time is that an extra has disappeared from a movie set. I'll keep you posted."

"Thanks," Nate said. He sank into a chair and laid his head against the backrest, his eyes wide with disbelief. "No," he cried. "No. No."

LATER NATE WANDERED OUT onto the roof garden. He had contacted Sylvia, told her he was back, and repeated his conversation with Detective Spaulding.

He sipped another scotch and sighed. At least the alcohol dulled his senses for a little while. When he looked at his watch, he wanted to cry. She had been missing for twenty hours. So many things could happen in that much time. *Emma, where are you?*

As he looked out over the placid water of the lake, he tried to connect with Emma's mind. If she did have a sixth sense, maybe she was trying to contact him, to tell him where she was. Over and over he tried to still his turbulent thoughts, but he couldn't concentrate, kept visualizing Emma unable to see, maybe injured, maybe… He gave up in frustration then felt someone staring at him. He turned to see Tracie inching her way toward the gate.

"Tracie, when did you last see Mrs. Winberry?" he asked.

She looked at him out of the corner of her eye. "Yesterday morning. I watered the plants today. Do you want me to keep on doing it?"

"Yes, please." *Emma would want her plants cared for. She'll be angry if I don't see that they're watered.*

"How about the ones in the atrium?" Tracie whispered.

"Huh?" Nate realized the girl had asked him something, but he didn't know what.

"Do you want me to water the plants in the atrium, too?"

"Yes, yes."

"Will Mrs. Win be gone long?" the girl asked, a worried expression on her face.

"No." He hesitated. "She'll be back very soon." His mind blotted out any other possibility.

Tracie nodded, picked up the watering can and walked timidly into the atrium.

Nate felt the feline eyes staring. He turned to see Hope looking at him, her head cocked to one side. "Mew," she said softly. The sound seemed to convey an understanding, as if the animal felt his distress.

"Mew," she said again, then sat and began licking her paw.

NINETEEN

MR. NATE IS WORRIED. I can tell. Something happened to Mrs. Win. She wasn't supposed to go away until Thursday. That's what she said. But maybe I got the day wrong. She's the only one who's been nice to me. I hope she's okay.

Uncle and Laura just went out. This is my chance to look around—see if I can find any money. Don't know how long they'll be gone, so I'd better hurry.

The desk—that's the first place I'll look. Nothing in this drawer but blank paper and envelopes. This middle drawer is locked. I better not try to pry it open or they'll know.

Here's a letter tucked in this corner. No name on it. God, it's a threat! That sounds bad. Uncle's in some kind of trouble, maybe something crooked. Wouldn't surprise me. He's kind of shifty.

Gotta figure a way for me and Hope to get out of here. Maybe I can find some jewelry in Laura's dresser that I can sell.

Oh, oh. The key in the lock. They're back. Better get in my room—fast.

TWENTY

EMMA HAD NO IDEA how long she had lain on the hard concrete floor. The dampness seeped into every joint of her body. She had screamed and called for help until her voice dwindled to a croak. She floated in and out of consciousness. Saw a pitcher of water suspended above her, a drop at the lip. She opened her parched mouth, but the drop didn't fall. "Water," she groaned. Still, the drop hung just out of reach.

Then a vision of a fat, juicy strawberry came into view. Again she reached for it, to no avail. She moaned and tried to get into a comfortable position, but she could hardly move.

A sound brought her back to the present. What was it? Emma wasn't sure. She shivered then realized how thirsty she was. No matter how many times she bit down on her tongue, no saliva filled her mouth. She ran her tongue over her sore lips and felt bumps forming between the cracks.

Oh great! That must have been duct tape on my mouth. Don't they know I'm allergic to that stuff?

How ridiculous that sounds. How could they know?

Why am I thinking of such nonsense? I have to figure a way out of here.

A skittering noise caught her attention. Rats!

"Stay away, rodents. I'm warning you." The sound of her rasping voice startled them and they ran, but she knew they would be back. What could she do? She was helpless.

Find the wall, a voice within said.

Is that you, Guardian Angel? What did you say?

Find the wall.

The wall. Certainly. She had no idea how large the room was. When she had screamed, she heard her voice bounce back like an echo. It seemed like a large cavernous space, but there had to be a wall somewhere.

She was stiff and sore, her hands tied behind her back with rough heavy twine, her ankles tied together with the same binding. She lay on her right side.

If I can turn on my back and pull up my knees, maybe I can scoot backwards to the wall. With a heave, she rolled onto her back. Every part of her body ached. *No time to think about pain. Think of the rats. Think of water. Think of your family.*

Oh God, if I don't die here, Nate will surely kill me for getting into this fix. Why didn't I listen to him?

She managed to bend her knees and, with all the strength she could muster, scooted backwards. After a few minutes of that, her backside was rubbed almost raw. *No good. There had to be another way.*

All right, Emma Winberry, think. If she turned back on her side and raised her feet behind her, she just might be able to untie the rope around her ankles.

"Damn! I'm not as agile as I used to be," she muttered. The skittering sound again. The closer it came, the more determined she was. She rolled over, then grabbed and groaned until she was able to reach one end of the rope with her right hand. *Now, if I could just get the other end with my left hand, I might be able to untie it.*

She struggled and pulled until her hands were sore and she was exhausted. Her head grew woozy; she lay there and seemed to float. Her mind took her out of the cavernous space and into the starry night. She felt free, her arms waving in the cool breeze, her legs free of their bindings. She dozed fitfully, then woke suddenly as a furry creature brushed against her arm, her nostrils assaulted by the rank odor of the rat.

"Get away!" she said in a voice barely audible. I've got to get free, got to get out of here.

Find a wall, the voice said again.

How can I find a wall when I can barely move? Think, think, she told herself.

You've been practicing yoga, the voice said.

It's been a while, Emma thought, but I'm still fairly flexible. She made a mental note to sign up for the yoga classes advertised at the local health club, that is, if she got out of here alive. Of course I will!

Again she rolled onto her back and lay there, panting. It was such an effort. Skittering. Closer. With grim determination she arched her back and began moving her bound hands toward her buttocks. Perspiration streamed down her face.

Her long limbs and narrow hips worked to her advantage. As she struggled, she realized she would have to lay her hands flat against the floor. She pulled the binding apart as hard as she could. It stretched just enough to maneuver her hands, but, oh, did it hurt.

Oh God! I'm going to cut off the circulation if I pull any harder.

Just a little more, the voice said.

Emma gave a tug. She managed to flatten her hands, the palms against her body, the outside scraping on the concrete. Then she pushed them downward, rocking her body from side to side. She grimaced as, with each move, she felt the skin of her knuckles tear. She moaned, took a deep breath, and moved a little more.

Finally she reached the position she wanted, her hands under her buttocks. She flexed her knees up to her chest and pulled her hands under her backside.

With her waning strength, she managed to sit up and release the tension on the bindings. Then she twisted her hands to their original position and let the blood flow back into her fingers.

Again she grew lightheaded and short of breath. *If I only had a drink of water.*

The skittering of the rats came closer.

"Move, Emma, move!" she commanded. She sat for a moment panting. Now she should be able to reach the rope around her ankles. She stretched. Yes! She had it! Her bleeding, shaking fingers fumbled for the knot. She pulled and pushed the rough fibers until she felt them begin to loosen. As a rat touched her foot, she pulled the end through. Her legs were free! She kicked at the rodent and heard it run away.

Emma cried out with joy and relief. She didn't care that her hands were bleeding, that her body ached all over. But she still had one more maneuver. She took a few deep breaths, remembering the yoga moves, then slowly, one leg at a time, squeezed her legs through her hands and arms. Now, at least, her hands were in front of her. She raised them to her face and pulled off the blindfold.

Everything was still pitch black. She realized that she didn't have her contacts, but she should still be able to see light, if there was any.

Okay, she told herself. Stand up. She got into a kneeling position, then slowly pushed against the concrete with her bound hands until she was upright.

Her head buzzed; she felt herself swaying. She couldn't even put her arms out for balance. All she could do was widen her stance, her feet as far apart as possible. She bent over slightly until the wooziness passed.

Then, like a blind person, she held her hands out in front of her and slowly began to creep along.

TWENTY-ONE

Nate jumped every time the phone rang. It was either Sylvia or one of her brothers wondering if there was any news.

"I'll call when I hear something," he said in an exhausted voice. "Please don't call me. Every time the phone rings I think it may be the police with news." He didn't want to sound rude, but he was beside himself with worry.

He looked at the half-empty bottle of scotch. He'd better not drink any more. Had to be clear-headed when Detective Spaulding called. He couldn't bring himself to think that perhaps he wouldn't call—perhaps they would never find Emma—perhaps... Raised voices from the roof garden caught his attention. What's going on out there? Nate walked unsteadily into the atrium. He could just make out three figures next door, Tracie and her aunt and uncle in a heated argument.

None of my business, he thought. I've got enough problems of my own. But he cracked the atrium door and hid behind one of Emma's huge plants.

"I told you I don't want any animals in the house," a male voice shouted.

"But she's keeping it in her room. You said it would be all right. The kitten got out by accident." Mrs. Evans's placating tone.

"Please, Uncle," Tracie pleaded.

"I'll give you one more chance. If I see that cat loose anywhere in the house again, out it goes. And I mean it!"

Nate watched the two adults walk into the condo. Tracie sat

on a bench, her head bowed, the furry ball clutched in her arms. He could just see her thin shoulders heaving. He shook his head, closed the door and walked into the silent living room.

In the dark, he tripped over a stool, threw himself onto the couch, and began the longest night of his life.

EMMA STUMBLED OVER what felt like chunks of concrete, but, with concentration, she managed to keep from falling. She tried calling with the little voice she had left and listened for the echo. Something told her she was getting closer to a wall. She tried to maintain the same direction, but it was difficult in the dark.

What's that sliver of light? A target. She walked faster. It looked like it was coming from a window, but it was only a thin straight line.

Finally her hands touched what felt like wood. It was a window—boarded up. She pounded on the boards, but they didn't budge.

Don't waste your strength, the inner voice said.

No, I mustn't, she thought. Don't have much left.

At least she had a wall to guide her. But which way should she go, right or left?

Right, go right.

Okay, Guardian Angel, right it is.

She crept along the wall until she came to a corner. She could feel the uneven edge. Maybe I can cut through this rope, she thought. She began sawing the thick fibers around her wrists along the rough corner.

"Ouch!" She kept scraping her arms against the concrete, but ignored the pain and the trickle of blood. Emma kept on rubbing until she felt the fibers begin to fray. Harder! I have to get free.

The sounds of the rats gave her an added adrenaline rush. She gave a vigorous pull and her hands parted. "Oh God, thank You." She rubbed her wrists and felt the grooves where the rope had pulled. No time for that now. She could walk faster, using both hands as she guided herself against the wall.

Another corner. Cautiously she felt around it, then looked—a window. In the distance moonlight shone through a clouded window. Emma almost ran toward the light.

Suddenly she realized she was in a small room. A shabby mattress lay in the center surrounded by boxes and crates. The smell of sweat and rotting food assailed her nostrils. Lights danced before her eyes as exhaustion and dehydration claimed the last of her energy. She fell onto the mattress as blackness engulfed her.

Emma was dreaming of her comfortable bed at home, the soft fluffy pillow, the ceiling fan casting a gentle breeze on her body.

What was that? Someone was bumping against the bed. Hesitantly she opened her eyes and squinted.

A dark figure loomed over her, silhouetted against the light coming from the window.

TWENTY-TWO

"HEY, LADY, WHAT you doin' in my bed? This ain't the house o' the three bears and you sure ain't Goldilocks. Get out'a here, now!"

A bright flash of light made Emma squeeze her eyes shut as the memories of the past hours flooded into her consciousness. Her head throbbed; her lips burned; her entire body ached. She just managed a whisper. "Please, help me. I'm hurt."

The dark figure shone the flashlight over her body.

"Holy shit! You bleedin'. What happened to yer mouth?"

"Water…"

"Okay, hang on. I got some right here. It ain't too fresh, but it's wet."

Gently he held Emma's head up and pressed a glass to her lips. The water smelled of sulfur, but, to Emma, it was manna from Heaven. She grasped the glass and gulped the liquid, ignoring the pain in her raw lips.

"Oh," she sighed and leaned back on the mattress.

"How'd you git here?" the man asked.

Hesitantly Emma told him. "I was an extra in a movie—sitting in a box in an alley—abducted by thugs…"

"Ab what?"

"Abducted—taken—kidnapped."

"You mean you was snatched?"

"Yes. Please, call nine-one-one. I need help."

He shook his head vigorously. "Oh no. I don't have nothin'

to do with the police. I show you how to git out'a here an you on your own, lady."

"All right." Emma tried to sit up, but dizziness and nausea washed over her in a wave as she fell back.

"Come on. I'll help ya."

He grabbed her arm and pulled her up to a sitting position, then tried to help her stand, but her legs buckled.

"I can't," she whispered.

"Okay, okay. I carry ya. If ya don't mind a smelly old black man puttin' his arms aroun' ya."

His face was close enough for Emma to see a smile and kindly eyes. "You're my Knight in Shining Armor," she whispered as she raised her arms.

Gently he lifted her like one would a child.

"There ain't nothin' to ya. What kinda' low life did this to a helpless little old lady like you? I better take you someplace where you can git help."

Emma leaned her head against his broad chest. He smelled of sour sweat and dirt, but she didn't care. She didn't care that he had called her a little old lady. He was her savior.

She slipped in and out of consciousness as she felt his movements. Vaguely she heard a door open and felt fresh air wash over her aching body.

"There's a joint up ahead, open all night. I take ya there. Sam'll call for help. You be all right."

His voice sounded soothing and caring. After a while Emma heard another door open, then voices.

"Sam, this here lady needs help. She been snatched and she hurt. Call nine-one-one," the black man said.

"She don't look so good," another voice said. "Put her down on that bench and I'll call right away."

Emma felt the hard wooden bench as her Knight gently laid her down.

"You be okay now, ya hear?" he whispered in her ear.

"How can I thank you? What's your name?"

"No need for thanks. I ain't nobody." He squeezed her hand and was gone. Emma lost all track of time. She heard a siren in the distance; felt hands lifting her onto a stretcher; heard voices calling orders. "Blood pressure eighty over fifty—shock—dehydration. Start a liter of intravenous fluids..." She was safe now. *Thank you, Guardian Angel, for sending me my Knight.*

TWENTY-THREE

AT THE FIRST RING of the phone, Nate's eyes opened wide. His heart pounded so hard he could hear the blood rushing in his ears. He reached for the instrument, his hand trembling violently.

"Hello." He held his breath, steeling himself.

"Mr. Sandler, this is Detective Spaulding. Sorry to call so early, but I have good news. We found Mrs. Winberry."

Nate let out his breath with a sob. "Where is she? Is she—all right?"

"She's at Rush, in the medical complex. She's injured, but nothing serious. They're treating her for shock and dehydration, but the doctors say she'll be fine. I'm on my way to question her now."

"Thank God. I'll meet you there, Detective." Nate sat on the side of the bed, tears streaming down his face. "Sparrow, my little Sparrow. You're alive."

He looked at the clock—the hands pointing to five—picked up the phone and punched in Sylvia's number. James answered and said he would meet him at the hospital. Nate could hear Sylvia crying in the background.

He showered and dressed and was out the door in fifteen minutes. He needed a cup of coffee, but that could wait until after he saw Emma.

The emergency room was quiet. The night shift had efficiently triaged the stabbings, fevers, heart attacks and accident victims.

They were preparing to hand over the responsibilities of

saving lives to the next shift. A woman from housekeeping carefully mopped the floors, erasing any trace of the traumas of the night.

Nate hurried to the desk and looked into the tired face of a nurse making a note in a chart.

"I'm Nate Sandler. I'm here for Emma Winberry. Detective Spaulding called me."

"Oh yes," the nurse said. "She came in by ambulance a while ago. I think the doctors are about finished. Wait here a minute, please."

She disappeared through a glass door and into a cubicle surrounded by a privacy curtain. Nate wanted to run after her. He held on to the desk, suddenly feeling lightheaded.

Soon another tired professional with a stethoscope hanging around his neck approached Nate.

"Mr. Sandler? I'm Doctor Abowitz." He offered his hand.

"How is she, Doctor?" Nate gripped the hand with both of his.

"We have her stabilized now. When she came in she was severely dehydrated, blood pressure low. After two liters of fluids, she's much better. She's had a mild concussion and has a number of scrapes and bruises on her face, arms, and legs. Apparently she was tied up and her mouth covered with duct tape."

Nate winced at the picture the doctor's words painted in his mind.

"She claims to be allergic to duct tape," the doctor continued. "So don't be alarmed by the pustules around her mouth. We've given her an antihistamine that should take care of it."

"All right. Please, let me see her."

The doctor nodded and led him into the cubicle. Nate stared at the inert figure lying on the bed looking so small and vulnerable. A dark red bruise spread down her left cheek; bandages encased her wrists and ankles. Big, angry-looking bumps circled her cracked, red lips.

"Sparrow," he whispered, dropping into a chair beside the bed.

"Nate?" she rasped. "Oh Nate, please forgive me." She opened her eyes and lifted her arms to him. Gently he embraced her; afraid to inflict more pain on her bruised body.

"Sparrow, there's nothing to forgive. I thought I had lost you. I'll never leave you alone again, ever."

"I'm okay," she croaked. "Really I am."

They stayed that way without speaking. Nate was afraid he would burst into tears. He brushed his hand against her unruly hair and felt a bump on the back of her head. She winced in pain.

A few minutes later a heavyset man in a disheveled suit walked into the cubicle. "I'm Detective Spaulding." He shook Nate's hand, the grasp strong and comforting. His face wore the map of many years of looking at pain and death. Dark circles under his eyes told Nate he had probably been up most of the night.

"Mrs. Winberry," the detective said softly, "can you answer a few questions for me?"

Emma opened her eyes and looked at the stranger then at Nate. She smiled. "I'll try." Her voice was little more than a whisper.

The detective sat next to Emma's bed across from Nate. He opened a small notebook, took a pen from his pocket and was about to begin when a thoughtful aide brought in two cups of coffee.

"Thought you might need this," she said.

The men thanked her and each took a generous gulp.

"Now, Mrs. Winberry, please start at the beginning and tell me everything you can remember. Take it slowly. We're in no hurry."

Emma blinked her eyes a few times, squeezed them shut, then opened them again. "I was an extra in a movie." She looked at Nate expecting a frown, but he smiled and nodded.

"I was in a cardboard box in an alley—supposed to be a homeless woman."

Nate held a cup of water to her mouth with a bent straw protruding. "Take a drink, dear."

She nodded and swallowed, then continued. "I heard a noise at the back of the box, thought it was rats. I was about to climb out when somebody grabbed me from behind and pulled me out of the box and through a broken window. The glass cut my arms."

She pointed to the water. Again Nate held the straw to her lips.

"Yes," the detective said. "We found some blood spattered on the floor of the abandoned building that faced the alley. Did you see who grabbed you?"

"No, they put a blindfold over my eyes and duct tape over my mouth. Then they tied my wrists and ankles." She stopped for a moment, breathing deeply.

"Go on," the detective said.

"They kept calling me Minnie. Then one of them pulled at my legs and said I wasn't Minnie. Do you know who this person is?" she asked the detective.

"No, but I'll try to find out. Is there anything you can tell me about them that would help in identification?"

"I listened to their voices; one was deep and heavy, the other high-pitched, and he talked with a lisp."

"Do you think you would be able to identify the voices if you heard them again?"

"Yes. I listened very carefully. My Guardian Angel told me to."

The detective looked questioningly at Nate who held up his hand and shook his head.

"They carried me outside and threw me on the floor of some kind of truck then drove to another building and just left me there, with the rats." Her weak voice cracked and she shook her head, unable to go on.

Nate held her hand and stroked it gently. "Can you let her rest now?" he asked the detective.

"All right. I'll be back later."

The nurse came into the cubicle. "We're ready to move her to a room now. Please wait outside."

As Nate walked into the waiting room, James came rushing in the door.

"She's all right," Nate said. "They're moving her to a room. Let's go get a cup of coffee and I'll tell you what I know."

Nate and James sat in the lobby of the hospital drinking black coffee and eating raisin nut muffins they purchased from the coffee bar.

Between bites, Nate told James all he knew.

James shook his head sadly. "Poor Emma. To think what might have happened to her." He shivered. "How did she get out of there?"

"I don't know. She was too tired to talk anymore. Detective Spaulding will be back this afternoon to ask her more questions. Come on, she should be in the room by now. Let's go up."

The weary night shift was busy giving reports to the day personnel who looked crisp and ready to face the challenges of working in a busy inner-city hospital.

The ward secretary directed the two men to a private room at the end of the hall. They tiptoed in so as not to disturb Emma, but found her awake and sitting up in bed.

"Hi," she said weakly.

James couldn't speak, just stared at her.

"Do I look that bad?"

"We've seen you look better," Nate said, giving her a kiss on the forehead.

"Give me a drink, please."

Nate held the cup while Emma slowly sipped from the straw.

"James," she said, "don't tell Sylvia how bad I look. The nurses will be in later to bathe me and do something with this hair." She tried in vain to smooth her errant locks. "And don't look so forlorn. I'm not going to die."

James took her hand and held it. "I know. You're a tough woman, a survivor."

"You bet."

They heard voices outside the room. A knock, then a nurse walked in carrying a clipboard, followed by three men.

"I'm Dr. Jepson," the most imposing member of the group said. "And these are my residents, and Miss Andrews the charge nurse."

The nurse smiled, nodded and checked the flow of Emma's IV.

"We've just been reviewing your case, Mrs. Winberry. You were lucky. Your injuries appear to be superficial, but I will order a brain scan and a few other tests to be sure. According to the ER report, you have a nasty bump on your head and a mild concussion.

"If you gentlemen will step out for a moment, we'll do a complete physical exam to rule out any other injuries."

Nate and James nodded and walked to a lounge area at the end of the hall. Large picture windows gave them a panoramic view of the Chicago skyline against a backdrop of bright blue sky. Down below, people scurried in and out of the doors of the medical complex like a stream of ants.

"How much misery and suffering is going on here at this very minute," Nate said.

"And how many miracles," James added.

"True."

The men sat, saying nothing, feeling the adrenaline rush of the past hour ebbing from their bodies.

A short time later, Dr. Jepson walked up to them. "My residents are completing the examination, but there don't seem to be any other injuries. We'll do a brain scan, a chest X ray and a complete blood work-up. If everything is normal, as I expect it will be, she can go home later this afternoon."

"Thank you, Doctor," Nate said. "You don't know how happy we are to hear that."

James nodded.

"I'm glad to be able to give you good news. Sometimes my job isn't so easy." He looked out the window. "Beautiful day out there. Go enjoy it."

As they reentered the room, a nursing assistant was preparing to take vital signs and give Emma a bath.

"Nate, did you call your brother?"

"Not yet. I'll do it as soon as I get home."

"What will you tell him?"

"That you were in a minor accident. I'd rather not go into details."

Emma nodded. "Now, both of you go home. And, Nate, please come back later and bring my glasses. I don't remember what I did with my contacts and can't see a thing."

TWENTY-FOUR

THAT AFTERNOON, as Nate entered the hospital lobby, he ran into Detective Spaulding.

"Detective, don't you ever sleep?"

"An hour here, a couple of hours there. One of these days it's going to catch up with me." The man carried a large Styrofoam cup filled with coffee and Nate noticed the slight tremor of his hands.

Emma had just returned from her CT Scan and chest X ray. She looked tired, but much improved. The bumps on her mouth and lips had shrunk in size; the angry redness had turned to a dull pink. The bruise on her cheek was turning from red to purple. Someone had combed her hair and dressed her in a gray hospital gown with an unrecognizable design.

She squinted, then smiled as she recognized the two men. Nate kissed her forehead and put her glasses on her face.

Emma adjusted them into position and sighed. "What a relief! Now I can see who's poking and prodding me. They've taken so many blood samples that I may need a transfusion."

Nate grinned. "That's my Sparrow talking. Your voice sounds better, already."

"I grew hoarse from yelling and calling for help. But nobody heard me in that awful place."

The men pulled chairs beside the bed. Nate held her hand, alternately kissing and stroking the bruised knuckles.

"I have your purse here," the detective said. "We looked through it, but found nothing to assist in the investigation. I believe your contact lenses are inside."

Emma brightened. "Now I remember. I got makeup in my eye and took them out. Thank you so much." She reached for her purse and clutched it to her.

"Are you ready to finish your story?" the detective asked.

Emma nodded. "After those two thugs left, I realized I was alone there. No, I wasn't exactly alone. I was kept company by a hoard of rats." She shuddered. "I knew I had to keep my wits about me, so I asked my Guardian Angel for help."

Detective Spaulding frowned.

"Don't ask," Nate said.

Emma went through the description of how she had wiggled through the ropes and untied her ankles, got the blindfold off and stumbled to a wall.

"That's what my Guardian Angel told me to do."

She glanced at Nate then at the detective, daring either one of them to contradict her.

"Then what did you do?" the detective asked.

"Well, I followed the wall 'til I came to a corner where I rubbed through the rope binding my wrists."

"And how did you get out of the building?"

Emma thought for a moment. Should she mention her Knight? He told her he didn't want anything to do with the police. The last thing she wanted was to get him in trouble.

"I finally found a door. The lock was broken, so I was able to get outside. I don't remember much after that. I saw lights in the distance so I started to walk toward them."

Detective Spaulding's eyes met hers. She felt he could tell she wasn't telling him everything.

She thought for a moment then added, "A street person found me and helped me to the diner. I guess I passed out there. The next thing I remember was being in the ambulance."

"Can you describe the street person who helped you? Man, woman, race, anything at all?" the detective asked.

"I don't remember much. A black man, that's all I can tell you," Emma said feeling guilty about lying.

"Okay," said the detective. "Some of our men are scouring the area right now. Unless those two left something behind, we don't have much to go on. Do you remember anything else they said that might give us a clue?"

Emma scrunched up her face trying to recall their exact words. "Well, one of them wanted to throw me in the river. Nice fellow. They both seemed very upset that I wasn't Minnie. Let's see, just what did the one with the deep voice say? Oh yes, he said 'I want what you took off that stiff in the alley.' When they realized they had the wrong woman, the one with the lisp said the boss wasn't going to be happy. They had better find Minnie, and quick."

"We've put word out on the street that we want to talk to this Minnie. Street people have a regular network. So far, no results." He rubbed his eyes with both hands and let out a deep sigh. "All right, Mrs. Winberry, if you remember anything else, be sure to contact me."

Shortly after the detective left, Dr. Jepson entered the room. "As I expected, all tests came back normal. Here is a prescription for the salve to use on your mouth. Everything should clear up within a week. Follow up with your personal physician."

He handed Emma the prescription, shook hands with her and Nate and hurried on to his next patient.

"Are those my clothes you have in that bag?" Emma asked.

"Absolutely."

"Oh Nate." She threw her arms around his neck. "Take me home."

WHEN EMMA WALKED IN the door, the first thing she did was check her plants in the atrium.

"Tracie watered them," Nate said, following her.

"Oh, you dear, sweet man," Emma said, swallowing the lump in her throat.

"I knew you'd be upset if I neglected them." He looked at her, his face suffused with love and relief.

"You're tired," she said. "Why don't you lie down. I'd better phone Sylvia and tell her I'm home."

Nate nodded and stretched out on the couch. Within minutes he was snoring. Emma took the phone and sat in her favorite chair in the atrium. She noticed a few brown leaves on the ficus, but everything else looked happy and healthy.

Her daughter answered on the first ring. "Mom? Is it really you? Are you okay?"

Emma never would get used to this caller ID. No one had any privacy anymore.

"Yes, dear, I'm home and I'm fine. So you can stop worrying."

"Oh." Sylvia let out a draining breath. "This entire episode has taken ten years off my life. Promise me you won't ever do anything like that again."

"You and Nate talk as if I planned the whole thing. All I was doing was taking a bit part in a B minus movie. It was only supposed to last two hours at most. Things just got—out of hand you might say."

"Well thank goodness it's over. Now you can forget all about it. Suppose we stop over this weekend for a short visit. Will you be ready for company?"

"Certainly. See you then." Emma thought about calling her sons but decided to wait until evening. Sylvia promised to call them both. She suddenly realized how tired she felt.

She sat back in the chair and looked out over Lake Michigan. Sailboats glided over the waves. Gulls swooped searching for a meal. A few clouds drifted lazily across the sky.

Forget about the whole thing, Sylvia said. But could she? What about this Minnie person? She was in danger, Emma felt it. She had to warn her, to find out what she had that someone was ready to kill for.

No, she reminded herself, it's not my problem!

Isn't it? the voice asked.

Do I have to take on the problems of all mankind? Wasn't that what Marley's ghost told Scrooge? Oh dear. She heaved a deep sigh. If I must, I must.

Perhaps if she went back to the diner, the owner might be able to put her in touch with her Knight. She had a better chance of making contact with the man than the police did. She would have to confide in Nate. He'd be upset about that, but she knew how to bring him around. She always had.

TWENTY-FIVE

THE FOLLOWING DAY while Emma watered her plants on the roof garden, she noticed Tracie playing with her kitten.

"Hi, Tracie," she called.

The girl walked over to the gate taking small mincing steps. "I'm glad to see you," she whispered. Then she looked at Emma's face and drew back in shock.

The rash on Emma's lips and mouth had dried and the skin was peeling leaving pink blotches in its place. The bruise on her cheek had morphed into a sickly greenish-yellow color.

"I was in a minor accident," Emma lied. "But I'm much better now, nothing serious. I want to thank you for taking care of my plants."

The girl shrugged. "It's okay."

"Why don't you come over? I took some muffins out of the freezer this morning."

Tracie nodded, opened the gate and came through, the kitten bounding after her.

Emma went into the atrium and returned in a few moments, followed by Nate carrying a tray with a pitcher of milk, two glasses, a saucer and a plate of muffins.

"Sit and rest," he said to Emma. "You're doing too much. Hello, Tracie."

The girl rewarded them both with a rare smile as Emma poured milk into the saucer and set it down on the floor. Hope crouched, the little pink tongue eagerly lapping up the milk.

"Call me if you need anything," Nate said walking back into the atrium.

"I missed you," the girl said, breaking off a piece of muffin and taking tiny bites.

"Thank you, Tracie. I like to think we're friends." Emma took a generous bite of muffin. She was glad she had added peanut butter to the recipe for more protein. She still felt so hungry, hadn't rebuilt her reserve. "How are things going?"

Tracie lifted one shoulder and played with the ring through her lower lip. "I hate it here. Laura and my uncle argue all the time." She hesitated for a moment then lowered her voice to a whisper. "I think my uncle's into something crooked. I saw a letter the other day. I'm afraid to stay here. I have to get away."

"What did the letter say?" Emma's curiosity was piqued.

"It was some kind of a threat. I have to leave before something bad happens."

"Where would you go, back home?" Emma asked, pouring milk into the two glasses.

The girl shook her head adamantly. "No way! I wish I could get my own place—away from everybody."

"You'd have to get a job in order to pay the rent and buy food. How old are you?"

"Seventeen. I'll be eighteen pretty soon. Then nobody can tell me what to do." She broke off more of the muffin and fed it to Hope.

Emma tried to visualize this girl on the street. She wouldn't last a week. "What kind of work would you do? You have responsibilities now, not only to yourself, but to your pet. She has to have food, clean litter, a place to sleep and visits to the vet to keep her healthy. That costs money."

Tracie looked down at the cat, her brows knit together in concentration. "I've been thinking about that." She let out a heavy sigh. "I'm not sure what I could do." She looked at Emma as if she might supply the answer.

"Did you finish high school?" Emma asked.

"Yeah. I was in an accelerated class. I got my diploma six months ago."

"That's helpful. What would you really like to do, I mean if you had your choice?"

"I dunno. I'm so mixed up. I have to think some more."

Emma took the girl's thin fragile hand in hers. "Remember this, I'm here for you. If I can help, just tell me. And, Tracie, promise me you won't do anything foolish, like running away. It would not be good for either you or Hope."

The girl's eyes met Emma's. She looked so vulnerable. "I promise."

"So what was the deep conversation between you and Tracie?" Nate asked as they sat in the living room perusing the newspaper.

"Typical teenaged angst," Emma said, deciding not to tell Nate about the threat Tracie claimed to have seen. There was no proof and he would just tell her to mind her own business.

"Here's a follow-up on that murdered inventor found in an alley. The police have no leads as yet..."

Emma didn't hear anymore—found in an alley. The words of the thugs flashed across her mind. Could her abduction and the search for Minnie be somehow tied in with this murder? She rubbed the gooseflesh on her arms.

"Nate, what did the paper say was missing from the man's body?"

"Two rings, one with a large diamond, the other a class ring he always wore. His wallet, money and expensive watch were untouched." He looked at her suspiciously. "Why are you asking?"

"It's something the kidnapper said when he thought I was Minnie. 'I want what you took off that stiff in the alley.' I have a strange feeling the incidents may be related."

"Oh no! Here we go again." Nate dropped the paper on the floor, leaned forward, his hands on his knees. "There's nothing you can do about it. Leave it to the police."

She looked at him, her eyes filled with concern. "We have to find Minnie. She's in grave danger."

"I think that bump on the head impaired your reason. How could we possibly find this street person?"

She hemmed and hawed then looked at him with a guilty expression. "There's something I didn't tell you or the detective."

He leaned back, closed his eyes and shook his head.

"Just listen to me before you scold. When I was wandering around that warehouse, I found a room where someone was obviously living. There was a mattress on the floor. I was so exhausted and so dizzy, I fell down on it and passed out."

Now she had Nate's complete attention. "Why didn't you tell us?"

"I'm coming to that. A big black man woke me and said I was in his bed and better get out. When he saw how weak and injured I was, he carried me to the diner and left me with the owner who called nine-one-one. The black man said he didn't want anything to do with the police. I suspect he may be wanted for some petty crime."

"When they search that warehouse, they're sure to find his 'living quarters,' " Nate said. "Emma, you should have told the detective."

"But he had absolutely nothing to do with the kidnapping. I was just trying to protect the man who saved my life."

Nate nodded and shrugged. "I can understand that."

"Can you? We have to contact him. He may know how to find Minnie."

"Oh no, absolutely not! Do I have to put a tracking device on you? Emma, please don't do anything without consulting me first."

Emma bristled, but said nothing.

"I don't like worrying myself to death over every crackpot idea you get in your head," he added.

"Well!" Emma got up from her chair and went into the atrium. She looked out over the lake. Whitecaps pounded against the shore. The sky filled with dark angry clouds. She felt the coming storm welling up inside her. Why was he treating her like a child? She knew what she was doing, didn't she?

After she had cooled down, Emma walked back into the living room. Nate dozed in the lounger. Quietly she opened the front door.

"Where are you going?" he asked in a concerned voice.

Emma bowed her head. "Do I have your permission to get the mail, My Lord?"

"I'll get it," he said, deliberately ignoring her sarcasm. "Sit down and rest. You still look tired."

Emma gritted her teeth. Suddenly she did feel tired, so tired. She went into the bedroom, threw herself on the bed and fell into a deep sleep.

When Emma woke, she felt better, but was still irritated with Nate. She decided to continue her little game, even though it did seem childish.

"Do I have your permission to prepare lunch, Your Eminence?" she asked, pursing her lips.

"Emma, come and sit here beside me."

She sat on the couch as far away from him as possible. He moved closer and put his arm around her shoulders.

"I'm sorry if I came across as a dictator."

She looked down at her hands clasped in her lap, her lower lip jutting out in a pout.

"You have no idea how I felt when I didn't know what had happened to you. The thought that I might never see you again drove me mad, Sparrow." He hooked his finger under her chin and turned her face up to his. His fingers gently stroked the bruise on her cheek.

She looked at him with her luminous eyes to see his eyes glistening. "Oh Nate, I'm sorry. I didn't mean to cause you so much worry and suffering. I promise not to do it again." She buried her face in his chest and hugged him as hard as she could.

He stroked her hair, her back and the healing scratches on her arms. "You're my whole world," he whispered, caressing her ear. "I can't let anything happen to you."

"Let's never quarrel again," she said.

"I'm sure we will, from time to time," he said. "But as long as we kiss and make up, everything will be all right." He kissed her forehead and the tip of her nose.

"My lips aren't ready for kissing yet," she said running her tongue over the rough peeling spots.

"They will be soon," he said, grinning. "I can wait."

TWENTY-SIX

I DON'T BELIEVE Mrs. Win was in an accident. She looks like somebody beat her up. My mother looked like that lots of times.

Where's Laura? Doesn't she hear the phone? Maybe I should answer it. No, let it ring. Where is she? I'll just pick it up and see if somebody says something.

"Evans there?"

"No. Want to leave a message?"

"Naw, I'll call back later."

He sounded tough. I've got a feeling something bad's going to happen. I better tell Laura about the phone call. After all, she let me keep Hope. And I better make some plans. Can't stay here much longer.

TWENTY-SEVEN

FRIDAY NIGHT EMMA slept fitfully, moaning and thrashing in her sleep. She felt Nate's hand patting her reassuringly and heard his voice.

"Shush, you're safe. Go back to sleep."

She drifted into a dream world—dark and foreboding.

HER HANDS AND FEET were tied; a huge rat was gnawing at the ropes. She tried to cry out, but no sound came. "Help." She heard a call from somewhere far away. "Help me." Suddenly Emma was free. She started moving toward the voice.

"Help me..."

"Where are you? Who are you?" she called.

Then she heard the deep voice of the thug who had struck her. "We're coming, Minnie. We'll find you." Emma curled herself into a ball to hide from them—the rats surrounded her with their scritch, scritch, scritch...

SHE WOKE BATHED in sweat, her heart pounding.

"What's wrong?" Nate asked in alarm. "Was it another nightmare?"

"Oh," she said feeling her heartbeat begin to slow down. "A terrible one."

She burrowed in Nate's arms where she felt safe. "Tied up— rats—someone calling for help—the thugs threatening Minnie. Oh Nate, we have to find her."

"Shush, calm yourself. There's absolutely no way we

can find this woman. What do you suggest, putting an ad in the paper?"

"Don't patronize me." She was desperately trying to control her emotions. "Just let me think."

"That's been known to lead to dire consequences," he said, lying back on the bed.

"If I could only contact the Knight," Emma mused.

"The what?"

"Oh, I forgot to tell you. The black man who carried me to the diner—I called him my Knight in Shining Armor."

"Very poetic. And how do you expect to find this elusive person?"

"Well—if I went back to the diner, the owner might be able to put me in touch with him."

"You sound very self-assured. What makes you think he would cooperate?"

"It's worth a try, isn't it?"

Nate let out a grunt and turned on his side. "You're not going anywhere without me."

"I didn't intend to, dear. You go back to sleep. If I do, I'll just have more dreams. I'm going to stay up, put on the coffee."

Emma sat in the atrium sipping a steaming cup. She felt stronger, almost back to normal. The headaches had subsided, her lips were better and the bruise on her cheek was fading. Amazing what being home can do for a person. Yes, this was home, here with Nate. She never wanted to be anywhere else.

Okay, Guardian Angel, how do I get in touch with the Knight?

She closed her eyes and waited for the answer that always came.

NATE WALKED OUT into the atrium yawning and holding a cup of coffee at a precarious angle. He grumbled as he sat in a chair opposite Emma and took a swallow. He squeezed his eyes shut and rubbed them with his free hand.

"You look like you're not quite awake," she said, grinning.

"I'm not. Somebody in that bed was tossing and turning and moaning all night." He gave her an exaggerated frown.

"I'm sorry. Maybe I should sleep on the futon in the study for a while," she said sheepishly.

"You'll do no such thing. I want you near me, want to listen to your breathing, to hold you. I don't mind a little lost sleep, not when I realize what you went through." He reached over and took her hand, held it to his lips and kissed it tenderly. "My little Sparrow."

"I love you, Nate Sandler, and I'll try not to cause you any more worry." She stroked his balding head. "Meeting you is the best thing that's happened to me in years."

"And you're the best thing that's ever happened to me," he said.

He sat back, drank his coffee and looked out over the lake. "It's going to be a nice day."

"Uh huh," she answered. "A good day for a walk along the shore, and then, a bit of shopping. I feel like myself again."

"Ah, shopping, woman's favorite pastime. As far as I know, you don't need anything. What is it you want?"

"I had an idea."

He groaned and looked at her with apprehension.

"Hear me out," she said, putting her cup down and leaning forward. "The Knight did save my life, and since he lives on the street, I thought I might buy him some warm clothes for winter. Maybe a couple of sweat suits, long underwear, wool socks, and a heavy jacket, cap and gloves. What do you think?"

"It would be a nice gesture. Show your gratitude. But how will you get these things to him?" He raised his eyebrows.

"We could leave them at the diner. The owner probably knows him."

"And if he doesn't, he may just keep the clothes for himself, or sell them," Nate said.

"It's possible, but I'll have to take that chance. I feel I must do something for the man. He's probably had to vacate that warehouse and find a new place to live—all because of me." She looked at Nate with pleading eyes.

"Okay, we'll go shopping."

"I knew you'd agree. Now, how about some breakfast?"

END-OF-SEASON SHOPPERS browsed the stores at Water Tower Place. Bargains on summer wear brought out young people and mothers towing boisterous children.

Emma noticed some people staring at her face. I should have worn a hat, she thought. They probably think I'm a battered wife.

As if reading her mind, Nate said, "Look at this, Emma, it's a great hat. I think it will look good on you."

The price tag showed a markdown from forty dollars to twenty. "Hmm." Emma fingered the soft navy-blue cotton. A wire in the brim allowed it to be contoured at different angles. She plopped it on her head, scrutinizing her reflection in the mirror sitting on the counter.

"What do you think? It hides the bruise on my face."

"It looks great," Nate said. "I like it."

"Sold." She left the hat on and found a salesperson.

"Now that you've bought yourself a present, we can get what we came for," Nate said, leading her toward a sporting goods store.

"I didn't intend on buying myself anything, but people were staring at me."

"Just your imagination," he said. "I like the way you look in that hat and, besides, you deserve something new."

"Of course I do. Now let's get the items on this list."

As Emma picked up two of everything, Nate took the excess out of her arms.

"My dear, this man probably lives out of a couple of

garbage bags. Socks, underwear and a sweat suit should be enough." He looked down at her, his lips twitching.

"You're right, as usual, but I think we should get a wool cap and mittens."

As the checker tabulated the bill, Emma fretted. "We should get more. I think my life is worth more than this, don't you?" She turned to him with an expression that dared him to disagree.

"Your life is priceless, Sparrow. Now we have one more stop." Lugging the parcels, he led her toward the phone store.

"What?" she asked.

"We're buying cell phones, one for each of us. That way we can always be in touch." His look gave her no room for objection.

"What's wrong with your old cell phone?" Emma asked.

"It doesn't work properly. Isn't reliable."

"All right." She had never wanted one of those irritating things, but now it seemed like a good idea. At a minimum, it would give her a sense of security.

TWENTY-EIGHT

EMMA PUT DOWN the phone and sighed. "Stephen wanted to come over but I told him Sylvia was coming. I don't think I'm ready for too many children just yet. I tried to be tactful, but I hope he doesn't feel slighted."

"They mean well," Nate said, handing her a cup of coffee.

"I know, but I'm still so tired; I need more rest."

"That shopping was too much for you, wasn't it?"

"No, no. I'm glad we did it, but I have to admit, it wore me out."

He sat next to her, sipping his coffee. "We're too old for this kind of excitement. I'll be glad when the opera season rehearsals start and we can go back to mishaps on the stage. They're much safer."

Emma laughed. "Remember when I first auditioned for the supernumerary role? I was so nervous. All I had to do was walk across the stage and put that darned pitcher on the table."

Nate shook his head. "You practically ran, then knocked it over."

"I was so embarrassed."

"I know, your face was crimson when you walked over and stood next to me. That's one of the things that attracted me to you. You made the most interesting faces."

Emma felt the laughter bubble up. "Humph, and remember the time I stepped in the horse manure in the triumphal scene from *Aida*?" Now she was laughing so hard tears streamed down her face.

They sat together for a long time, each with their own thoughts, smiling from time to time, reliving the happenings of the past few years.

The ringing of the phone interrupted their reverie. "Who is that now?" Nate said in exasperation.

"I'll get it," Emma said. "Hello."

"Emma," Gladys's voice boomed through the instrument. "We haven't talked in weeks. How is everything?"

Emma glanced at Nate and raised her eyebrows. "How much time do you have?"

"Why?"

"The past week has been more than eventful." Emma walked into the atrium, settled herself in a comfy chair and told Gladys the whole story.

"I don't know what to say." Gladys's voice reflected disbelief.

"You mean for once you're speechless?" Emma laughed.

"Are you all right?"

"Yes, yes, I'm fine. The police may never find those thugs, but since they were looking for someone else and they know I couldn't see them, it's unlikely they'll come after me."

"God, Emma, I can't believe this."

"Don't worry, Nate isn't letting me out of his sight. We even bought cell phones. There's nothing to do but wait."

"Be sure to call me if anything else happens," Gladys said, concern in her voice.

"I will. Love to Cornell and the girls. Bye now."

Emma found Nate in the kitchen whipping up an omelet.

"Smells good," she said.

"I figured after talking to Gladys you'd be hungry." He looked at the clock. "Only a half hour. Usually those calls last a lot longer."

She gave him a look out of the corner of her eye. At that moment the toast popped up. She buttered the slices as Nate expertly cut the omelet in half and dished it out.

THAT AFTERNOON Sylvia and James came over. They had left the boys with a sitter. Emma was glad of that. She wasn't sure she could cope with two rambunctious little ones.

The four adults had a pleasant visit and Sylvia seemed satisfied that her mother was on the mend. As they were leaving, she hugged Emma and whispered, "I never realized how much I love you, until I thought you might be gone from us." Her eyes filled with tears.

"Don't worry, dear. I'm not going anywhere and I'm safe and sound. Nate will see to that."

He stood like a sentinel, slipped his arm around Emma and nodded to Sylvia and James.

MONDAY MORNING dawned gray and rainy. Emma felt logy and very tired. Was she still feeling the effects of her ordeal? Probably. She had an appointment to see her own doctor for a follow-up in a few days. Maybe she needed a tonic of some sort.

She watched Nate pick up the ringing phone and listen intently. He frowned and gripped the instrument a little too tight.

"I understand," he said. "We'll be there."

"What?" Emma asked.

"That was Detective Spaulding. They've rounded up a few known felons and want you to come in for a lineup."

"But I didn't see them," Emma insisted.

"He knows that. He wants you to listen to their voices to see if any of them sounds familiar."

Emma nodded feeling her heart beat faster, her palms grow moist. "When are we supposed to be there?"

"Ten this morning."

"HOW ARE YOU FEELING, Mrs. Winberry?" the detective asked.

"You certainly look much better than the last time I saw you."

"I'm fine, thank you. A few days at home does wonders."

"Try not to be nervous. The men won't be able to see you. I know you were blindfolded, but something might spark a memory. We'll have each one say, 'I want what you took off that stiff in the alley.' That's what he said, wasn't it?"

"Yes," Emma said, feeling a wave of fear and uncertainty.

"Come this way."

He led them through the reception area. It didn't look anything like the police dramas on TV. It was rather quiet, a few people sitting at desks answering questions.

When they reached the viewing room, it was darkened. Emma drew back a moment, then stared at the large glass window. She felt so vulnerable.

"As I said, you can see them but they can't see you," the detective reassured her. "There are six men standing there. Does anything about any of them seem familiar?"

Emma looked closely at each one and shook her head.

"All right, number one," the detective spoke into the intercom, "step forward. Say 'I want what you took off that stiff in the alley.'"

Emma closed her eyes and listened closely as the man repeated the words. "No, not him."

They went down the line, each man saying the same thing, but none sounded like the men who had abducted her.

When the last one finished, Emma looked at the detective. "I'm sorry. It wasn't any of them. I'm certain of that."

"It was a long shot," Detective Spaulding said, "but I felt it was worth a try."

Emma hesitated for a moment. "Detective, I have a feeling that this incident is somehow related to the murder of that inventor a few weeks ago."

Nate grimaced.

The detective knit his brows together. "What makes you say that?"

"I have sort of a sixth sense you might say. Sometimes I know things without any explanation. And I'm usually right."

He looked dubious as he turned to Nate.

"I have to agree. I don't know how, but she is right a good percentage of the time."

Detective Spaulding ran his hand through his graying hair. "Without any proof or further leads, I don't see how we can connect the two."

"Have you found Minnie?" Emma asked.

He shook his head. "Not yet." His expression said they probably never would. "We searched that entire area and we did find the warehouse where you were held prisoner. There were bloodstains on one corner of the wall and on the floor. We might need a blood sample from you for comparison. I'll let you know if it's necessary, but we do need your fingerprints."

"That's probably where I rubbed off the rope," Emma said.

"Yes, we found that, too. Nothing else, I'm afraid. Forensics is examining the strands of rope to see if there's anything unique about it, but I doubt it," he said slowly, a look of weariness creeping into his face. "We did find evidence of someone living there, an old mattress, some crates, but the occupant was long gone." He looked directly at Emma. "Did you see anyone there?"

Emma fidgeted. "Not that I recall." She had a feeling the detective knew she was lying.

He continued to stare at her as if waiting for more information, but, forcing herself to maintain eye contact, she shrugged and said nothing.

"May I have a copy of the police report?" Emma asked, trying to remain calm though her palms were moist and she realized she was biting her healing lip.

"You should have gotten one."

"If I did, in all the excitement, I may have lost it." She gave him a smile, hoping she looked sincere.

"Tom," he called to an aide. "Make a copy of the police report in Mrs. Winberry's file, then get her prints, please."

When they were finished, Nate asked her, "Are you okay? You look a little shaky."

"I'm fine, just nervous. I'm certainly not used to being questioned by the police."

"Why did you want the police report?" Nate asked as they walked out of the station through a persistent drizzle.

"So I'll know exactly where they found me. I really don't remember much and probably couldn't find the place on my own. We have a parcel to deliver, remember?"

"Humph," he mumbled. He opened the car door for Emma, got behind the wheel and drove home without saying another word.

The phone was ringing as they opened the front door.

"Damn thing. Person can't have any privacy," Nate mumbled as he grabbed the receiver. "Hello." His tone was far from friendly.

"May I speak with Mrs. Winberry?"

"Who is this?"

"This is George Watkins from Consolidated Films."

"You're speaking with Nate Sandler. What do you want with Mrs. Winberry?"

"How is she?" the man asked timidly.

"Much better, no thanks to your security measures," Nate said, sarcasm rolling off his tongue.

"I just wanted her to know that we have taken care of the hospital bills."

"That's the least you can do. If anything more serious had happened, you would have heard from my lawyer and your company would probably be out of business."

"Mr. Sandler, we do try to keep the areas we're filming as safe as possible…"

"I don't want to hear any of your excuses. Never call Mrs. Winberry again for any roles in your films. Is that clear?"

"Yes, sir."

Nate hung up before the man could say another word.

"You certainly were rude," Emma said.

Nate let out a deep breath through clenched teeth. "He made me angry. Let's just try to forget this whole thing."

But Emma couldn't forget it. She knew her role was unfinished. And she hated leaving loose ends.

TWENTY-NINE

"NATE, WHERE IS that roll of brown wrapping paper? I can't seem to find it."

"Ah, I think I put it on the top shelf in the closet in the study. I'll get it."

He walked into the room, reached up, pushed a few things aside, and retrieved the paper. "What do you want this for?"

"I have to wrap up those clothes we bought before we take them to the diner," she said, holding a ball of heavy twine.

"Want me to help you?"

"No, no," she answered too quickly. "I can manage. You were going for a walk, weren't you? Didn't you say you needed something from the hardware store?"

He frowned. "You're not up to anything, are you?"

"Don't be silly. All I'm going to do is wrap a package. Now go on, get your exercise."

After Nate left, Emma took all the clothing they had bought and put it on the kitchen table. She removed the tags and stacked everything in a neat pile.

She thought for a moment, then poured a cup of coffee, walked into the study and sat at the desk. Resting her elbow on the surface, she cupped her chin in her hand and ruminated. She took a sip of coffee, pulled out a sheet of stationery and began to write.

To my Knight in Shining Armor,
Please accept this clothing as a token of my gratitude

for saving my life. The police have not found the kidnappers nor have they located Minnie. I know she is in
grave danger. Can you help me find her? You saved my
life, perhaps you can save hers, too. Please try. If you
do, call me, and we can arrange a meeting.
Goldilocks

She wrote her phone number at the bottom and tucked the
note in between the clothing, then, with some difficulty,
managed to wrap everything together and bind it with the
twine. Now, all we have to do is deliver it, she thought, and
hope for the best.

Emma looked at the police report. It stated the ambulance
had picked her up at Sam's Diner with an address on Canal
Street. Would she recognize this Sam? She had been pretty
woozy and disoriented, but it was worth a try.

That evening around eight o'clock Emma suggested to
Nate they go to the diner.

"Why now?" he asked.

"I wanted to wait until the supper hour was over. And I
thought we should go while it's still light out."

He nodded. "Okay, let's get this over with. Suppose the
same guy isn't there? Will you even recognize him?"

"We'll see, won't we?" She gave him an innocent smile.

Nate shrugged, picked up the package and followed her
out the door.

Michigan Avenue was crowded with tourists, shoppers,
people headed to the many hotels and restaurants in the area.
Everyone seemed to be taking advantage of the last pleasant
days of summer.

Nate turned west on Chicago Avenue to get away from the
traffic. He turned south on Clark Street to Randolph, then
headed west again. When he reached Canal, the area suddenly
changed. There were signs of urban renewal, but no one

walked the streets, only security lights illuminated the warehouses. Everything looked deserted.

"God, what a neighborhood," he grumbled. "This is not exactly the place I would choose to open a diner."

"There it is, on the right," Emma said. "I do recognize it."

Nate parked as close to the dilapidated building as possible. "I'm going to have to keep an eye on this car," he said, activating the alarm.

The scene reminded Emma of Edward Hopper's painting *Nighthawks*. It had the same lonely feel. Only two patrons sat at the counter, black men in overalls and heavy boots. They looked up suspiciously at the two white people.

Nate led Emma to the unoccupied end of the counter.

"What can I get you folks?" asked a burly man wearing a dirty apron, covering a black stained shirt. His grizzled hair framed a face wearing a map of years of hard living. A cigarette hung from his lower lip looking as if the ash would drop at any minute. He wiped the counter in front of them with a dirty rag. Nate frowned, stood back and kept glancing out the window at his car.

"Are you Sam?" Emma asked.

"Who wants to know?"

"Do you remember me?" She looked closely at him trying to recall if he was the man who had called for help.

"Can't say that I do. Why?"

"I'm the lady who was brought in here a little over a week ago. Remember? You called the police?"

"Jeez! You sure look different. I thought you were a goner. You okay?" His attitude changed from suspicion to genuine concern.

"I'm fine, thank you."

"The police were in here askin' questions, but I didn't know nothin'."

"I'm looking for the man who brought me in here," Emma said leaning forward.

Sam pulled back frowning. "What for?"

"I want to thank him. He saved my life."

The man seemed to relax. He threw his cigarette on the floor and ground it with his foot. "He stays pretty much to himself. Comes in once in a while. Don't know where he is right now."

Emma felt he was being evasive, but she didn't blame him. The way these homeless people lived, they had to be on their guard all the time.

"Could you give him this package the next time he comes in? I bought him some warm clothes for the winter." Emma turned to Nate.

He handed the package to Sam. The man held back for a minute, then reached for it.

"Okay, I'll keep it for him. But like I said, don't know when I'll see him again." He put the parcel under the counter.

"Thank you," Emma said as they hurried out of the diner.

The sun had set and the sky was beginning to darken.

"Let's get away from here. This place gives me the creeps," Nate said, opening the car door. He drove well above the speed limit until he reached the lights of Michigan Avenue.

THE FOLLOWING DAY Detective Spaulding called.

"Mrs. Winberry? I told you that we found evidence of someone living in the warehouse." He paused, but Emma said nothing.

"We found the fingerprints of a Jackson Baker, wanted for petty theft."

Still Emma waited.

"We also found your fingerprints on a broken water glass. How do you explain that?" His voice had taken on a hard edge.

Emma hemmed and hawed. "I don't remember anything clearly. I had a concussion, you know. I passed out once or twice—fell on something. It could have been a mattress.

Maybe I knocked over the glass? I was so thirsty, Detective, I really don't remember." She felt that he didn't believe her.

"All right," he said. "But if you do remember anything, no matter how insignificant, call me."

"I will." As she hung up the phone, she dropped into a chair resting her head against the backrest. *Oh Guardian Angel, this is getting so involved. Help me, please…*

THIRTY

EMMA BEGAN to wonder if she would ever hear from her Knight. Two weeks had passed since they left the package at the diner. The police still had no leads. She knew the more time that passed, the less likely they were to find the kidnappers. She decided to put the entire matter out of her mind and get on with her life.

As fall approached, Emma and Nate looked forward to the auditions for supernumeraries at the Midwest Opera. They felt comfortable with the prospect; they were veterans, and they enjoyed helping the newcomers relax.

One crisp morning Emma walked out onto the roof garden to pick a few of the remaining tomatoes. She saw Laura Evans gripping the brick wall and staring out at the lake.

"Good morning, Laura," she called.

The woman hesitated, then turned to Emma and gave her a halfhearted greeting.

"How is Teresa? I haven't seen her lately." Emma worried about the girl, fearing she might follow up on her threat to run away.

Laura slowly shook her head as she stumbled toward Emma. Her eyes reflected a look of helplessness.

"Come and sit for a while," Emma said. "Is something wrong?"

Like a mechanical doll, Laura sat in a chair next to the patio table. She seemed oblivious to the question, her eyes glassy, as if she were drugged.

"Are you all right?"

"I don't know." The woman put her elbows on the table and held her head in her hands. "Teresa is becoming more and more withdrawn. She stays in her room all day with that cat. She hardly eats anything, only comes out to feed the animal and clean the litter box. Then she takes a few bites of anything that happens to be available." She raised her eyes to Emma as if searching for an answer. "I try to keep nutritious snacks around, but I'm afraid she's determined to starve herself." She took a deep breath and looked across the lake.

"This isn't working out. We'll have to send her back to her parents. I can't handle the responsibility and my husband takes no interest in her at all." Laura shrugged in a helpless way, as though she believed there was no way out of her trouble. "Lately he's been upset about something, but won't tell me what. I think it has something to do with his work."

Now that she had unburdened herself, she looked around as if just realizing where she was. "I'm sorry to lay this on you. I have no right to do that."

"It's all right," Emma said. "I wish I could help." She felt there was something else, something the woman wasn't saying.

"No one can, I'm afraid. I never even inquired about your accident. Were you badly hurt?" She looked at Emma as if searching for some signs of injury. "Teresa was concerned. You're the only one she seems to connect with."

"It was minor. I'm fine now. I wish I could do something for the girl. She seems so unhappy."

"Perhaps her parents should put her in some sort of home," Laura said. "Oh, I don't know."

"She told me she would soon be eighteen and would like to go out on her own," Emma said.

"Huh? Where would she go? She has no money, no job. She wouldn't last long, would she?" She looked at Emma as if asking for an answer.

"When is her birthday?"

The woman looked surprised. "I don't even know."

"Maybe we could take her out somewhere, as a celebration," Emma suggested.

Laura shrugged and looked out at the lake again. "The water looks so inviting, doesn't it?"

Oh God, Emma thought. I hope this one isn't suicidal.

After Laura went back home, Emma thought about them—what a strange trio. Laura seemed worried and preoccupied. Tracie had real psychological problems. The only thing keeping her together was the kitten. As for Mr. Evans, Emma barely knew him. He rarely came out of the condo and then merely nodded or ignored her.

I wonder what he does for a living, Emma thought. I get very negative feelings from him. Could he be involved in something illegal, as Tracie had suggested? All right, Emma Winberry, that's enough. He's probably an overworked businessman having difficulty coping with the stress. Wasn't that the way of life these days?

"Emma," Nate called. "How about going out for lunch? We can try that new coffee shop down the street."

"Coming." Mind your own business, she told herself.

Think of Nate and the children. That's all that really matters.

A FEW DAYS LATER Emma woke with a feeling of trepidation. Something is going to happen. I know it. She tried to chalk it up to her wild imagination, but experience told her otherwise.

"What's the matter now?" Nate asked, peering over the newspaper, his glasses perched on the end of his nose.

"I'm just restless."

"Why don't I believe you?" He frowned and went back to the news.

"I think I'll do some baking," Emma muttered, half to herself. She started puttering around in the kitchen, searching for a new recipe and upsetting the flour canister. White powder spilled over the butcher-block table and onto the floor like winter snow. "Damn!"

She jumped when the phone rang. Heard Nate answer it. Covered with flour, she walked into the living room and listened.

"Who is this? Is this some kind of joke? Goldilocks?"

Emma froze, then grabbed the phone out of his hand.

"Hello, this is Goldilocks. Is this my Knight?" She waved the startled Nate away.

"Yeah, that's me," the deep male voice said. "Got your note. Thanks for the clothes."

"I'm sorry you lost your cozy home. It was my fault," Emma said.

"That's okay. Was gettin' to be time to move anyway."

"Can you help me find Minnie?" Emma asked. She saw Nate's eyes widen, a look of surprise spread across his face.

"Maybe yes, maybe no. What you want her for?"

"She's in danger. Those men are still out there and they're ruthless. They won't hesitate to kill her for whatever it is they want. I believe they've already killed one man and they almost killed me." That was the best she could do. It was up to him now.

"I'll try. And I ain't no Knight in shinin' armor. Name's Jake."

"And you can call me Emma."

"I think I like Goldi better." With that he broke the connection.

Emma turned to face her irate partner.

"What was that all about?"

"Well," she hesitated, biting down on her bottom lip. "I put a note in the bundle of clothing and left this phone number. I really didn't think he'd call, but he seems to be the only link to Minnie."

Nate shook his head and let out a loud breath, his cheeks puffing out. He rubbed his hand over his forehead. "I thought you were going to drop that." He gave her a frigid look.

"I can't! I tried, but it won't let me go." She looked at him with fire in her eyes.

"All right. All right." He knelt beside her and took her in his arms.

"You know how I've been plagued with this," she said, laying her head on his shoulder. "My whole life long."

"I know, I know." He rubbed her back in a circular motion. "We'll try to find this Minnie, if at all possible." He went into the kitchen, came back with a towel and wiped the flour off her face.

She looked up at him and managed a smile as she saw the look of understanding on his face.

"You are special," he said. "Maybe that's why I love you so much." He kissed her neck, her cheek, then her mouth. "You taste like flour," he murmured. "Why don't we go into the Jacuzzi and wash it off?" He gave her a lascivious grin.

She couldn't help but laugh as she got up and followed him, all thoughts of baking forgotten.

THIRTY-ONE

A FEW DAYS LATER Jake called again. "Hi, Goldi. I talked to Minnie. No way she gonna meet you. Don't trust nobody."

"Did you tell her that her life is in danger?" Emma knew she was right to worry about Minnie, but how could she make these suspicious street people understand?

"She say why should she believe you? Maybe you want that ring for yourself."

So she did take the ring. But which one? There had to be something in one of those rings that someone was willing to kill for.

"If she won't meet me, will she at least talk to me on the phone?"

"Don't know. She havin' trouble with her leg now. Got some sores."

"What's wrong with her leg?" Emma asked.

"She got it cut off in a accident a few years back," Jake answered in a matter-of-fact tone.

"Oh, does she have an artificial limb?"

"A what?"

Emma realized he didn't understand her language. "A fake leg, made out of wood or plastic."

"Oh yeah. She got one o' those. Found it in the trash outside the County Hospital."

"You mean she picked up any old leg that someone threw out?" Emma was confounded. How could anyone live like that?

"Heh, heh. That's Minnie for ya. It don't fit too good. That's why she got sores. She stuffs newspapers and rags down inside. Holds it up with some old suspenders. She walks real funny, but she get around." He was chuckling into the phone.

"Jake, you tell her if she agrees to see me, I'll try to get her fitted with a leg made specially for her. Then she won't get any more sores."

Now how am I going to do that? Emma wondered.

Take her to Stroger County Hospital, the voice said.

Of course. They take care of the indigent.

"I tell her," Jake said. "But I ain't sure she buy that."

"Do the best you can, Jake. Bye now."

Emma walked into the kitchen, took the bowl of strawberries out of the refrigerator, and began eating them, one after the other.

"What's with this strawberry craving all of a sudden?" Nate asked. "We just bought those."

"I don't know. Since that experience in the warehouse, I can't seem to get enough of them." She looked at him feeling confused and unsure of what had really happened to her. "I remember seeing a ripe strawberry, but it was always just out of reach. I thought I was going crazy."

"Oh, Sparrow, I can't begin to imagine what you went through. I'll get a case of strawberries if you want them. Come here."

She nestled in his arms. "I need your understanding, especially now. Something is going to happen. I feel it. Something bad." She trembled as he held her tight.

"It's all right, I'm here. You're safe." He stroked her hair, her cheeks and kissed the tip of her nose. "Why don't you make some cookies? We're going to Stephen and Pat's tomorrow. The kids love those treats." He cocked his head to the side giving her an inquiring look.

"Good idea," she said, taking a deep breath. "I was going to make muffins, but I'll make cookies instead, double the recipe so there's sure to be enough. And will you get another quart of berries, please?"

Nate kissed her and was off in minutes.

As Emma assembled the ingredients, she listened to a light classical station on the radio trying to elevate her mood. But deep down she sensed trouble.

Guardian Angel, help me. Give me the strength to face whatever comes. I know it's there, waiting to pounce. She felt a warmth envelope her and knew, as always, that her Angel would be there.

THIRTY-TWO

LAURA DIDN'T SEEM to care when I told her about the phone call. She's taking some kind of pills. Sleeping a lot. Yesterday she walked right by me and didn't see me. Maybe I'm disappearing. Maybe I'm shrinking away. I'll just be a pile of dust. Isn't that what it says in the Bible?

Who is that staring at me in the mirror? That girl is so skinny. Her skin is all dried out and her hair looks like straw. That's not me. It's some kind of trick. But sometimes I feel weak. I better start eating more. Gotta keep up my strength for when I get out of here. Got to think of Hope. If anything happens to me, Uncle will just throw her out on the street.

I don't feel hungry anymore, but I better force myself. Get a glass of milk. My hands are shaking. Oh, oh, I spilled some on the floor. Better clean it before Laura sees it.

Maybe I'll go next door and get some of those tomatoes and those leaves. They taste good, all spicy. I wish I had one of Mrs. Win's muffins.

I have to take better care of myself. I have to think of my pet...

THIRTY-THREE

EMMA WENT OUT onto the roof to tend to her plants. The weatherman predicted storms with high winds and she wanted to be sure everything was secure.

She spotted Tracie intently engrossed in a project. It was the first time Emma had ever seen her interested in anything other than the cat. From time to time the girl reached down to a plate on the ground, picked up a morsel of food, and put it in her mouth.

I've never seen her do that before, either, Emma thought. "What are you doing, Tracie?"

"I'm drawing," the girl muttered putting pencil strokes on a pad of paper.

"May I see it?" Emma asked.

Tracie stood up and walked to the open gate. With a belligerent expression on her face, she handed the pad to Emma.

"Well, this certainly is interesting. What exactly is it?" Emma stared at the intricate design.

"It's going to be a tattoo, as soon as I get enough money," Tracie said, her expression resolute and determined.

Emma cringed at the prospect of a needle penetrating that delicate skin over and over. She let out a breath.

"Come and sit down, Tracie."

The girl walked over and plopped herself in a deck chair. Hope curled her body around Emma's legs.

"Why do you want to do this to yourself?" Emma asked. "I'm really trying to understand."

The girl shrugged. "Because I can and nobody can stop me." She pursed her lips and rubbed the scars on her forearms that were barely healed.

Emma felt the sorrow emanating from the withered figure.

"How about some lemonade? I have a fresh pitcher in the fridge."

Tracie nodded and went back to refining her design. Emma walked into the condo and returned in a few moments with a tray of lemonade and cookies, and a saucer of milk for the kitten.

Tracie had closed the tablet and was looking out over the lake. Emma watched her as she reached for an oatmeal cookie and began to bite into it.

"What else do you have in that tablet? May I look?"

"If you want."

Emma leafed through the pages, amazed at what she saw. "Why Tracie, these drawings are wonderful. You have a real talent."

Sketches of Hope in various poses leapt off the page; a scene of the lake with boats dotting the surface; then one of a turbulent storm, waves crashing against the shore.

The drawings became more disturbing as she went along until Emma saw one of a figure of a man slashed with red marker.

Tracie pulled the tablet away. "That's enough," she whispered. She finished her lemonade, took another cookie, nodded to Emma and went back through the gate.

Emma sat for a long time trying to understand the workings of that troubled mind. I'm out of my element here. I'd better call Bertie and get some advice.

She went into the house when the thunder started rumbling.

EMMA COULDN'T GET that disturbing sketch out of her mind. That evening she called her daughter-in-law and described the drawings.

"She was working on an intricate design for a tattoo she intends to get. The thought of it made my skin crawl."

"Hmm," Bertie said, "some of these kids think of their bodies as an artist's canvas—the tattoos, the piercings, the branding—are all ways to decorate themselves and defy society."

Emma's ears pricked up. "Did you say branding? Like in cattle?"

"Yes. It's so sad that they go to such painful extremes."

"Oh my God." Emma gripped the phone tighter. "She let me look through the rest of her drawings. Some of them are very good. The girl does appear to have talent. But they gradually became more and more turbulent. There was even a male figure slashed with red marker."

"It certainly sounds like that girl has a deep-seated resentment against someone, probably male, either her father or her uncle, maybe both." Bertie hesitated for a moment. "I wonder if she was abused by either of them?"

"Oh Lord," Emma said. "I never thought of that. She also has marks on her forearm that look like cuts. I asked her about it, but she said she scratched herself on a nail." Emma paced, feeling more upset by the minute.

"Don't believe that," Bertie said. "She's probably cutting herself. I've seen so many of them."

"Why?" Emma asked. "Why do they do it?"

"Because they have control and the physical pain is easier to cope with than their emotional upheaval. Pain releases endorphins in the brain and some of these unfortunates actually claim that it gives them a high."

"Oh no, I don't understand any of this," Emma said.

"She needs professional help," Bertie said. "And if she doesn't get it, she may do something more desperate. I can give you a referral."

"Thanks, dear. I'll have a talk with her aunt."

"Let me know what she says."

LATER EMMA SAW Laura and Tracie sitting on the roof garden. They appeared to be deep in conversation. Tracie held Hope in her lap, stroking the soft fur.

Emma went about her business, tending her plants in the atrium. The fig tree bore three tiny immature fruit. Maybe they'll ripen, she hoped. The thought of picking a ripe fig from her own tree made her mouth water.

Loud voices drifted across the roof. Emma cracked the door to listen.

"No, I won't!" Tracie shouted. "You can't make me!"

"Don't raise your voice to me, young lady. You can pack your things and leave this house any time you want," Laura shouted back.

"Wait 'til my uncle comes home. I'll tell him what you said." Tracie held the kitten close and stomped into the house.

Laura rose from her chair, walked over to the railing and stared out at the lake.

Emma opened the door, watering can in hand, and walked outside. "Good evening, Laura."

The woman slowly turned, as if in a trance. "Oh, hello."

"How are you?" Emma asked.

"Better not to ask." She heaved a deep sigh, thought for a moment, then seemed to make a decision. She walked toward the gate and looked at Emma. "Can I talk to you about something?"

"Of course. Come on over." Emma put the watering can down, sat in a comfy flowered chair and motioned Laura to do the same.

"You've raised children."

Emma nodded. "Three."

"I never had a child of my own. I don't know the first thing about babies, much less rebellious teenagers." She let out a breath and hung her head.

"I know Tracie is a handful," Emma said. "She'd be a challenge for the most experienced parents."

"I've had it," Laura said. "Either the girl goes, or I do."

Emma studied the woman. She seemed to have aged considerably since they moved in, barely a month ago. Deep furrows creased her cheeks. Puffiness around her eyes indicated a chronic lack of sleep. Her thin lips never wore a smile.

"Have you talked with your husband about the girl?" Emma asked.

"Humph, my husband. I think I've seen him a total of three hours in the past week. He's never home."

"Is he away on business?" Emma prodded.

"Monkey business, I think." She looked directly at Emma.

"I'm getting worried. He's suspicious of everything, doesn't talk about his work like he used to."

"What exactly does he do?"

"I don't even know anymore." She played with a loose button on her shirt, twisting and turning it. "He used to be in the antiques business—had a partner. One of them would travel to Europe and the East Coast to buy antique furniture and jewelry at estate auctions. They'd bring the pieces back here and store them in a warehouse. They opened a store on north Clark Street and were doing quite well for a while." Her eyes took on a look of concern. Was it fear? Emma wasn't sure.

"Then something happened." Laura's voice dropped to a whisper. "He started getting phone calls at all hours of the night. He never gave me any explanation, but I know he was worried, and—afraid. His partner disappeared a few months ago. I don't know where he went. He left the country and never came back.

"I think my husband's involved in something illegal. I'm frightened." Her eyes took on a wild look.

What can I do to help this woman? Emma thought. *Guardian Angel, give me a hand here.*

"Have you talked to him about it?"

"I tried but he just got angry and told me to stay out of it. He had everything under control. But checks started to bounce and when I went to the bank, they told me he had closed the savings account." She put her hand on her chest and took a number of deep breaths.

"Then, all of a sudden, there was a lot of money. I saw packs of hundred-dollar bills in his dresser drawer. When I asked him about it, he threatened me. Said if I interfered, I'd be sorry. I never saw that money again." She didn't seem to realize that tears were flowing freely down her face.

Emma handed her a tissue. She sniffled and wiped her eyes.

"I'm sorry. I didn't mean to burden you with my troubles, but you're a good listener."

Emma took her hand. "Sometimes all it takes is talking about a problem for the solution to come. Have you contacted Tracie's parents about her?"

"I tried, but they're in the middle of a divorce and want nothing to do with the girl. I don't know what to do, where to turn."

"I spoke with my daughter-in-law about Tracie. She's a social worker dealing with troubled teens. Tracie's cutting herself, isn't she?" Emma looked into the woman's eyes.

She nodded. "It's sick. I found a bloody razor and saw the bandages on her arms. When I confronted her, she became belligerent. She said it was her body and she could do anything she wanted."

The woman seemed to shrink, as if willing herself to disappear. Again she looked out over the placid lake. "It looks so inviting," she whispered.

"Tracie needs professional help," Emma persisted. "My daughter-in-law can refer her to a psychiatrist. Can you get her to go?"

"I don't know. And you know what? I don't care."

Without another word Laura got up and walked slowly across the roof and into her house.

Emma shook her head. More trouble is on the way. Of that, I am sure.

THIRTY-FOUR

"Hurry up, Emma, or we'll be late," Nate called from the bedroom.

"I'm coming. We have plenty of time. The movie doesn't start for an hour. It'll only take us fifteen minutes to get to Navy Pier." She walked out of the bathroom patting her hair, held stylishly in place with a new foaming pomade to keep her unruly locks in place.

"How do you like my new hairdo?"

"Looks great. Now come on." Nate balanced impatiently from one foot to the other.

She stood pouting. "You didn't even look at it."

"I did." He stood back. "A vision of loveliness. Now let's go."

"That's it," she muttered, suppressing a smile. "The honeymoon's over."

"This is the end of summer," Nate said. "The Pier will be crowded, especially since the storm is over. I want to get a good seat."

They walked to Michigan Avenue and boarded a bus heading south. Half the passengers disembarked at Navy Pier.

"See?" Nate said, taking her hand and joining the parade of people walking out onto the promenade.

"Remember when this was just what the name said—a pier?"

"Sure do," Emma answered. "My father used to take us out here on a Sunday to see a ship or two at the dock. That was it, plus a few shanties that sold fried seafood, nothing more."

She looked in awe at the South Dock lined with restaurants, tourists and locals walking along, laughing and taking photos. A juggler stood at the side tossing red and yellow balls in the air. Children watched waiting for him to drop one. Three boats lined the dock advertising dinner cruises, sight-seeing, and more.

They walked into the Family Pavilion, past numerous shops, and joined the line waiting for tickets to the Imax Theater. Emma felt as giddy as a child every time she put on the three dimensional glasses. They brought her right into the action on the huge screen.

Pictures of deep-sea creatures advertised the realistic oceanic adventure. Emma and Nate sat in the center section and donned the 3-D glasses as the movie began.

Whales and dolphins cavorted in an ocean she could almost feel. When a great white shark hurled itself head-on into camera range, its mouth agape, rows of deadly teeth lining the sides, the children in the audience screamed. Emma cringed and gripped Nate's arm. He held her hand tightly, as if protecting her from the shark and anything else that threatened her.

After an hour and a half of sea creatures consuming one another, the lights turned on and the babbling horde streamed out of the theater.

"I must admit, that was a bit scary," Nate said.

"A little, I felt like shark bait. That was more than enough for me. Speaking of bait, I'm kind of hungry," Emma said.

"Me, too. Let's stop at one of these outdoor restaurants and grab a bite."

Emma cringed at the word, still visualizing the sharp teeth of the predator.

"There's a place with a few empty tables," Nate said, leading Emma to the Dock Side Café.

They sat down and looked at a chalkboard on the outside wall advertising the specials of the day.

A teenaged server came up to them. Her multicolored hair

stood out all over her head, looking like iridescent pink and blue spikes. It reminded Emma of Tracie's hair, but that was where the resemblance ended. This girl was well-fed and brimming with health. She took a pencil from behind an ear decorated with so many earrings there was little flesh exposed. "What'll you guys have?"

Nate frowned and looked down at the menu. "I'll have a burger, medium rare, fries and a beer."

Emma looked up at the board—fish sandwiches and deep-fried shrimp. After that movie, she decided against seafood. "I'll have a grilled cheese and iced tea, please."

"Gotcha." The girl bounced away to a tune only she could hear.

Nate slowly shook his head and rolled his eyes. "If that's a sample of the younger generation, God help civilization."

They sat back enjoying the view: excursion boats filling with people; colorful crowds walking back and forth; children chasing pigeons and squealing with delight.

When their order arrived, they began eating and enjoying the breeze that blew off the lake. Suddenly Emma froze. She dropped her sandwich on her plate and stared.

"What?" Nate asked.

She held up her hand and listened to snatches of conversation at a table behind them.

"The bawth's really mad," said a lisping, high-pitched voice.

"We gotta find that dame." A low, gravelly voice.

"Shoulda dumped…"

"Shut up." The voices dropped to a whisper.

"Nate, those two behind us. I recognize the voices," she whispered. "I'm sure they're the men who kidnapped me. Don't turn around," she said as he began moving his head. "We mustn't let them suspect anything. Call Detective Spaulding, hurry." She clutched her trembling hands together.

He nodded. "Give me the camera from your purse," he whispered.

With difficulty, Emma extracted the small digital camera and handed it to him.

"I'm getting a refill," Nate said loudly. "You want anything?" He stood and walked into the interior of the restaurant. Sliding behind a doorway where he was obscured from view, he took a good look at the two men. One was thin and wiry looking with dark hair hanging in his eyes. He kept flipping his head giving him the appearance of someone with a tic. The other was overweight and looked out of condition. His belly spilled over his belt. His face wore a scowl; a wispy beard hung down his chin.

Nate felt a deep rage well up inside him. These two had hurt his Sparrow. He wanted to run out and attack them, beat them, but he knew he had to think rationally. He took a deep breath, pulled out his cell phone, and punched in Detective Spaulding's number. The voice that answered was someone else.

"I must speak with Detective Spaulding immediately. It's urgent."

"I'm sorry sir, he isn't in right now. This is Officer Thomas, can I help you?"

"This is Nate Sandler. The two men who abducted Emma Winberry a few weeks ago are here, in a restaurant at Navy Pier. Mrs. Winberry recognized their voices." Nate's voice rose in pitch with every word.

"I'm familiar with the case. Just where are you? There is security at the Pier. I'll contact them."

"We're in the outdoor section of the Dock Side Café."

"Okay. Stay put."

Nate flipped the phone closed. He knew he had to get their picture. He aimed the camera, but there were too many other patrons in the way. His hands trembled when he walked out toward Emma.

He motioned her to move aside, then said, "Smile," as he framed the two men in the viewfinder and clicked.

"That guy'th wavin'. Takin' pictures," high-pitched voice said.

The heavy one looked up and scowled. "So what? Everybody takes pictures."

"But he pointed the camera at uth."

"Hey, did you take our picture?" the heavy man asked. His scowl deepened.

"Hell no. Why would I want your ugly face? I took the lady's picture," Nate said, barely keeping his temper in check.

"Gimme that camera," the man said, getting up and swaggering toward Nate.

The other patrons looked around at the sound of raised voices. Some of them moved back.

"Officer," Emma called looking wildly around hoping to spot one.

"Leth get outta here," Squeaky Voice said.

Nate slipped the camera to Emma and grabbed the neck of his empty beer bottle. He stood defiant, daring them to try something.

Most of the surrounding patrons had vacated their tables, standing at a safe distance to watch the drama.

The two looked around. When they saw they were the center of attention, they ran out onto the Pier and mingled with the crowds.

"Oh Nate, they got away," Emma said in despair.

"Not to worry. We've got their picture."

When the police arrived, Nate explained what happened. They knew it was impossible to follow the two now.

"I got a picture on the digital camera," Nate said. "And, those two beer bottles," he pointed to the vacated table, "have their prints on them." He felt quite proud of himself.

"Good thinking, sir. Maybe you should be on the force," one of the officers said, smiling.

"No thanks, I'm too old for this kind of excitement."

The policemen bagged the beer bottles. "I'll have to ask you for that camera, Mr. Sandler. You can come down to the station tomorrow to pick it up."

"Okay," Nate agreed. He was clasping and unclasping his fists, still in an adrenaline rush.

Emma removed the camera from her purse and handed it to the officer.

"Here's a receipt," he said, scribbling on a notepad.

At that moment the server with the multicolored hair ran up to the policemen. "Those guys didn't pay," she whined. "Aren't you gonna go after them? I'm responsible for the tab."

"Don't worry," Nate said. "Add it to my bill."

She looked at him in wonder. "That's awful nice of you."

"I'm just a good guy."

"Thanks, mister." She gave him a smile that lit up her face, tabulated the bill, and handed it to Nate.

He gave her a generous tip and watched her prance away.

"Well," Emma said. "There's hope for the younger generation yet."

THIRTY-FIVE

THE FOLLOWING DAY Nate and Emma went to the station to retrieve their camera. Detective Spaulding greeted them with a smile. He looked more rested than he had previously. A fresh haircut gave his face a neat appearance. His eyes almost twinkled.

"That was nice work you two did," he said with a nod.

Nate beamed at the compliment.

"We ran their fingerprints through the system. Came up with Alton Montgomery and Bernard Gordon, AKA Bubba. The prints confirmed their identities and the picture coincided with their mug shots. They are well-known to the police. My men are searching their last known addresses."

"Will I have to testify in court?" Emma asked, biting her lip and twisting her hands.

"Yes, I'm afraid you will, Mrs. Winberry. Are you okay with that?" He raised his eyebrows.

"I guess so. Certainly. They can't get away with snatching people off the street," she said, jutting her chin forward.

He nodded, then frowned. "One thing bothers me. They've only been convicted of petty crimes—mostly stealing small things, no large sums of money, certainly nothing as sophisticated as kidnapping. We have to find out who's paying them, who's behind the whole thing."

"How are you going to do that?" Emma asked, wide-eyed.

The detective smiled. "That's my job. Leave it to me. Here's your camera, and thanks for your help." He took the digital camera out of his desk drawer and handed it to Nate. A yellow evidence tape hung from the strap.

"By the way, after we printed the picture of the two, we deleted it. Sorry…"

"Their ugly faces are imprinted on my mind," Nate said, clenching his teeth. "I'll never forget what they look like, as long as I live."

THAT EVENING another late-summer storm lashed the city with its fury. Emma watched from the atrium. She could see huge waves crashing against the shore. The cars on Lake Shore Drive crawled. The wind howled like a wounded animal. Rain came down with such force that Navy Pier disappeared from view.

"What a strange feeling," Emma said as Nate came up behind her. "It seems like we're floating, suddenly disconnected from the earth."

"It does, doesn't it?" he said, snaking his arms around her. She wiggled closer.

"I have a bad feeling," she said, turning her face toward his.

"Now what?"

"I'm not sure, but something else is going to happen."

"Well, I can't argue with you. You're right most of the time. I thought this might be a good time for a romantic interlude."

"Oh Nate." She threw her arms around his neck and covered his face with kisses.

As his hands began exploring her body, the phone rang. "Damn!" he said. "Don't answer it."

"I have to." She pulled away from him, regret registering on her face.

"Hello."

"Goldi?" the familiar voice asked.

"Jake, yes, it's me."

"I talked to Minnie again. She says okay, but we gotta meet someplace where there ain't no police."

"What about the diner?" Emma asked.

"No. She wants to meet on the street."

Emma shook her head. Why were they so suspicious? Didn't the woman realize what kind of danger she was in?

"All right. Let me know when and where." She hung up the phone and turned to Nate.

He stood back, his arms folded, a look of resignation on his face. "I suppose I'll have to forget about amour until this thing is resolved."

Emma gave him a helpless look and shrugged just as a bolt of lightning hit the lake followed by a deafening crash of thunder. The entire condo was plunged into darkness.

"Nate!" Emma shouted.

"Here I am. Don't be frightened. Stay where you are, I've got a flashlight here, somewhere."

He fumbled around until Emma heard a click and saw the circle of light. She slowly let out the breath she was holding. "That was a little scary," she said, grasping his arm.

"It's all right. That lightning must have struck a transformer. We'll probably be without power for a while."

Another streak zigzagged across the sky followed by a thunderous crash.

"Get away from the windows," Nate warned.

"I'm worried about my plants out there."

"Never mind the plants. Come and sit here on the couch." He pulled her down beside him. "Isn't this nice? Very romantic."

Emma snuggled against him, hardly in the mood for romance. She didn't like storms, the electricity in the atmosphere made her skin feel like bugs crawling all over her.

Rain pelted the windows, sounding like pebbles being hurled by an angry god. The wind howled like all the demons of hell.

Emma snuggled closer, picked up her head and listened. "What's that sound?"

"The rain hitting against the windows," Nate said, squeezing her tighter.

"No." She pulled away. "It sounds like it's coming from the door." She got up and inched her way toward the front door, Nate right behind her.

"Someone's trying to open the door," he whispered.

Emma felt the hairs on the back of her neck rise.

"Stay here. I'll be right back," Nate ordered.

Emma flattened herself against the wall next to the door and listened. It sounded like someone was inserting something in the lock. She was glad she had fastened the chain.

A minute later Nate returned carrying a ball peen hammer. "Who's out there?" he shouted in a threatening voice.

The sounds stopped.

"I said who is it, and what do you want?"

Mumbling from the other side. Nate checked the chain and opened the door a crack. He shone the light directly into the eyes of a surprised burly man.

"I have a weapon. If you don't tell me what you're doing here, I'll call the police. Emma, get the phone."

The man held up his hands. "Wait a minute, mister. I got the wrong place. I can see that. Was lookin' for Evans."

"He lives next door. How did you get up here? This is a secure building. Unless someone buzzed you in, you couldn't open the front door."

"Uh, I made a mistake. I'm going right now."

He turned and ran toward the stairwell, stumbling in the dark. They heard the door to the stairway open, then close.

Nate blew out a breath then turned to Emma, his hands shaking.

"Shall we call the police?" she asked.

"He'll be long gone before they get here. I think it's time I had a talk with our neighbor. Your intuition may be right, my dear. He's into something shady."

THE NEXT MORNING the sun shone on a cleanly washed world. The electricity had come on sometime during the night; the appliances' buzzing was reassuring.

Emma went out on the roof to view the carnage the storm had done to her plants. A few pots lay on their sides, soil seeping out from the tops, but most had weathered the storm. She set about cleaning the mess while Nate went next door.

He returned a few minutes later. "Evans is out of town, his wife said. She seemed frightened when I told her what happened. She said she would tell him as soon as he gets back. He has some explaining to do, both to me and to the Condo Association." He frowned, then picked up a broom with more force than was necessary, and proceeded to help with the cleanup.

Emma looked out over the lake. The storm had passed, but another tempest was brewing.

THIRTY-SIX

JAKE CALLED BACK a few days later. "Minnie say Saturday night at Clark and Polk Street. There's a lot where you can leave your car. A little way down Clark a charity gives out suppers to folks like us. We be there."

Emma let out a breath puffing out her cheeks. "What time?"

"'Bout six."

Emma continued to hold the receiver to her ear, but soon heard only the dial tone. "I swear, I don't know why I get involved in all this," she mumbled.

Nate put down the book he had been reading and asked the question with his eyes.

"We're to meet them at Clark and Polk Streets at six on Saturday."

"Any particular reason for choosing that spot?"

"Someone distributes food to the homeless."

He shrugged. "I suppose that's as good a reason as any."

ON SATURDAY, Emma paced, unsure of what she would say to gain this woman's confidence. "Let's dress down," she said, looking through her closet for something appropriate.

"I wasn't going to wear a suit and tie," Nate said, pulling on a pair of old slacks and a washed-out T-shirt with an un-identifiable logo.

"Do I look the part of a conspirator?" he asked, a twinkle in his eye.

"You look like a bum," Emma said, giggling.

"I'll have you know this is the exact outfit I wore when I used to wash my own car."

"Good, maybe you can get a job at the local car wash. I heard they were hiring." She gave him a smile and received a frown in return.

Emma found an old pair of jeans and slipped a blue and white striped shirt over it. "Is this okay?"

"Fine. Let's not let anybody see us leave the building. They'll think we're vagrants."

"It's nobody's business," she said with a snort.

"I'm glad to hear you say that, my dear. You should take your own advice."

She gave him a look that would thaw an ice sculpture, turned, and walked out the door.

As they left the building Emma looked up at the leaden sky threatening another storm and wondered if it was a portent of more trouble.

When they arrived at the appointed spot, Nate parked the BMW in the northwest corner of the lot in the very last space, next to an oversized SUV.

"I suggest you lock your purse in the trunk," he said, getting out and surveying the area.

She did, then stood and looked around.

"It appears that someone plans to build a high-rise on this spot," Nate said. He stared at the architectural rendering of a towering structure that didn't seem to fit in with the area. "Now what do we do?" he asked, turning to Emma.

"Let's walk down the block to the food dispensary truck. See? There's a line of people waiting for a handout."

"Do we get in line with all the rest?"

Emma looked at him in exasperation. "This is a serious matter, Nate Sandler. We're trying to save someone's life here."

"Don't sound so melodramatic, my dear. Perhaps if we just stand here next to this building, they'll seek us out."

"Hmm," Emma said, looking closely at the line of people. Men and women stood patiently waiting, all dressed in shabby clothes, all with despairing expressions on their faces. Did she even remember what Jake looked like? She had been only half-conscious when she met him.

"Oh look, those two coming from the corner. That has to be them. Look at the way she's walking, poor thing." Emma shook her head in wonder that the woman could navigate as well as she did.

A big, burly black man dressed in old torn jeans and a tight black T-shirt accompanied a diminutive white woman. Her gait identified her immediately as Minnie. Her right leg pumped precariously up and down in the ill-fitting prosthesis. She had to swing the leg in a wide arc to the side for the foot to clear the ground. She wore a man's worn shoe on the large prosthetic foot and an athletic shoe of unknown vintage on her own smaller one.

As they joined the queue, Jake looked around and nodded when he spotted Emma. He whispered something to the woman. She raised her head and looked up at Emma and Nate. An old straw hat with a faded flower dangling at the side covered her head. A few strands of hair escaped from the sides, the same color and fiber as the hat.

She wore men's trousers cinched at the waist with a piece of rope. A man's shirt with the sleeves cut off covered the top of her, a button missing from the center. She had tucked it into the trousers. Emma could only guess at its original color. A pair of suspenders rested on her shoulders, their ends disappearing into the trousers. Jake had said she needed these to hold up the artificial limb.

"Oh Nate," Emma whispered. "What a disaster."

He simply shook his head as they waited for the pair to get their packets of food. The meal consisted of a sandwich, an apple and a carton of juice. Some of the people ate their food on the spot; others tucked it into their belongings as they scuttled away.

Jake grabbed Minnie's hand and pulled her toward Emma and Nate.

"Hi, Goldi," he said, a broad smile showing a gold tooth in the center. "You look pretty good." His expression radiated warmth as well as a sense of resignation to life's enigmas. "This here is Minnie."

Emma's eyes widened as the breeze blew the odor of sweat, urine and something unidentifiable into her face. She swallowed, trying desperately not to react, but she couldn't help taking a step backwards.

"I'm happy to meet you," Emma said, deciding whether or not she should shake hands. Was that speck on Minnie's hat moving? Finally she forced herself to extend her hand.

Minnie chose to ignore it and looked at Nate. "Who's this dude? You a cop?"

"No, no," Emma said. "This is my friend, Nate Sandler. He watches over me, don't you, Nate?" She turned her eyes to his.

"You bet I do," he said.

"She's your woman," Jake observed. "That's good. You can trust them, Minnie. I feel it in my gut."

"Humph. I don't go for those feelings. Where can we eat? I'm hungry."

"My car is in the parking lot, over in the corner," Nate said, pointing. "That gray one."

Emma poked Nate in the ribs with her elbow, frowned and gave him a slight shake of her head. How many vermin would they leave in the cushions? She gave a sigh of relief at Minnie's response.

"I ain't sittin' in no fancy car. Let's go behind it. We can sit on the railing."

As they walked into the lot, Minnie shook her head and frowned. "See," she said, pointing to the sign. "They put a new building up here and the fancy folks won't want that food truck no more. Always pushin' us out." She perched herself on a low railing and attacked the packet. Within minutes she had wolfed down the sandwich, taking gulps of juice between bites. "Dry," she croaked.

"You want somethin'?" Jake asked, looking at Emma and Nate.

"No thanks, we ate before we came," Emma said. "In fact, I brought some muffins along in case you're still hungry."

"Yeah, I could go for one," Minnie said, shoving the last bite of bread in her mouth.

Nate opened the car door and took out the bag of muffins. He was careful to lock it again.

"Ain't takin' no chances, huh?" Jake said with a grin.

"Not with this car."

"Smart man. What kinda' muffins, Goldi?"

"Banana nut."

"Oh boy, lemme have one," Minnie said, grabbing a soft, moist muffin from Nate's hand. She took a generous bite. "Ain't had nothin' this good in years." She reached for another. Between the two of them, they ate the entire bag within minutes.

"Ah, that's better." Minnie looked questioningly at Emma. "What you want to see me about that's so damn important?"

"I believe your life is in danger," Emma said.

Minnie laughed. "Who'd want to hurt me, an old bag lady?" She became pensive. "My life ain't worth much anyway. Don't have no place to make good muffins like these here." She pointed to the empty bag.

"You may have witnessed a murder and you might have taken something of value from the murdered man."

"Who told you that?" The woman pulled away hunching her shoulders, a frightened look crossing her face.

"Jake told you I was kidnapped by two thugs, didn't he?"

She nodded.

"They thought I was you. They won't stop looking until they find you. They want whatever you took from the dead man in the alley." Emma looked closely as Minnie's expression became more fearful.

"I didn't take nothin'." She shook her head adamantly.

"Minnie, listen to me. They left me to die, tied up in an abandoned warehouse with only rats for company. God only knows what they'll do to you if they find you."

"I think you better listen to the lady, Min," Jake said. "She make sense."

Emma persisted. *Guardian Angel, help me get through to this woman.*

"You did take a ring off his finger, didn't you?" She made eye contact with Minnie and held it.

"How'd you know that?"

"The newspaper said that two rings were missing. The man had money in his wallet and wore an expensive watch, but only the rings were stolen. Did you take them?" Emma held the eye contact until the woman sighed and looked away.

She shook her head vigorously. "I only took one. Them guys took the other one. Didn't have time to take nothin' else. Heard the sirens comin' and I hightailed it as quick as I could."

"Did you see the two men, Minnie? This is very important."

The woman nodded. "I seen 'em skulkin' in the alley, seen 'em hit the guy. I didn't see their faces too good, but they seen me. They ran, too, when they heard the police comin'."

Emma let out a breath she didn't realize she was holding. Her energy drained away with it.

"The police gonna arrest me for stealin'?"

"No, I don't think so. If you give back the ring, they won't charge you." Emma had no basis for this remark, but it seemed like the only thing she could say at the moment.

"Why should I believe you?"

"Because you have no one else to believe," Emma said with an authority she didn't feel.

"I like that ring. It's pretty. It shines nice."

"May I see it?" Emma asked.

The woman hesitated, as if she were trying to decide.

"Go on, Min, show it to her," Jake said, giving her a nudge.

She frowned at him then rolled up her pant leg and plunged her hand down into the gaping prosthesis. She pulled out an old lace handkerchief with embroidered thread unraveling around the sides. Hesitantly she handed it to Emma.

In the waning light Emma unwrapped the faded hanky to reveal a class ring, the name of the school and the year inscribed on the side. A semiprecious stone sat in the center. There didn't appear to be anything unusual about it.

"Suppose," Nate said, "we hand this over to the police without telling them where we found it."

"But it's mine," Minnie protested.

"I'll give you a receipt," Nate said, pulling out his wallet. He took out five twenty-dollar bills and placed them in Minnie's outstretched hand. "How's that?"

Her eyes widened. "I couldn't get half that much from a fence." She grinned revealing a huge gap between her front teeth. She grabbed the bills and shoved them down into the prosthesis.

"Minnie," Emma persisted, "can you go somewhere that's reasonably safe, a shelter maybe? Just until the police find these thugs?"

Minnie frowned, then looked at Jake.

"She's right, Min," he said, nodding.

"I'll think about it. Now, you told Jake you'd help me get a new leg that fits good," she said, looking at Emma.

"Yes, I did."

"You gonna keep your promise?"

"Certainly. How can I get in touch with you?"

"Jake'll call ya. Now we gotta go. Been here too long."

"Call me next week, Jake," Emma said.

"Sure, Goldi, sure." He looked at Nate and grinned. "Bye, Baldie."

Nate frowned, then laughed and raised his hand in a salute.

The food truck had gone, leaving the street deserted in the approaching dusk. Jake and Minnie walked down the sidewalk, Minnie hobbling, looking as if she might fall with each step. They disappeared into an alley.

"And how do you propose to keep that promise?" Nate asked, running his hand over his head as he unlocked the car door.

"I have no idea."

THIRTY-SEVEN

EMMA AND NATE looked at the ring from every possible angle, but could find nothing different about it. There was no secret inscription on the inside, no special markings. It was just a class ring like any other.

"Do you think this stone is more than it appears to be?" Emma asked.

Nate made a face and shrugged. "It looks just like the one in my class ring." He walked over to the end table, opened the drawer, and took out a magnifying glass.

"Hmm."

"What? Did you find something?" Emma leaned over his shoulder and squinted through the glass.

"It looks like there's a little bit of glue or something sticky in this corner," Nate observed.

"Maybe the stone came loose and he glued it back in place."

"Or, maybe, he took it out for some reason."

"Oh Nate, now you're playing detective." Emma grinned, caught up in the mystery.

"Let's go in the kitchen where the light is better and pry up this stone," he said.

"Do you think we should?"

Nate gave her a look, shrugged, then walked into the kitchen. He put a clean white dishtowel on the table and placed the ring on it.

"Isn't this tampering with evidence?"

"Sure, but we're already guilty of withholding information

from the police. We can say the stone fell out." He raised his eyebrows and pursed his lips. "Emma, get me a razor blade from the bathroom, and don't cut yourself."

"I'm not a child," she said, straightening her back and hurrying into the bathroom. "Ow! Damn!" She came out with the blade, sucking her finger. "Don't say a word."

He laughed as he took the blade and gently poked at the gluelike substance in the corner. After careful prodding, he was able to pull it away, leaving a tiny space. He put the edge of the razor blade into the space and put gentle pressure on it. One side of the stone came loose and Nate pushed the instrument farther underneath until the stone popped out. He slowly turned the setting over and a tiny microchip fell out on the towel.

"Well, well. So this is what those two were after. Whatever's on this chip, someone was willing to kill for it."

Emma stood still, wide-eyed, her mouth open.

"Get me a pair of tweezers," Nate said, "and an envelope. And put a Band-Aid on your finger. You're bleeding on the floor. Emma, did you hear me?" He gave her a gentle nudge.

"Yes, yes." She hurried out of the room holding the injured finger.

Later they sat in the living room staring at each other. "What do you think is on there?" Emma asked, brimming with excitement.

"Haven't got a clue. But, since the man was an eccentric inventor who made a bunch of claims, it could be plans for something valuable or some exotic dream, like a spaceship or a UFO."

"Oh, now you're making fun. What shall we do with it?"

"Since it's ten o'clock at night, I suggest we go to bed. Tomorrow morning we'll call Detective Spaulding, and we'd better have a good story to tell him. I have a feeling he's not going to be too happy with our meddling in his case."

"Nonsense, we've already helped him. We identified the two thugs and we found Minnie. The police haven't been able to do that."

Nate got up from his chair, stretched, and headed for the bedroom. "You forget, Sparrow, that he'll want to know how we found Minnie. We didn't just happen to bump into her on Michigan Avenue. You'll have to tell him about Jake. It's time to confess your little transgression and ask for forgiveness."

He put his arm around her and guided her to the bed.

"I suppose you're right," she said, yawning. "All this intrigue is tiring. Let's go to sleep."

But Emma couldn't sleep. She tossed and turned, listening with envy to Nate's even breathing. He let out an occasional snore. She got up, pushed her feet into her fuzzy slippers and walked into the atrium.

A heaviness lay inside her. Every time she closed her eyes, she saw Minnie. She could be anywhere from fifty to seventy. It was hard to tell. How does one end up on the street? Emma wondered. What was her life like? Did she have family? How had she lost her leg? So many questions, but no answers.

You must find out more about this woman, the voice inside of her said.

Now listen, Guardian Angel, am I responsible for everyone's problems? Tracie, Laura, and now, Minnie?

Life has been good to you, Emma Winberry. You must give back to others less fortunate. You have the gift.

Ah yes, the gift. "You're right," Emma said out loud. "I am a most fortunate woman. I realize that and I must help others."

"Now you're talking to yourself, hum?" Nate came up behind her.

She jumped. "You shouldn't sneak up on me like that."

"And who were you talking to?"

"The spirits," she said in a low, menacing voice.

"Come back to bed. It's lonesome in there all alone."

In the moonlight she could see the longing on his face.

She got up, climbed in bed and snuggled into his embrace. They kissed; they touched, and soon forgot about everything else but each other.

WHEN NATE CALLED the police station the following day, Sunday, the officer on duty told him that Detective Spaulding wouldn't be in until Monday morning.

"Is there anything I can do for you, sir?" the man asked.

"No thank you. I'll call tomorrow. Just leave him a message that Emma Winberry and Nate Sandler want to see him about an important matter."

Ending the call, Nate turned to Emma. "Now that that's done, we have this entire day to ourselves, for a change. What is your pleasure, Madam?" He made a deep bow and gave her a lascivious grin. When he straightened up, he grimaced, grunted and rubbed the small of his back.

"You're not a young buck anymore," Emma said. "Be careful of your back."

He grabbed her playfully in his arms. "I was pretty good last night, wasn't I?" He nibbled her ear and her neck.

"Nate, stop that. Act your age." She gave him a reprimanding look but broke into a giggle.

"That wouldn't be any fun now, would it?"

"I'll fix breakfast," she said, "and you check the Sunday paper for something we might enjoy."

Nate gave her a pat on the rear as she sauntered into the kitchen. When she came back carrying two mugs of coffee, Nate had the newspaper spread out on the floor, section by section.

"Here," he said, "the last concert of the season at Millennium Park. It's a lovely day, promises to be a perfect evening. How does that grab you?"

She raised her eyebrows as she handed him his coffee. "Sounds perfect."

They spent the rest of the day reading, relaxing and talking with their respective families. Nate called his brother in Florida.

"Rachel says he's behaving himself. He lost ten pounds, is going to cardiac rehab, and eating the right foods. I wonder how long that will last?"

"Maybe he's learned his lesson," Emma said.

"I know my brother. By the way, he wants to know when we're both coming for a proper visit."

"As soon as the weather cools off down there. It's been bad enough here. Summer in Florida is definitely not my thing," she said.

Emma walked to the window watching the street below. The strip of land east of Lake Shore Drive bordering the lake was alive with activity—families walking, joggers, cyclists. They looked like puppets bouncing on strings. An armada of sailboats raced across the water. A mad rush of humanity attempted to squeeze the most out of the waning days of summer.

"WHAT TIME DOES the concert start?" Emma asked.

"Outdoor concerts always start at dusk, you know that," Nate said. "If we get to Millennium Park about seven, we can spread our blanket on the lawn and walk around a bit. It's supposed to be a nice evening and this program will draw a lot of people." Nate looked at the announcement in the newspaper.

"'Elena Consada,'" he read aloud, "'the Spanish soprano who captured the world by storm with her dramatic voice and continental flair, will sing selections from operas by Puccini, Verdi, and Massenet. Her voice has the same remarkable quality as that of Rosa Finelli who recently retired from the operatic stage.'"

"Well," Emma said, "that's quite a recommendation. I hope she lives up to it."

Emma went about cleaning the kitchen, remembering her encounter with the tempestuous soprano, La Finelli, at a performance at the Midwest Opera. She had certainly been difficult to deal with, carried almost as much baggage as Tracie. I wonder what happened to her?

When it was time to leave, Nate took a bottle of champagne out of the refrigerator, wrapped it in a towel, and put it carefully in a small picnic basket. Emma smiled as she wrapped two plastic flutes and nestled them next to the bottle. She tucked another container inside.

"Music always sounds better while one is sipping champagne," Nate said, winking at Emma. He carefully laid the blanket on the top of the basket.

They boarded a bus on Michigan Avenue, disembarked on Randolph Street and joined the crowd on their way to the Music Pavilion on Columbus Drive.

"Look at all these people," Emma said.

"I told you this would be a popular event," Nate said. "Now do you believe me?"

The flower petal-shaped steel performance shell looked like a surreal sculpture. The rays of the setting sun reflected off the surface like sparkling jewels.

"Here's a spot," Nate said, walking onto the turf of the egg-shaped area. He put down the basket and spread the blanket on the ground.

"Isn't it great that there are so many wealthy people like the Pritzker family who donate huge sums of money to make all this possible?" Emma mused. She looked up at the netlike structure creating a dome over the entire area.

"What a feat of engineering," Nate said. "Who would imagine that those pipes provide a state-of-the-art sound system?" He shook his head in wonder. "Do you want to walk around?"

"No. Someone might steal our spot and our champagne," Emma said. "See how the area is filling up? I'm going to sit right here and guard our goodies."

Nate laughed. "Speaking of which, I'd better open that

bottle before the concert starts. We can't have corks popping in the middle of an aria."

He opened the champagne and poured two glasses. "To us," he said, touching her glass with his. "A great pair."

"I'll drink to that." Emma laughed as she sipped the wine, bubbles tickling her nose.

"What else did you put in here?" Nate asked.

"Some strawberries," she said, giving him an innocent look. "They go well with champagne."

She sat comfortably in the lotus position. As she promised herself in that warehouse, she had been practicing yoga and this pose became second nature. She sipped the bubbly, savored the juicy berries, and looked around at the crowds of people: families with children of all ages, young couples gazing into each other's eyes, older couples talking amiably.

Her gaze stopped at a pair directly across from them. "Nate, look—those two—the woman in the red halter top and black shorts. That man. Isn't he our neighbor, the elusive Mr. Evans?"

Nate turned. "It sure is. And that is definitely not Mrs. Evans. I'll try and catch up with him at the intermission." Nate rubbed his chin and frowned as he watched the two. "On second thought, this might not be the right time to approach him about questionable people at our door." He shook his head. "There's something shady about that man."

Evans and his playmate seemed oblivious to anyone around them. His hands explored her body with familiarity. She twisted and squealed. They began kissing passionately just as the announcer walked out on the stage.

"Ladies and gentlemen, we are happy to present to you tonight a new star in the firmament of music, Elena Consada."

The audience greeted the singer with enthusiastic applause.

Emma watched as the two composed themselves, he wiping off lipstick, she rearranging her scanty top.

"Miss Consada will begin our program with a zarzuela from her homeland."

More applause filled the night air as the buxom, dark-haired beauty walked onto the stage in a shimmering gown of black sequins. She held up her arms, bowed to the audience and burst into a lively Latin melody.

During the intermission Emma looked around, but Evans and his playmate were nowhere to be seen.

"I'll bet Laura thinks he's still out of town," Emma said in disgust. "What a distorted family they are."

"That man is as mysterious as the Scarlet Pimpernel," Nate said, pouring the last of the champagne. "Hey, that's a great title for a story, *Golidocks Meets the Scarlet Pimpernel.* I'll bet it would be a best-seller." He threw back his head and laughed. "I'll have to run it by Cornell."

"Very funny." Emma frowned. A sudden breeze off the lake sent a chill through her. Was she somehow going to be involved with this nasty man as well as all the others?

THIRTY-EIGHT

MONDAY MORNING Nate and Emma arrived at the police station at nine. Emma felt nervous about this interview. She noticed a peculiar smell, something unfamiliar—was it sweat, vomit, or mold?

The sound of a woman shouting came from behind a closed door. Emma felt so many conflicting vibrations in this place. She wanted to run out the door but, at that moment, they were called into Detective Spaulding's office.

"Good morning," she said, giving him a broad smile though her limbs felt a little shaky and she kept her hands tightly clutching her purse.

Nate nodded.

"Have a seat," the detective said. A cup of coffee sat on his desk in a spot where it apparently remained most of the time. Rings of the spilt brew made a circular pattern on the metal desk. He grabbed the cup and took a swallow, made a face and put it down. "Cold. Now, what do you two have to tell me?"

Nate looked at Emma. "I'll start," she said. She fidgeted for a moment until she was as comfortable as possible on the hard wooden chair. She took a deep breath and blew it out. The detective sat back, waiting.

"I didn't exactly tell you everything about my experience in the warehouse." She looked at him expecting some sort of reprimand, but he said nothing, simply stared at her in his unnerving manner.

"About that room with the mattress?" Emma continued, "I

did fall onto it and lose consciousness, but the occupant found me. He was very kind and he carried me to the diner where the owner called nine-one-one." Emma felt like a child caught playing hooky.

"And why didn't you tell me this before?" Detective Spaulding asked, his brows knit together.

"Well…" Emma wiggled around in the chair trying to get comfortable. "He said he didn't want anything to do with the police so I figured he must have a record. And, since he wasn't involved in the kidnapping, I didn't think it was relevant."

"Mrs. Winberry. Let me decide what's relevant."

Emma jumped at his tone. "I'm sorry."

"Detective," Nate said, "she was just trying to protect the man."

Emma looked at him and began taking rapid short breaths; she caught herself just as spots began dancing before her eyes. Calm down, she told herself. She took a deep breath, then another and began to relax.

Detective Spaulding waited a moment, then said, "Go on. I suspect there's more to this confession."

Emma looked at Nate for moral support. He took her cold hand in his and gave it a squeeze.

"Well…" She hesitated again searching for the right words. "I decided to give him a gift, for saving my life." She leaned forward. "He did save my life, Detective."

Spaulding sat back, his lips twitching. "Yes, he did. Go on."

"We bought him some clothing for the coming winter and left the package at the diner. A short time later he called to thank me. I thought that was a nice gesture."

"Wait a minute. You say he called you."

Emma nodded.

"How did he get your phone number?"

"Oh, I left a note in with the clothes telling him that Minnie was in danger and, if he knew her, he should let her know. I left my number."

"And did he identify himself as Jackson Baker?"

"He told me to call him Jake. He said he did know Minnie and would try to find her."

Emma stopped. Her mouth was so dry she could hardly speak. "Might I have some water?"

"Sure. You want coffee?" He looked at the two of them. They shook their heads. He pressed a button on the phone and said, "Bring two cups of water in here, please."

An aide came in carrying two paper cups. He handed one to Emma and the other to Nate.

After Emma downed half of the cool water, she continued. "Jake was as good as his word. He found Minnie and gave her the message, but she was suspicious and refused to contact me." Emma was animated now as she told the story. "Jake said that Minnie had lost her leg in an accident and was wearing an old prosthesis she found somewhere."

The detective shook his head; his face softened in a hint of a smile.

"So I told him if she agreed to meet with us, I'd see she got a proper limb."

"You certainly are taking a lot of responsibility here, Mrs. Winberry. How do you propose to do that?"

"I'm not sure, but there must be agencies to help homeless people."

Nate put his hand on Emma's arm. "I'll finish the story," he said, taking an envelope out of his pocket. "We did meet the woman Saturday night and convinced her to turn over the class ring she took from the body of the dead man. She claimed she saw the two men strike the inventor on the head and take the other ring."

Detective Spaulding scratched his head and looked at Nate in disbelief. "She told you that?"

"Yes. She saw two men in the shadows, but couldn't identify them. They all scattered when they heard the sirens. The only thing she had time to take was the class ring."

He withdrew a folded piece of paper from the envelope and carefully placed it on the desk.

The detective unfolded the paper to reveal the ring with the stone removed and the microchip tucked into the setting. He raised his eyebrows in a question.

"The stone was loose and, with a little bit of prodding, it came off," Nate said, shrugging his shoulders.

Detective Spaulding scowled and shook his head. "Whatever information is on this chip is what those thugs were after. You know, you two are guilty of tampering with evidence." He looked at Emma and Nate with a stern expression. "You should have come to me as soon as you made contact with this woman."

Emma sat up straight, her eyes wide. "Detective, do you really think she would have been so forthright with the law? I brought her banana-nut muffins."

"And for that she just handed you the ring?"

Nate bit the side of his cheek and gave the detective a sheepish look. "I gave her a few bucks. She certainly looked like she could use them."

The detective let out a whistle. "All right. You've done well here, but, I'm warning you both, no more interference. Is that clear?"

"Absolutely," Nate said.

"There is one more thing," Emma said. "My promise to Minnie about the leg."

Detective Spaulding thought for a moment, then scrawled a phone number on a notepad. "Call Father Michael at St. Andrew's Parish. He works with a lot of indigents and should be able to help." As they were leaving, Emma turned around.

"You will let us know what's on that microchip, won't you?"

He gave her a look that said, "Don't even go there." Nate took Emma's hand and hurried her out of the office.

THIRTY-NINE

A FEW DAYS LATER, Jake called again. "Goldi," his worried voice said, "Minnie's missin'."

"What do you mean missing?"

"Nobody's seen her since last Saturday. She usually sleeps at one o' them shelters, but she ain't been to none of 'em."

"Oh dear, I warned her to find a safe place. Is there anywhere else she might have gone?" Emma asked, a feeling of trepidation creeping up her spine.

"Don't think so. Hope nothin's happened to her."

"So do I. Keep me posted, Jake."

"Now what?" Nate asked as he walked into the room.

"Minnie's nowhere to be found." Emma paced from one end of the room to the other. "If those thugs got hold of her…" She couldn't finish the sentence. She looked at Nate with a pained expression.

"Sparrow," he said, taking her in his arms. "There's nothing you can do about it."

"Maybe it's my fault. Maybe they saw her with us. Maybe…"

"Stop it," he commanded. "It's not your fault. No one was watching us, we checked that, remember?"

She nodded wiping away the tears that sneaked from the corners of her eyes. "She's in trouble. I feel it." *Oh Guardian Angel, help.* Emma began sniffling.

Nate held her, patting her back until she regained control.

"Go lie down for a while," he said. "I'll start dinner."

Before he reached the kitchen the phone rang again.

"Hello."

"Mr. Sandler, this is Detective Spaulding. I think we've found Minnie."

"Where is she?"

"At the moment she's at Stroger Hospital. Somebody worked her over pretty good. She refuses to give them her full name or tell them anything about herself. Says she's Minnie and will only talk to someone named Goldi, the Muffin Lady."

Nate laughed and shook his head. "That sounds like her."

"I remembered Mrs. Winberry saying she brought Minnie muffins. Where does the Goldi come in?"

"It's a long story. Suffice it to say that the street people identify Emma by that name."

"Nothing surprises me anymore," the detective said. "Can you and Mrs. Winberry meet me at the hospital? I want to question her, but she won't talk."

"We'll be there in a half hour."

Nate turned to see Emma's frightened eyes staring at him from the bedroom doorway. "Come on, we have to go to Stroger Hospital."

"Minnie?" Emma ran out of the bedroom and grabbed Nate's arm. "Is she all right?"

"Stop worrying, she's tough. But she refuses to talk to anyone but the Muffin Lady."

"Oh the dear sweet thing," Emma said, smiling. "Let's get going." She reached for a sweater. The cool weather had arrived suddenly, putting an end to the brutal heat wave.

Emma felt such a wash of relief that she almost danced out the door. Nate followed, a look of resignation on his face.

The evening rush hour made their trip to the hospital longer than they anticipated. The Emergency Room bustled with activity. Gurneys, with half-conscious patients waiting for transport, lined the corridors. They spotted the detective talking with one of the nurses. He gave them a rare smile; his face looked almost handsome.

"This is Goldi," he said, introducing Emma to the nurse.

"I'm certainly glad you're here," the frustrated nurse said. "To say that this patient is difficult is the understatement of the year. She says her name is Minnie, nothing else."

"What happened?" Emma asked.

"A patrolman found her under a bridge at the Chicago River. Apparently someone got a little rough and stole her prosthesis. She tried to hop, but fell and rolled down an embankment. That's where we found her."

"Take your hands off me! I don't want no more cleanin' up!" The angry voice came from one of the cubicles ringed by a curtain.

"That sounds like Minnie," Emma said, grinning. "Let me talk to her."

"Gladly," the nurse said, leading them into the cubicle. The bedside stand held a basin of dirty water, a white soap scum around the edges. A towel and wash cloth lay on the floor. The sour, decaying smells of the street lingered in the confined space.

"Goldi. Am I glad to see you. Tell these folks to leave me alone. They keep washin' me." Minnie pushed at the hand trying to comb her unruly hair.

Emma winced at the red swollen eyes and the bruises on her thin, frail arms. She looked so vulnerable.

"That's enough, Agnes," the nurse said to the aide. "We'll let the detective and this lady take over."

"They took my leg away," Minnie whined. "And then they hit me, over and over."

"Who was it?" Emma asked.

"Two rough lookin' guys. Think they was the same ones killed that guy in the alley. Grabbed me when I was goin' to the shelter for some grub."

Minnie stopped for a moment and took a breath. "Then they pulled me into some bushes. Said if I didn't tell 'em where the ring was, they was gonna kill me." She looked like a helpless child sitting up in bed, her hands and face washed, a clean hospital gown covering her frail body.

"It's all right, Minnie. You're safe now," Emma said, sitting down beside her.

She gave Emma a distressed look. "I had'a tell 'em I gave it to you. I ain't no snitch, but they was gonna kill me."

"Just exactly what did you tell them?" Detective Spaulding asked.

"Who's he, the fuzz?" Minnie asked, looking at him suspiciously.

"His name is Detective Spaulding. You can trust him. He's okay," Emma said.

Minnie shook her head. "Never trusted no police."

"Answer his question, Minnie, what did you tell them?"

"That I gave the ring to the Muffin Lady, and the dude with the fancy car." She gave Emma a look of remorse. "I ain't no snitch, but I didn't wanna die."

"Of course you didn't. But they still don't know who we are, so we're perfectly safe," Emma said, trying to sound convincing. But were they?

"Did you get a good look at them?" the detective asked.

"You bet I did."

"I'll want you to come down to the station and look at some pictures," he said.

"How am I gonna get there? I ain't got no leg." Minnie looked desolate.

Emma's heart went out to her. This woman was living on the edge of society. Any change in her existence could be disastrous. "We'll drive you there." She gave Nate a sweet smile and ignored his responding frown.

"How am I gonna walk?"

"The nurse will give you a pair of crutches. Can you use crutches?" the detective asked.

"'Course I can. Used to have 'em before I found my leg." She grumbled and mumbled. "Where's my clothes?" she called out to anyone within earshot. "I want out of here!"

"The doctors want to take some X rays," the detective said.

"Oh no. I'm okay, just sore. Wanna get out o' here."

The aide came in with a set of clean clothing.

"Them ain't mine," Minnie insisted.

"Yours were filthy and falling apart. I took these from our store of miscellaneous clothes," the woman insisted, handing them to Minnie.

"Won't wear 'em." Like a petulant child she folded her arms over her nonexistent bosom. "Want my own."

Detective Spaulding had reached the end of his tether. "I'll be at the station. Bring her along as soon as she's ready." Nate nodded watching the detective hurry away from this difficult woman.

He turned to her, his patience also at an end. "Now listen, if you want our help, you had better put these clothes on and stop complaining. Otherwise we'll simply leave you here and they'll put you back out on the street."

Minnie frowned at Nate and humphed. "Well get out so's I can get dressed. You'll help me, won't you, Goldi? I'm hurtin'."

Emma nodded as Nate walked out of the cubicle.

WHEN NATE REACHED the desk, he saw the nurse chuckling. "Not the easiest person to deal with, is she?"

"Do you have to put up with a lot of this kind of behavior?" Nate asked.

"You'd be surprised. She's typical of some of these street people. No matter how much we try to help them, most refuse and go back to their old lifestyles."

"I can't see what could be comfortable about it," Nate said, shaking his head.

"Neither can I, but that lifestyle is familiar and they're entitled to live as they please," she said, taking a folder from the desk. "I would like to fill in these items. Do you know her last name? Next of kin?"

"I have no idea," Nate said. "All we know her by is Minnie."

"She refuses to give us any more information than that. I'll have to file this along with all the others known only by their first names." The nurse put down the folder and looked at the clock. "Time for my break, and I sure need it."

Nate commiserated with the woman as she walked wearily down the hall. This would not be his choice of work, but, thank goodness, someone wanted to do it.

After a protracted length of time, Emma emerged from the cubicle followed by Minnie. She hobbled painfully on a pair of crutches, as a therapist fiddled with them.

"Let me adjust those one more notch," the therapist said.

"Leave 'em alone. I like 'em like this," Minnie insisted.

"All right." The woman held up her hands in dismissal and walked away.

"You have to sign this release," the ward secretary said as Emma and Minnie walked toward the desk.

Minnie squinted at the paper, then signed with an X.

"What is your full name?" the secretary asked.

"Minnie Smith."

She received a look of disdain from the woman behind the desk. "I'll file this with the thousand other Smiths. And, you have to go out in a wheelchair, hospital policy. If you just wait a minute, I'll call transport."

"I ain't sittin' in no wheelchair. I can walk with these crutches."

Minnie smirked and followed Emma and Nate out the door. When Nate brought the car up to the Emergency Room entrance, Emma saw the backseat draped with the blanket he kept in the trunk.

He's always prepared, she thought as they assisted Minnie into the car. She sniffed. It would take more than one bath to remove the smell from this woman.

WHEN THEY ARRIVED at the police station Minnie looked with compassion at the people sitting on benches waiting to be seen. She seemed to recognize someone, but didn't acknowledge the woman. Detective Spaulding ushered them into an interrogation room. It looked sterile with only a metal desk and a few chairs. Light came through a barred window. Emma shivered, remembering all the TV shows she had seen with criminals being questioned for hours by intimidating officers.

"Sorry to bring you in here," the detective said, "but every place else is occupied at the moment."

Minnie frowned. Emma could see she wasn't comfortable here at all.

"Now, Miss Minnie," Detective Spaulding said in a placating tone, "I'm going to show you some pictures. If you see the men who beat you, point them out."

Minnie sat back exuding an air of importance. She looked at the sheet of six faces then leaned forward, squinting through her swollen eyes. "That's them," she said, pointing to two men.

"Are you sure?" the detective asked.

She turned to him with an irate expression. "Are you callin' me a liar?"

"Absolutely not. I just want you to be certain."

"That's them all right. They hit me and took my leg and now I can't walk no more. They gotta be the same guys hit that man in the alley, 'cause they knew about the ring."

"Okay. Did you notice anything else about the men, something unusual in the way they talked?"

"Yeah," she said, her mouth agape. "One of 'em lisped. I

know what that sounds like. My kid brother used to talk like that. Had to have talkin' lessons."

"Very good, Minnie, you did well," the detective said.

"What's gonna happen to me now?" she asked.

The detective thought for a moment. "We can call Social Services and they'll find a place for you."

"No!" she said emphatically. "Don't want no nosey social worker askin' a bunch o' questions. I like my privacy." She hugged herself.

"What about that Father Michael you told me about?" Emma asked the detective.

"I heard about him," Minnie said. "He helped some folks I know."

"All right," he said, "I'll give him a call."

After a rather long phone conversation, Detective Spaulding assured Emma and Nate that he would have someone take Minnie to Father Michael's and they were free to go.

"WHY ARE ALL the windows open in this car?" Emma complained. "I'm chilly."

"I'm airing it out. In case you didn't notice, there was a decidedly unpleasant odor from that woman."

Emma didn't disagree. *Better not antagonize him,* the inner voice said.

"Let's stop for a bite. I'm in the mood for Chinese," Nate said pulling into a parking spot just as someone vacated it.

They walked into the traditionally red-and-black decorated atmosphere that dominated most Chinese restaurants. Emma breathed in the smells of garlic and curry. She looked at some patrons deftly picking up vegetables with chopsticks. *I must learn to do that.*

As they waited for their order, Emma shook her head. "When I think of what might have happened to that poor woman…" She didn't finish the sentence, just gave Nate a despairing look.

"Well, it didn't. So stop worrying about her. I'm sure she'll be well taken care of." He gave her a look that said, "Stay out of it."

Emma made a mental note to check up on her. She did have Father Michael's phone number. At that moment their order arrived. They both realized they were ravenous. Without another word each grabbed for an egg roll and the hot mustard sauce. Minnie and Father Michael could wait.

FORTY

A FEW DAYS later Bertie called.

"How are you feeling?" Emma asked, remembering how tired and queasy she had felt during her first trimester of pregnancy.

"The morning sickness is passing. I only throw up every other day now." Bertie laughed, an almost musical sound. "I called to ask about that poor girl next door. I haven't been able to get her out of my mind."

"I saw her a few days ago," Emma said. "According to her aunt, she stays in her room most of the time. I spoke to Laura about the psychiatrist, but she shrugged me off. Said she didn't care."

"It sounds like she needs help as much as the girl. I remember your telling me about the sketchbook. An art therapist just joined our staff. She might be of some help."

Emma remembered the disturbing drawings, the reflection of that girl's tortured soul. She sighed. "I'll try and talk to her about it, but don't expect too much." She felt helpless in this situation.

"I know. Sometimes it's easier for them to hold the grief and pain inside."

"Thanks for your concern, dear. Give my love to Martin. Talk to you soon."

Now, Guardian Angel, how am I going to approach Tracie? She bit down on her lip, screwed up her face and thought, but no insights came. I'll think of something, I always do.

That afternoon Emma spotted the girl on the roof, playing with the kitten. She grabbed a muffin from a plate on the kitchen table and hurried out the door.

"Hi, Tracie," she called. "I haven't seen you in a while."

The girl looked up in alarm, picked up the kitten and clutched it to her chest.

"I thought you and Hope might like to share a muffin." Emma opened the gate and extended her hand holding the golden brown confection. Hesitantly, Tracie limped toward her, wincing in pain.

"What's wrong, dear?" Emma asked, looking closely at her.

"I—fell," she whispered.

"Come on over and sit with me for a while."

Tracie looked back for a moment, as if expecting to see someone. Then she followed Emma and slowly sank into a deck chair. She began to take tiny bites of the muffin, breaking off small pieces for her pet.

"Put her down and let her run around," Emma said. "I'm sure she needs the exercise."

Again the girl looked around anxiously. "My uncle doesn't like her to be loose."

"This is my property, not your uncle's." Emma closed the gate. "There, she can run and explore to her heart's content."

Tracie gave Emma what passed for a smile as she put the kitten down. The animal immediately scampered away exploring the various potted plants.

"Why don't you tell me what really happened?" Emma took Tracie's hand and noticed fresh bleeding at the edge of the fingernails.

The girl pulled her hand away and folded both of them in her lap. She looked down in despair. "I have to get away," she whispered.

"You didn't really fall, did you?"

She shook her head.

"Was it your uncle?"

Again Tracie looked at the condo next door; an expression of fear spread across her pitiful face. "He drinks a lot. He gets mean when he's drunk."

"Did he hit you?" Emma asked, trying to control her anger.

Almost imperceptibly the girl nodded. "Laura, too," she whispered.

Oh that man, Emma thought. I'd like those two thugs to get a hold of him.

"They're fighting more and more," the girl continued, "something about money." She turned frightened eyes to Emma. "I'm afraid of him."

"Listen, Tracie, my daughter-in-law is a social worker. She runs a support group that meets every week for young people like you. Maybe if you went to a couple of meetings, you might be able to decide what to do. I'm certain she could help you."

Tracie made a face and vehemently shook her head.

"Don't say no so quickly. Think about it. You might make some friends." She cupped the girl's chin in her hand and raised her head until their eyes met. "Everybody needs a friend. Will you just think about it?"

"Okay." Tracie scooped up the kitten and walked painfully back next door.

Oh, Guardian Angel, something's going to erupt over there. I know it. Help me to get that girl out in time.

FORTY-ONE

EMMA WATCHED the weather channel—"cooling temperatures, into the forties tonight…" Time to pick the last tomatoes of the season, she thought with regret.

"Damn," she said as she dropped an armful of dead leaves on the floor of the roof garden. I knew I should have brought out a garbage bag. Didn't realize so many of the plants were spent. She crouched down behind a huge planter and scooped up a handful of debris.

The door to the condo next door opened and Emma heard a whispered male voice apparently talking on a cell phone. She hunkered down low and moved close to the brick wall. It was Evans, his voice barely above a whisper.

"My men…close to finding…merchandise…little more time…"

She peeked from behind the planter and saw Evans flip the phone closed and begin to pace and swear, slamming his fist into his hand. As she watched him, the hairs on the back of her neck bristled. She felt the evil emanating from the man as he stomped into the condo.

A few minutes later Tracie peered out the door and inched her way onto the roof. When she saw Emma, she walked over, a terrified expression on her face.

"Tracie, has something happened?" Emma felt the fear.

"Uncle is real mad about something. He scares me." The girl's slight frame trembled.

"Come and sit down," Emma said. "I'll get you a muffin."

She hurried into the condo and came out with a tray of milk and muffins.

"Where's Hope?" she asked.

"I left her in my bedroom. She's hiding under the bed." Tracie reached for a muffin and simply held it in her hands as if it gave her a sense of security.

"Now," Emma said, sitting down beside her, "tell me what he's so angry about."

Tracie shook her head. "He didn't know I was listening. I opened the door, just a crack." She shivered. "He was talking to somebody on the phone. First I thought it was about business, something about money." She reached for a glass of milk and took a swallow, then hesitated. "He said the guys were looking for somebody named Goldi, the Muffin Lady. It didn't make any sense. Maybe I didn't hear right." She looked at Emma, a question on her face.

Emma froze. He was talking about her! What did Evans have to do with all this? Oh my God, he might be behind the whole thing. But why?

"Where is he now?" Emma asked, her throat so dry the words came out in a croak.

"He went out. So did Laura. Don't know where. I better get back and lock myself in my room." The girl walked back next door, clutching the muffin and glancing around suspiciously.

Emma sat, unable to move. What if he finds out who I am? Nonsense, how could he? I hope he doesn't see that muffin Tracie took back with her. I'd better not make any more until this whole mess is solved, if it ever is.

When she finally got up the strength to go inside, she was just able to make it to the nearest chair before she collapsed into the soft cushion.

"Emma, what's wrong? Are you all right?" Nate asked, walking in from the study.

She shook her head.

He hurried over to her. "Tell me. You're shaking like a leaf."

"Evans," she mumbled. "He's involved."

"Involved in what?" He grabbed her arms and gave her a gentle shake. "You're not making sense."

She shook her head and just sat there, trembling.

Nate poured an ounce of brandy in a glass and handed it to her. "Drink."

She took a swallow and started choking. After a glass of water and the rest of the brandy, she was coherent enough to tell Nate what she overheard and her conversation with Tracie.

"Maybe she misunderstood," he said, trying to sound reassuring, but the furrow between his eyes deepened.

"No!" She shook her head so hard the water sloshed out of the glass she still clutched in her hand. "I felt it. It's here in my head. The man is somehow involved in my kidnapping and this whole business with that murdered man. We have to tell Detective Spaulding."

"Just simmer down. He'll think you're crazy. You have no proof of anything, just a few overheard words. Think about how it sounds, Goldi, the Muffin Lady?"

Emma sat back, the adrenaline rush beginning to recede. Maybe the whole thing was a misunderstanding. After all, Tracie was in the bedroom, listening through a closed door. She got off the chair and went into the bedroom to lie down. She needed to think about this.

For the next few days Emma peered out the door to the roof garden, looking cautiously around before venturing out. She jumped at every unfamiliar sound.

Then Detective Spaulding called. "We have the two felons in custody," he said. "My men picked them up at Union Station. They were planning a little trip."

"Do I have to come down and identify their voices?" Emma asked, clutching the back of a chair.

"Yes, you do," the detective said. "We have their picture

that you took and their fingerprints as well as your signed complaint, but we'll arrange for you and Minnie to come in for a lineup."

Emma's hands grew cold and damp. "Did they tell you who planned the whole thing?" she asked with a feeling of trepidation.

"No."

"Well I think I know. It was my next-door neighbor."

Silence from the other end. Then Detective Spaulding said, "Mrs. Winberry, I think you had better come down here and explain that last statement."

As THEY WALKED INTO the station, Nate shook his head, grumbling, "This is a waste of time. He's not going to believe you."

"Maybe so," Emma said, jutting out her chin, "but I feel it's my duty to tell him what I heard and what Tracie said. Besides, Evans is a domestic abuser."

Nate held up his hands in a gesture of helplessness.

Detective Spaulding acknowledged them with a nod as they walked into his office. "Want some coffee?"

They shook their heads. He held the same stained cup, cracked along one side. It had long since outlived its usefulness. Emma made a mental note to buy him a new one.

"Now, what is it you want to tell me about your neighbor?" He looked at Emma with raised eyebrows.

"He's an evil man," she said, "mean and surly and he cheats on his wife."

"Unfortunately, that's not a crime, Mrs. Winberry," the detective said, looking at Nate.

"I overheard him talking on a cell phone; he didn't see me; I was hiding behind a planter." She noticed the detective raise his eyes to the ceiling. This isn't going well. I'm telling it all wrong.

"You see, I was tending my tomato plants on the roof garden. When I heard him whispering, I ducked down and listened. I have very acute hearing." She could see the look of exasperation on the man's face.

"Go on," he said. "What did you hear?"

"Snippets of conversation. It sounded like he needed more time to get the merchandise."

"That could have related to his business."

"When he finished the call, he was mumbling to himself and seemed very angry. Then his niece came out and told me she heard him talking about finding Goldi, the Muffin Lady."

Detective Spaulding put down his cup and stared at her. His eyebrows almost met each other.

"That's me, Detective. Jake and Minnie call me Goldi the Muffin Lady, because I brought them muffins."

The overworked detective heaved a deep sigh. "That's hardly evidence we can use against him. It's hearsay and doesn't mean anything. The niece could have misunderstood."

"How many Goldi's are referred to as the Muffin Lady?" Emma asked, a defiant look on her face.

"I don't know the statistics on that," he answered.

Emma shook her head and clenched her fists. "Did those thugs tell you who the boss is?" she persisted.

"No, they didn't know his name. He contacted them through an intermediary, but they didn't know his identity, either. They used a cell phone and called a certain number, another cell phone we were unable to trace. The money was sent to a post office box in one of their names."

"Well, can't you trace the money?" Emma asked. "They're always doing that on TV."

Detective Spaulding let out a deep sigh. "I wish it were that simple. There's a world of difference between television and real life. We did everything we could, but they claim to have spent the money."

"Come on, Emma, we've wasted enough of the man's time," Nate said, standing and moving toward the door.

"He physically abuses his wife and niece," Emma said, determined to have her say.

"How do you know that?"

"They told me, and I saw the bruises. They're afraid of him."

"How old is the niece?"

"About seventeen."

"They would have to report the abuse themselves. Give me the man's name and I'll see if he has a record." He took a notepad and pencil and looked at Emma. His expression had definitely softened.

"Maurice Evans. According to his wife, he used to be in business with a partner importing antiques from Europe and selling them in a shop on the North side. But the business was failing and his partner is gone."

She continued after a moment. "The wife told me that he suddenly seemed to have a lot of money and wouldn't tell her where it came from, then became very angry when she asked him."

At that moment the door opened and an officer stuck his head in. "Detective, we need you up front."

"All right. We're finished here." He turned to Emma. "Thanks, Mrs. Winberry. I'll look into this. If you notice anything else suspicious, let me know. And try to encourage the wife and niece to come in."

His expression told Emma that he wanted to believe her. She gave him her most gracious smile as she and Nate walked out the door.

Nate took her arm, and guided her to the car.

Guardian Angel, she prayed, *help me through this, please.*

FORTY-TWO

EMMA RUMMAGED THROUGH her purse searching for a scrap of paper. Finally, in an act of utter frustration, she emptied the entire contents of all three compartments on the kitchen table.

"What's the meaning of all this?" Nate asked, leaning against the door and suppressing a grin.

"I'm looking for something." She examined a number of old receipts and threw them in the garbage. After a thorough cleanout, she held up the sought-after sticky-note, a triumphant smile on her face.

"And what, pray tell, is written on that note that precipitated all this frenzy?" Nate asked.

"Father Michael's phone number."

"Why?" His smile turned to a question.

"I just want to know how Minnie's doing, that's all."

"Hmm." Nate shook his head and walked into the living room.

Emma punched in the numbers and heard a woman's harried voice answer, "Rectory."

"Is Father Michael there?"

"He's very busy right now. Can I help you?"

"My name is Emma Winberry. I'm a friend of Minnie."

"Who?" the woman asked, an impatient tone in her voice.

"The homeless woman with the missing leg. I wondered how she's doing."

She heard a sigh from the other end.

"Causing a great deal of trouble if you ask me. All she

does is complain about her leg. Says someone promised her a new one."

Emma grimaced. That someone is me, she thought. "Is there any way I might speak with Father? I may be able to help."

"Hold on a minute. I'll see if I can find him."

A soft male voice came on the line, "This is Father Michael." Emma identified herself and asked if she could help.

"Oh," he said. "You must be the Muffin Lady."

"Yes, I suppose I am."

"The problem is, Mrs...."

"Winberry."

"Mrs. Winberry, we're very shorthanded at the moment. One of our volunteers had surgery and another is out of town. We don't have anyone to take Minnie to Stroger Hospital for an evaluation. You said you might be able to help?"

"Of course, Father. We can take her." Oh boy, Nate's not going to like this.

"Splendid. I'll make the appointment and call you back. And, you must bring us some of those muffins Minnie has been raving about."

"I will, Father." She gave him her phone number and thought about how best to approach Nate.

When she turned around, she saw him standing in the doorway frowning at her, his arms folded across his chest.

"I have a feeling you just committed us to some mission of mercy without consulting me first."

He tried to look stern, but Emma saw his lips twitching.

"Nate," she cajoled, "I promised that woman a new leg and Father Michael has no one to take her to Stroger Hospital and I told him we would." She raised her huge gray eyes to him with a most appealing look.

"Don't bat those eyes at me, Sparrow. I know all your conniving ways." He wrapped his arms around her and gave her a loud smacking kiss. "We can consider it community service."

FOR THE NEXT FEW DAYS Emma looked out at the roof garden searching for either Laura or Tracie but saw neither. As she listened to the haunting prelude to *Tristan and Isolde* that sets the tragic tone of the opera, she almost felt the grief next door. She worried about what might be happening to both women. But a call from Father Michael temporarily took her mind off the neighbors.

When she and Nate arrived at the rectory, Minnie was ready and waiting for them. She wore a clean cotton dress, belted at her trim waist. A dark blue jacket, worn but clean, kept her warm. Her hair looked as if it had been washed, it was parted on the side and held in place by two pink barrettes.

Emma looked at her in surprise and nodded her approval. As they headed to Stroger Hospital, Minnie complained all the way, bemoaning the loss of the prosthesis that had served as a compartment for what she termed "her valuables."

"What did you do with the ring, Goldi?" she asked.

"We gave it to the police." No matter how many times Emma had told the woman her correct name, she insisted on calling her Goldi. Now just the sound of the name filled her with fear.

"Can I get it back when they're done with it?" she asked sheepishly.

"Now Minnie, you know that ring didn't belong to you. It belongs to the dead man's family," Emma answered giving her a sideways look. Emma watched Nate shake his head. She could imagine the thoughts going through his mind.

"What was so special about it anyway?" Minnie persisted.

At that point, Nate interrupted. "The police are investigating. They haven't said anything yet."

Emma took the hint and said nothing further, but she made a mental note to ask Detective Spaulding about the microchip.

Nate dropped them off at the clinic entrance. "Call me on my cell phone when you're finished," he said. "I have that meeting with the Opera Chapter. We need to finalize the plans for the fund raiser."

The clinic was jammed. Minnie limped on her crutches as Emma tried to clear a path through the mass of people, some grumbling, others swearing, but most accepting their lot.

"Do we have to wait 'til all these people go first?" Minnie whined.

"We have an appointment with a specific doctor," Emma said, making her way to the reception desk. She took the note from Father Michael out of her purse and handed it to the busy woman thumbing through stacks of files.

"We have an appointment with Dr. Gupta," Emma said, giving the note to the woman.

"Down the hall to the Physical Medicine Department," the woman said, handing the note back to Emma and pointing.

"What's Physical Medicine?" Minnie asked. "We just come to pick up a new leg."

"It's not that simple," Emma said, wading through people standing in line at a door marked Laboratory. I hope we don't have to go there, she thought.

Minnie limped along, occasionally pushing someone out of her way with a crutch.

"Be careful," Emma warned.

Minnie ignored her.

The Physical Medicine Department was relatively quiet. It was cleaner than the general waiting room—no smell of sweaty bodies or dirty baby diapers, only the lingering scent of Lysol. A few people sat in chairs against the wall, most of them amputees.

The receptionist looked at Minnie and whipped out a form from one of the folders piled on her desk.

"We have an appointment with Dr. Gupta," Emma said.

"So do all of them." She pointed to the men and women

waiting patiently, some of them sleeping, some reading, some simply staring into space.

"I need some information," the woman said. "Name of the patient?" She looked from one woman to the other.

"Minnie."

"Come on, honey, your full name, your real name."

Minnie heaved a sigh and shook her head. "Minerva Walden."

"Address?"

Emma said, "St. Andrew's Parish House," and gave her the address and phone number.

"Next of kin?"

Minnie hesitated before answering. "Ain't got nobody."

"Put my name," Emma said and gave her the information.

"You have a Social Security number, don't you?"

"I used to have one, but it got lost. Don't remember it."

"Okay." The woman looked down at Minnie's missing limb. "You're a Right BK."

"A what?" Minnie screwed up her face taking the woman's words as an insult.

"Below the knee amputation. You got a knee, haven't you?"

"Yeah," Minnie said, flexing her knee a few times.

"All right," the woman said, slipping the form into a manila folder and writing Minnie's name on the side. "Sit down over there. We'll call you."

They sat on chairs that seemed purposely designed for discomfort. The backs were too low, the seats unpadded.

"Minnie, put your crutches behind the chair so you don't trip anyone," Emma said.

"I ain't used to crutches no more," Minnie grumbled. She did as she was told and leaned her head against the wall, apparently oblivious to her surroundings. Within minutes she was asleep.

I suppose she's used to sleeping wherever and whenever she can, Emma thought fidgeting in the chair. She took a paperback book out of her purse but closed it after reading the same page three times.

Her eyes scanned the people around her. A young boy sat in a wheelchair; both his legs were missing above the knee. What cruel twist of fate left him so disabled? He held a video game in his hands, fingers flying across the keys.

A man with an arm missing kept rubbing the short stump. Emma had heard about phantom limb pain and wondered if he could still feel his missing fingers.

Minnie soon woke, shaking her head as if to orient herself. "I used to have a real job," she said, surprising Emma. "I worked in an office. Made pretty good money in them days." She looked down at her hands, at the arthritic nodules deforming the joints. "Used to have nice hands, too."

Emma refrained from commenting. If the woman wanted to talk, she was ready to listen.

"I had a little girl," Minnie whispered.

Emma's eyes widened.

"Her name was Penny and she was just as purty as a shiny new coin. Had red hair and big blue eyes." She turned to Emma with a look of unutterable sadness.

"What happened?" Emma asked.

"The drink. I lost my job. They took my Penny away from me. Said I was an unfit mother. Put her in a foster home—never saw her again—my shiny new Penny." Huge tears coursed down the woman's lined face.

Emma put her arm around Minnie and held her close.

"It was for the best. I couldn't take care of her proper, but every day I think about her, wonder what kind'a woman she grew up to be. Today is her birthday." She screwed up her face. "At least I think it is. Used to have it wrote down and stuck in my leg with all my valuables 'til them thugs got ahold of me." She looked into the distance and thought for a moment.

"My Penny's forty years old. Hope she's happy."

"Ms. Walden, Dr. Gupta will see you now," a nurse called.

They trudged into the tiny office littered with papers, journals and books. The thin dark-skinned man looked tired and overworked. He smiled wanly at Emma and Minnie.

"Sit down and let me see your leg," he said with a clipped Indian accent. He pulled up the right side of Minnie's dress and examined the limb. "Well, whoever did this surgery did a good job. There's plenty of padding on the stump. We should be able to give you a nice fit." He smiled at the women, turned to a desk and wrote out something on an order sheet.

"Here is your prescription. Go to the Prosthetics Department and they will measure you and give you a sock to wear. It is important that you keep the swelling down so the limb will fit properly."

"Don't I get the leg now?" Minnie asked.

The doctor smiled. "No. It has to be specifically made to fit you. That way you will walk normally and won't get any sores. The nurse will show you where to go."

They left the office and were directed down the hall to a door marked PROSTHETICS. Inside Emma saw artificial arms and legs on tables, in corners, some being worked on by technicians. Computer screens showed images of residual limbs. A technician was busy putting in precise measurements.

Emma waited in yet another uncomfortable chair as a young man took Minnie into a cubicle to be measured. Emma heard her complaining, but the prosthetist said nothing. He had undoubtedly heard it all before.

EMMA LOOKED OFF into the distance as she and Nate rode home. They had taken Minnie back to St. Andrew's after the prosthetist took the measurements and gave her an elastic sock to wear. She was to return in two weeks for a fitting.

"Oh Nate, it was heartbreaking," Emma said. "That poor woman."

"I'm sure that most street people have a tragic tale like that one," Nate said.

I wonder where her daughter is, Emma thought. I'll call Bertie. She may have some connections. "It would be great if we could find Penny," Emma said, looking at Nate.

"Now what? Did your Guardian Angel tell you where she is?" he asked, a sarcastic note in his voice.

"Don't berate my Guardian Angel. She's helped me out of many a jam."

"How do you know it's a she?" he asked, suppressing a grin.

"That's the way I envision her. Actually Guardian Angels are genderless." Emma spoke with authority, jutting out her chin.

"I see." Nate said nothing more as they pulled into the underground garage of their building.

FORTY-THREE

EMMA COULDN'T GET the picture of Minnie and her red-haired Penny out of her mind. She dreamed of a child of that description playing and laughing with other children.

The next evening she called Bertie.

"How are you feeling, dear?" Emma asked.

"Much better. The morning sickness is gone and I feel more energetic. The only problem now is that I'm ravenous. I'm keeping careful tabs on my weight." Her lighthearted laugh always brought a smile to Emma's face. "Are you calling to tell me that Tracie is coming to my group?" Bertie asked.

"Unfortunately not. I told her about it and she said she'd let me know, but I haven't seen any of my neighbors in days."

"Hmm," Bertie said. "I hope there's no trouble there."

"I have a feeling there is, but right now, I can't do anything about it," Emma said.

For the next ten minutes Emma told Bertie as much about Minnie as she wanted her to know: the missing limb, the homelessness, Father Michael, and Penny.

"Is there any way to find this woman's daughter?" Emma asked.

"You haven't given me much to go on. Her name is Penny Walden, probably Penelope. And I have her approximate date of birth. Was that in Chicago?"

"I presume so. Minnie didn't say."

"And Minnie's full name is Minerva Walden?"

"Yes."

"Was there a husband?"

"She didn't say that, either, but I doubt it."

"Let me see if I can find a birth certificate and we'll take it from there. I love sleuthing." Bertie giggled.

"So do I," Emma said. "Bye now."

WHEN EMMA SPOTTED Tracie on the roof garden, she hurried outside to talk with her. She considered grabbing a muffin but thought better about it.

"Hi, Tracie."

The girl jumped at the sound of Emma's voice. "Oh, hi," she said turning her face away.

"Is anything wrong?" Emma asked, noticing the bruise on Tracie's neck.

"No, no," the girl answered too quickly.

"Is your aunt at home?" Emma asked, clutching her fists and pursing her lips.

"Yeah."

"Tell her I would like to speak with her, now." Emma's tone had its effect. Tracie hurried into the condo and, a few minutes later, Laura emerged.

Emma noticed the heavy makeup, too much for a summer day. A filmy scarf was wound around her neck and trailed behind her.

"You wanted to see me?" she asked.

"Yes. I want to talk to you about Teresa. Can you sit for a few minutes?"

"I, I don't have much time, I have an appointment. What about Teresa?"

"I've noticed a lot of bruises on her."

Laura hesitated, looked back at the condo, then turned to Emma. "She's been falling down. I think she's weak from not eating. We're making arrangements to send her back to her parents. Now I have to go."

"Laura, wait a minute." Emma reached out to her, but the woman pulled away. "Is your husband abusing her, and you too?"

"I think you should mind your own business," Laura said and hurried back into the condo.

That woman is frightened, Emma thought. I wonder if he threatened her? *Oh Guardian Angel, please tell me what to do.*

EMMA TRIED TO CONCENTRATE on preparing the deck for the coming winter. Yellow and russet-colored mums blazed in pots that previously held succulent tomatoes. She pulled off a few dead leaves then decided which plants had to be moved into the atrium. The night temperatures plunged with each passing day. I'd better not wait any longer, she thought. As soon as Nate gets back from the store, I'll ask him to help me.

The phone rang, pulling her back into the house. "Hello."

"Mrs. Winberry, this is Detective Spaulding."

"Detective, I've been thinking about you. Have you found out what was on that microchip in the ring?"

"I believe I'm the one who's supposed to ask the questions," he said, a light tone to his voice.

Humph, after we found it for him, the least he could do is tell us something, Emma thought.

"It's an ongoing investigation, so I can't tell you much. But I will say there was information on that chip that some people might kill for."

"Well, that's not saying much, but it's something." Emma made a face. Her innate curiosity was definitely not satisfied.

"The reason I called," the detective continued, "is to tell you that I checked on your neighbor, Maurice Evans."

"Yes?" She was all ears now.

"I shouldn't be telling you this, but, since he lives next door to you, I thing it's advisable that you take precautions. He's been charged a number of times with crimes ranging from robbery to extortion, but, because of lack of hard evidence, he was never convicted. Keep this information between you and Mr. Sandler only. And, if you see anything suspicious, call me."

"I will, Detective, and thank you."

Emma paced back and forth wringing her hands and muttering. "What a mess. When I lived in Brookfield, I had decent, friendly neighbors. Now, in this expensive area, we have criminals."

When Nate came home, he found her punching down bread dough. Chocolate chip and oatmeal cookies cooled in plates on the counter.

"To what do we owe this cooking frenzy?" he asked, kissing her on the neck. "Are you planning to open a bakery?"

"Detective Spaulding called. We have a criminal living right next door."

"What?"

"Evans. He's been charged with a number of crimes, but never convicted. I told you he's evil. The detective said we should be careful."

"Hmm." Nate frowned. "They were supposed to do thorough background checks on all prospective buyers in this building. I'm not happy about this. We have a big investment in this place. Don't have any further interaction with those people, Sparrow. We'll see what happens."

"I'll tell you what's going to happen," she said, pounding down the bread dough so hard that flour flew around the kitchen like a snowstorm. She ignored the mess. "Someone is going to get hurt, or maybe worse."

"Who?"

"Either Tracie or Laura. I know it."

FORTY-FOUR

EMMA'S FEARS materialized the next day. She sat out on the roof garden taking advantage of an early fall afternoon. Her floppy hat protected her eyes from the sun as she watched the gulls and listened to their raucous calls. A few small waves rippled across the otherwise placid lake. In the distance she could see the giant Ferris wheel at Navy Pier turning slowly in its never-ending circle.

Emma had her cell phone on the chair beside her. Since the detective's call about Evans, she never went outside without it.

Suddenly she heard raised voices.

"No, please," Tracie pleaded. "Don't hurt her!"

"I told you to keep this damned animal away from me. She pissed all over the rug. Out she goes."

He held the struggling frightened kitten by the scruff of the neck and marched toward the fence surrounding the roof.

Oh my God, Emma thought. He's going to throw that cat right off.

Tracie clung to the man's body trying desperately to reach her pet. "No!" she screamed as he raised the hand with the writhing animal above his head.

Emma watched everything as if in slow motion: the raised arm, the pitiful animal, Tracie's dilemma.

In a desperate leap Tracie threw herself at Evans, sinking her teeth into his arm.

"Ow!" he yelled, turning to her with blazing eyes. "You little bitch!"

She raised her knee and kicked him in the groin. Evans doubled over dropping the kitten on the deck. The animal ran to the gate, crawled underneath and hid behind one of Emma's flowerpots.

Emma got up from the chair, unsure what to do. The girl is in danger. I must help her. But her body refused to respond. Her feet remained glued to the roof. She watched, helpless, as Tracie looked around for a means of escape. Evans pounced on her. Emma almost felt the blow as his clenched fist slammed across the girl's cheek, knocking her to the deck. She lay there weeping, her hands covering her bloody face.

An adrenaline rush spurred Emma into action. She ran to the gate. As Evans raised his fist again, Emma shouted, "Get away from her. I'm calling nine-one-one." She held up the cell phone and gave him a menacing look.

He glared at her. "Stay out of my affairs, lady, or you might regret it."

Did he just threaten me? Emma thought, gritting her teeth.

Evans looked down at the prostrate girl and snarled, uttering words Emma couldn't hear. He turned and stomped into the condo.

Emma opened the gate and ran to Tracie. "Are you all right?"

The girl looked up. Her face was covered with blood. The blow had ripped the ring out of her lower lip leaving a deep gash. The left side of her face began to swell. "Hope?" she whispered.

"She's all right. She's hiding at my place. Come on, we have to get you to a hospital."

She helped the girl to her feet and half dragged her across the roof. "Nate, Nate," she called.

"What's all the fuss…?"He took one look at Tracie, ran out and lifted the girl in his arms.

"Evans," Emma said, gritting her teeth.

"The bastard! Get a wet towel, Emma." Gently he lay the

weeping girl on the couch, oblivious to the blood seeping into the fabric.

"We have to get her to a hospital," Emma said. "That lip is split wide open and her jaw is terribly swollen."

"Get an ice pack from the freezer," Nate said as he held the towel against Tracie's damaged mouth.

Emma placed the pack against the girl's jaw as Tracie winced in pain. "Hope?" she asked again.

"I'll lock her in the atrium. She'll be safe there." Emma filled a dish with water and put some vermiculite in a pile on the atrium floor. Then she found the trembling animal, picked her up and crooned softly to her. "There, there, you're safe now." She carried the kitten to Tracie for a moment. As the girl clutched her pet, it mewed pitifully.

"Now that you see she's safe, give her to me and I'll lock her up. Then we'll get you taken care of."

Nate drove to Northwestern Hospital as fast as the traffic allowed. Tracie whimpered in pain as Emma held her in her arms. Emma heard him cursing, his hand slammed against the steering wheel as they sat in an unending line of cars.

When they reached the Emergency Room, Nate left the women in the car and rushed inside to get help. He returned with a nurse and an orderly pushing a gurney. He lifted the girl gently out of the car and placed her on the litter. Emma went with Tracie into the Emergency Room as Nate parked the car.

They pushed the girl into a cubicle where a young resident immediately came to her side. "Hi, I'm Doctor Carson. What happened here?" he asked, removing the towel from Tracie's lip.

"She was assaulted by her uncle," Emma said, clenching her fists and gritting her teeth. "I saw the whole thing."

The doctor let out a breath and shook his head. "Lie still. I'm going to shine a light into your mouth. Can you open it?"

"Oh," Tracie moaned as she tried.

"It's okay," he said as he gently probed the line of her jaw. She cried out in pain.

"Well, young lady, I think your jaw is broken and that's a nasty split in your lip. We'll get an X ray first."

He turned to Emma. "Did she have a ring through her lip? I noticed a stud in her tongue."

"Yes, she did."

"This is what we call a pull-through injury. It causes a lot of tissue damage. She'll need a plastic surgeon to avoid a disfiguring scar. Are you a relative?"

"No, I'm her next-door neighbor. She's staying with her aunt and uncle." Emma wanted to say more but checked herself.

"What's her name?" the doctor asked.

"Tracie Adams."

"Tracie," the doctor said, bending close to the pitiful girl. "The nurse will take good care of you. Her name is Sandy. We have to draw some blood from your arm and give you some intravenous fluids and antibiotics so you don't get an infection. Okay?"

Tracie nodded.

"I'm going to order an X ray of your jaw and call in a specialist. I'll be back in a few minutes."

He spoke to the young nurse who had accompanied him, instructing her to start an IV. Then he motioned Emma out of the room. "You say she was assaulted?" he asked.

"Yes, I saw her uncle strike her—with a closed fist." Trembling with rage, Emma related the chain of events. "I've seen bruises on both her and her aunt. The man is a beast."

"We'll make out a police report. In the meantime, we need someone responsible for this girl to sign consent forms."

"You can call her aunt, Laura Evans." Emma rummaged through her purse. "Here's the number."

Emma and Nate sat in the waiting room, only a few people around them. This is so different from the county hospital,

Emma thought. She looked at the clean floor, saw no noxious spills, smelled no odors. They might have been in the waiting room of a doctor's office.

An hour later, Laura rushed in, her face a mask of fear. As soon as she saw Emma and Nate she hurried over to them. "What happened? Where's Teresa? Is she badly hurt?"

"Sit down, Laura," Emma said. "They took her to X ray. She may have a broken jaw."

"Oh God," the woman said, burying her face in her hands. "This is all my fault. I should have sent her away long ago. I had a feeling something like this would happen." The woman's hands were shaking so that she almost dropped her purse.

"Laura, I can read the fear in your face," Emma asked. "What is it you're so terrified of?"

She looked at Emma, her eyes wide, one of them twitching uncontrollably. She looked around. Then lowered her voice. "I overheard a phone call. Between my husband and someone I didn't recognize. I was on the extension in the bedroom."

"What did the man say?" Emma urged her on.

Again Laura looked around as if expecting to see someone. "He said, the police picked up your boys. Then Maurice said that they don't know who he is, only call him 'the boss.' Maurice was nervous, I could tell. I know that tone in his voice all too well." She stopped for a moment and began wringing her hands.

"What next?" Emma prodded.

"The man said, 'You have forty-eight hours to get the merchandise or I call in your marker.'"

"That was it?"

"He hung up, but the threat was implied." She sighed deeply, apparently relieved to have told someone.

"The staff called the police," Emma said. "You'll have to tell them everything." At this point she felt no pity for Laura, allowing this abuse to continue for so long. "Come to the desk. They need information."

Laura nodded and followed Emma to the admitting department. She had a frightened look in her eyes, like that of a caged animal, as she answered the questions and gave them Teresa's parents' phone number. She drew an insurance card from her purse and handed it to the woman behind the desk.

"Teresa is still covered by her parents' policy, thank God."

At that moment a man came up to them and identified himself as Officer O'Connor. They sat in an isolated corner and Emma repeated the incident. Laura winced as Emma described her husband's brutality. Then Laura gave her statement of the abuse.

"Tell him the rest," Emma said.

"But," Laura said, "it has no bearing on the beating."

"Tell him the rest!" Emma insisted.

"All right." She repeated exactly what she had heard on the phone.

"Officer," Emma said, "I suggest you contact Detective Spaulding from the Violent Crimes Division. This information is significant to one of his cases."

He gave Emma a quizzical look.

"Please."

He made a note. "Now I need to interview the girl."

A nurse accompanied him into the cubicle.

Laura looked at Emma. "I'm going home to pack right now. I've decided to leave. I don't feel safe in that house any longer."

"Where will you go?"

"To my sister in California. I never want to see Maurice Evans again."

"But what about Teresa?"

"She's not my problem. And, frankly, I don't care what happens to her. I just want my freedom."

Emma couldn't believe the callousness of Laura's words—or was the woman so terrified that she could think of nothing else?

"I know these people my husband borrowed money from will come after him. They're the ones who were looking for him the night of the storm. I heard the man at your door. And if they don't find Maurice, they may take it out on me." She began to tremble. "You must think I'm a terrible person, but I'm terrified."

"Did you speak to Teresa's parents?" Emma persisted.

"Yes." Laura looked down at her hands. "They don't seem to care about her, either. They're bogged down with legal problems and pretty much said she's on her own. She'll be eighteen in two weeks, a legal adult." Then she looked up at Emma. "I'm sorry. She isn't even my niece."

At that moment Officer O'Connor returned. "The girl is hardly coherent. She can't even sign a complaint against her uncle, so I'm signing it. We'll get a squad over there and pick him up."

"He isn't there," Laura said. "He left a little while ago."

"I'm still sending someone over there."

Laura began to tremble. "I have to go now," she said and hurried out of the Emergency Room without even seeing Tracie.

Emma sat in a daze trying to digest all she had just heard. Laura was leaving, the police were looking for Evans, the loan sharks were circling, and Tracie was all alone.

FORTY-FIVE

WHEN EMMA AND NATE returned home, the police had just finished searching the condo next door. Officer O'Connor saw them and came over.

"He's gone," he said, "and so is Mrs. Evans. She packed her things in a hurry and left." He handed Nate a card. "If you see any activity here at all, call the station. And keep your doors locked."

"Thanks, officer, we will." Nate ushered Emma into the atrium and locked the door.

"I don't know about you, but I need a drink." He took the bottle of scotch from the cabinet and poured a generous amount into a glass. He looked at Emma, the bottle poised over a second glass.

She nodded. "Yes, but not quite so much, and add a little water, please."

They drank in silence. "I'm going to bed," Nate said when he took the last swallow. "I suggest you do the same."

"In a minute." Emma stared into space. *Guardian Angel, what's going to happen next?*

Be cautious, the inner voice said. *It isn't over, yet.*

THE FOLLOWING DAY Emma and Nate arrived at the hospital at ten. Tracie lay as still as death, looking like a lost child. Her jaw had turned an ugly purple; her lip oozed a bloody fluid through the bandage. An intravenous dripped steadily into her arm; a tube snaked into her right nostril delivering a white suspension, drop by drop, into her stomach.

Emma took the girl's hand gently in hers. The eyes opened to slits. When she saw it was Emma, they widened expectantly.

"Hope is fine," Emma said. "She's adjusting to my house. I put a bed for her in the atrium and bought her a ball with a bell inside."

Tracie tried to smile, but grimaced in pain.

Emma sat beside the bed holding the girl's hand. The eyes slowly closed again.

Nate stood at the window looking down at the traffic speeding by. "This is too much like your brush with death," he said, his hands gripped in tight fists.

Emma went up to him and put her arms around his waist. "I'm sorry to have gotten you involved in all this. I seem to draw these troubled people to me like a magnet."

He turned and clutched her a little too tightly. "As long as I don't lose you again." They stood that way for a long time.

Later the medical team made their rounds. A tall kindly man introduced himself as Dr. Palmer, a plastic surgeon. He sat beside the bed and took Tracie's hand in his.

"Hi there, young lady. I'm the man who's going to make you beautiful again." His smile was genuine. Tracie gave him a pleading look.

"I know you can't talk, so don't even try. Just listen." He nodded at Emma and Nate. Then turned his attention back to his patient.

"I studied your lab reports. You're quite anemic and some of your readings are abnormal. You haven't been eating enough to keep a bird alive, a small bird." He lifted her forearm, a bone covered with a thin layer of muscle and skin. He looked at the scars on her arm, but said nothing.

"We'll have to tune you up first before we take you to surgery or you won't heal. I'll do some fancy stitching on that lip and also wire your jaws shut to give the fracture time to heal."

Tracie winced at his words. A few tears escaped from the corners of her eyes. The doctor took a tissue and dried them.

"We'll also give you a pint of blood to put some color back in your cheeks. Don't worry, I've been doing this sort of thing since before you were born, so I'm pretty good at it. I'll write orders and see you tomorrow."

He patted her hand, rose from the chair and looked at Emma giving her a slight nod of his head. She followed him out of the room.

"Are you a relative?" he asked.

Emma shook her head. "I'm the only friend she has. Her parents refuse to come here, her aunt has left for California, and her uncle is wanted by the police." Emma gritted her teeth. She felt so helpless.

He shook his head. "Poor little thing. Her condition right now is quite serious. Her lab readings are so abnormal that it would be dangerous to put her under anesthesia at the present time. How long has this girl been neglected?"

"I really couldn't say. Her aunt told me she was hospitalized for anorexia before she came to live with them. I've tried to get close to the girl but…"

"I know," the doctor said. "Some of these problems are so deep-seated that it's impossible to understand everything that's going on. I'll order a psychiatric consult, but not until her physical condition improves. We'd better get social services involved, too." He shook his head. "I wish it were as easy as stitching up her lip."

Emma nodded, feeling the burden of this sudden responsibility. But she couldn't abandon the girl; it would be unthinkable.

THAT EVENING Emma got a call from Bertie. "I'm making some progress," she said, a tone of pride in her voice. "I actually found Penny's birth certificate."

"Well, I guess that qualifies you as a super sleuth." Emma could hardly keep her voice positive.

"What's wrong?" Bertie asked. "You sound down."

Emma sighed and told her daughter-in-law all that had happened.

"My God," Bertie exclaimed. "That poor girl. What's going to happen to her?"

"I have no idea. It's too tragic to contemplate."

"So many of these kids end up suicidal," Bertie said.

"That's what I'm afraid of. Only that pet keeps her going."

"And you."

"I'm trying, but I can't take care of her."

"We'll think of something," Bertie said. "Now let me see if I can find Penelope Walden."

DISTURBING DREAMS invaded Emma's sleep. Maurice Evans held Tracie's limp body over the wall of the roof garden. Emma tried to call out, to stop him, but no sound came. She woke just before he let go.

Nate found her sitting in the atrium sipping warm milk and gazing at the turbulent waters of the lake. She kept glancing at the condo next door.

"Dreams again?" he asked, sitting next to her and rubbing his hand gently down her back.

"Uh huh. Oh Nate, what's going to happen to that girl?"

"I haven't a clue, my dear." He gave her a questioning look.

"I certainly hope you weren't thinking of taking her in."

"Of course not. That thought never entered my mind." But she had thought about it, long and hard. If she were still living in the house in Brookfield, she might consider it, even get Maria involved—Maria. Suddenly a light bulb popped on.

"You know, I wonder if Maria and her family would consider taking the girl under their wing, just until she gets on her feet, I mean. They're such a loving, caring family, something Tracie's never known."

"Whoa. That's asking a lot." Nate looked dubious.

"There's no harm in asking, is there? Now that one of the daughters is married, they have room, and they all have big hearts. I'll bet Maria would take one look at Tracie and consider her a challenge to her culinary skills. She would be compelled to fatten her up." Emma gave Nate such a pleading look that he began to laugh.

"You may be right. Now come back to bed. I'll hold you until you fall asleep and protect you from all the bad things in this world."

He put his arm around her and led her to the bedroom. She rested her head on his shoulder, but fears of Maurice Evans kept creeping into her mind.

FORTY-SIX

THE FOLLOWING DAY Father Michael called. Emma was still shaken over the happenings of the past two days, but she tried to cover her nervousness.

"Mrs. Winberry, I have a favor to ask," he said in his persuasive voice.

Oh dear, I can't get involved in any more. "Yes, Father?" she replied.

"Mrs. Walden has an appointment with the Prosthetic Department at Stroger Hospital. My volunteers are all busy preparing for a fundraiser for the parish. I was wondering if you might be able to take her?"

Emma rubbed her face and glanced at Nate. He looked up from the newspaper, a grim expression on his face.

"Just a minute, Father." She turned to Nate. "Can we take Minnie for her fitting?"

He thought for a moment. "I suppose. We don't have anything else planned for today."

She smiled her gratitude. "Yes, Father. What time?"

ON THE WAY TO the hospital Minnie complained, as usual: they woke her too early in the morning, insisted she bathe every day, made her help in the kitchen.

"Minnie," Emma said. "You look wonderful, well-fed, well-dressed, your hair neatly combed. What more do you want?"

"I wanna get outta there. Too many people telling me what to do."

"As soon as you get your leg you can go anywhere you wish. You can get a job, rent a room somewhere, or go back on the street. The choice is yours."

Minnie sat in a pout. She obviously didn't like any of those choices.

"Maybe," Emma said softly, "you can even find your daughter."

Minnie's eyes widened. She sat up straight. "What'd ya mean?"

"My daughter-in-law is a social worker. She found Penny's birth certificate and is looking for her foster parents."

"Who told her to do that?" Minnie asked, becoming agitated.

"I did."

"You got no right."

"No, I suppose I haven't. Maybe I'm just an old busybody. But, if she does find Penny, you will have another choice. Either contact her or not. It's up to you."

For a moment Minnie looked hopeful, then she covered her face with her hands. "She wouldn't want a mother like me. I'm a failure at everything." She shook her head.

"I think you're a very brave, independent woman. If you took that determination of yours and put it to good use, who knows what you might accomplish."

WHEN THEY ARRIVED HOME, Nate took Emma's arms firmly in his hands and looked at her, a stern expression on his face. "Sparrow, until this mess is over with those people next door, I do not want you on that roof garden unless I'm with you. Is that clear?"

"You sound so serious."

"I am serious. I don't like what's been happening and I don't want you in any danger." He pulled her close, his arms around her slim body and kissed her neck. "I almost lost you once, I won't chance it again. Promise me?"

She looked up at him, planted a kiss on his chin and whispered, "I promise."

The next afternoon Nate went to a meeting of the Opera Chapter. "I should only be gone for an hour or so. How about going out to dinner tonight?"

"Sounds good to me."

After he left, Emma decided to call Maria.

"Hallo."

"Maria, it's Emma."

"Emma, we no talk in such a long time. I miss you."

"I miss you, too, my friend. I need to ask a big favor of you."

"For you, anything."

Emma hesitated clutching the phone. What if she says no? "This is a really big favor."

"Well, if you don't tell me what it is, I can't say yes or no."

"Do you remember my telling you about that young girl next door?"

"*Si,* poor little thing. How is she doing?"

For the next half hour Emma poured out the whole sordid story.

"*Madonna mia!* And what's gonna happen to her?"

"I don't know. If I still lived in Brookfield, I would take her with me, but things are different now."

There was silence on the other end for a moment. "And this is the favor, right?"

"Would you ask your daughter? If you could take her for a few weeks, just until they take the wires off her jaws. Right now she can't talk or even eat. It's so sad."

"I talk to my daughter, Carmela. You know, my granddaughter, Connie, got the whole downstairs, with two beds. There's plenty room here. Don't worry. We take her."

Emma breathed a sigh of relief as she hung up the phone. One problem solved. She walked out into the atrium and looked at the sky. Huge clouds rolled in over the lake. Hope curled herself around Emma's legs, mewing for attention. Emma reached down and stroked the animal. She had forgotten to tell Maria about the cat. *I'll tell her later. Oh dear, I don't even know if Maria likes cats.*

As she looked out over the roof garden, she noted with satisfaction that she had pulled out all the annuals and taken in all the tender plants except…Damn! *I forgot to take in that lovely coleus. I promised Nate I wouldn't go out there, but it'll only be a minute.*

She grabbed a sweater and opened the door. A brisk wind chilled her, almost pushing her back inside. Hope took the opportunity to dash out.

"Get back here," Emma scolded. She took the coleus and put it in the atrium then went out to retrieve the cat. Emma muttered as she watched the animal squeeze herself under the gate and run around the roof next door.

"Hope, get back here," Emma called. "Tracie isn't there."

Slowly the door of the condo opened and a large rough-looking man stepped out. He looked at Emma through small, beady eyes set deep in a puffy face. He reached down and grabbed Hope by the scruff of the neck.

"You lookin' for this, lady?" Hope struggled and mewed, but he held her fast.

"Yes, that's my cat. Would you give her to me, please?"

"First you answer some questions." His tone was menacing. "Where's Evans?"

"I have no idea," Emma said, trying to remain calm.

"Wrong answer. I'll ask again. Where's Evans?"

Emma had had enough of these thugs pushing her around.

Without thinking of the possible consequences, she opened the gate and stalked toward him reaching for Hope. With his free hand, he grabbed her arm in a vise-like grip and twisted it behind her.

"Ow! You're hurting me."

"I'm askin' one last time. Where's Evans?"

"And I'm answering one last time. I don't know where he is, but I do know the police are looking for him."

The man looked at her through squinting eyes; a look crossed his face. Was it fear? "Why?"

"Because he beat his niece within an inch of her life. Put her in the hospital. Big brave man." Where was all this bravado coming from? *Guardian Angel, you had better be here.*

"Are you his missus?"

"Good heavens, no. I live next door. Now if you will please give me my cat, I'll go home and you can go about your business."

"Not so fast, lady. I want some answers."

"And I don't have any. Now—let—me—go," she said between gritted teeth.

He twisted her arm tighter.

"Ow!" she yelled.

"Emma?" Nate's beloved voice. "Emma, what's going on?" He ran out onto the roof garden brandishing a pistol. "Take your hands off her or I'll blow your head off."

By the tone of his voice, Emma believed him. But where did he get the gun?

The thug pulled Emma closer. "You'll have to shoot her first."

At that moment Hope twisted her lithe body, unsheathed her sharp claws, and sank them into the man's neck.

"Ah!" he shouted, letting go of Emma. She turned, and in a fit of fury, kicked him in the groin as hard as she could. He sank to his knees, groaning. Emma grabbed Hope and ran to Nate. He didn't move, just kept the gun aimed steadily at the man writhing on the ground.

"Emma, get the wire we used to tie up the tomatoes."

"Where did you get the gun?" she whispered.

"Never mind. Get the wire."

She ran into the atrium, locked the cat in the house and ran out again, wire and wire cutters in hand.

"Hold this pistol pointed at this noble member of society while I tie him up," Nate instructed.

The man was still groaning as Emma hesitated. She had never held a gun in her life. When she finally found the courage to take the weapon, her hands shook so she was afraid she might drop it, but she held it tight.

"Hey, that hurts," the man complained, straining and trying to pull away, as Nate twisted the wire around his wrists.

"Don't move or she'll shoot you. All I have to do is pull you over to my property and I have every right to protect myself," Nate said.

He pushed the man over and tied the wire around his ankles. When Nate finished, the thug looked like a pig trussed for market.

"You got no cause to do this." He let out a string of expletives that made even Nate lift his eyebrows.

"Emma, give me the gun and call Detective Spaulding. But first, give me that rag you use to wipe out the cat's litter box. I want to stuff it in his foul mouth."

Emma stood for a moment rubbing her hands down her arms and across her chest and abdomen in sweeping motions.

"What on earth are you doing?" Nate asked, keeping one eye on his captive.

"Getting rid of his negative energy." Her hands continued sweeping her body. "I feel like a bulky sweater that has collected lint. I have to get rid of it."

Nate rolled his eyes and shrugged then turned his full attention back to the piece of scum on the ground.

AFTER THE POLICE had cuffed and loaded the intruder into the squad car, Detective Spaulding sat in the living room, a cup of coffee in one hand and a pad of paper and pen in the other.

"Now, tell me exactly what happened. And, Mr. Sandler, I presume you have a permit for that gun?" He raised his eyebrows at Nate.

Nate opened the drawer to an end table and produced the document. "Right here." He handed it to the detective who looked at it and nodded.

"When did you get that gun?" Emma asked, her eyes wide with astonishment.

"After you were kidnapped, my dear, I wasn't going to take any chances."

"And why didn't you tell me?"

"Because I knew you would react exactly the way you are right now."

"Do you know how to use it?" she persisted.

"Absolutely."

"Okay," the detective said, "let's get back to what happened here. Tell me everything."

After Emma and Nate finished their tale, he said, "I don't know how you two do it, but you seem to be involved in every aspect of this case. I presume this guy is a muscleman for the loan sharks looking for Evans. By the looks of the way he tossed the condo, I doubt that he found anything of value on the premises."

"He's probably the one who tried to break in the night of the storm," Nate said.

"Since we've been so instrumental in assisting you with this case, can you at least tell us what's on that microchip that people are willing to kill for?" Emma asked.

"I guess I can tell you that much. As you probably read in the newspapers, Mr. Porter was an inventor. He claimed to have modified an engine that would run for an indefinite amount of time on a cupful of fuel. The plans are on that chip. Our experts are checking it out now. Incidentally," he leaned forward, "this information is for your ears only."

He put down the coffee cup, put his pad and paper in his pocket and looked around. "Nice place you got here. I hope your next neighbors are better than the last."

When he was gone, Nate looked at Emma, his face a mask of frustration and disappointment. "Why didn't you keep your promise to me? Why?"

She bit down on her lip, feeling such guilt. "The weather was threatening and I noticed that I forgot to take in one of my favorite plants. When I opened the door, the cat ran out, and, that's when things happened." She gave him such a look of contrition that he smiled.

"You're going to learn to use this gun, Sparrow. Now don't balk. It's not that difficult. Okay?"

She nodded and turned away. *Oh Guardian Angel, help me. I don't like weapons, but I had better do as Nate says before he decides I'm not worth the aggravation.*

FORTY-SEVEN

THE FOLLOWING WEEK Tracie's condition had stabilized enough for surgery. Emma and Nate sat at her bedside, waiting. Tracie's eyes reflected the fear and despair she felt. She had asked for her aunt by writing the question on a notepad. Emma painfully told her Laura was gone and did not intend to return.

Tracie then wrote, "What will happen to me?"

"Don't you worry," Emma said. "We'll work something out." She patted the girl's hand, talked about the kitten and casually mentioned her friend, Maria. She said nothing about her tentative plan for Tracie to stay with her nor did she mention the intruder. No need to burden this girl with any more baggage.

After an interminable wait, the surgeon walked into the room. His demeanor inspired confidence. Tracie looked at him as if he were a god.

"Well, young lady, we have a telephonic consent for surgery from your mother. Are you ready?" He took her hand, felt the pulse at her wrist, then nodded. "Nice and strong. You're coming along just fine."

Tracie smiled.

"Let me explain just what I'm going to do." He sat next to her bed and took a pad of paper and pen from his pocket. He drew a simple picture of a slightly open mouth without the lips.

"I'll attach what are called arch bars on the outside of your teeth, top and bottom, right above the gum line."

Tracie winced. Emma tried not to.

"Don't worry, you won't feel it. When I have your jaw in the correct alignment, I'll attach wires to little nobs on the arch bars to hold it in place." He drew them on the pad and showed it to Tracie and Emma. Nate looked over his shoulder.

"You understand?" he asked.

Tracie nodded slightly, a tear sneaking from her eye.

"Good girl. And, while you're asleep, I'm going to remove all that hardware from your pretty face as well as that ring in your navel. Don't think I didn't notice." He winked at her. "And I'll stitch up those holes in your ears so that you won't even see them. Okay?"

She nodded, attempting a smile.

"And I sincerely hope you won't be tempted to replace any of them after you've healed." He looked down at her like a father looking at a recalcitrant child.

Slowly she shook her head from side to side.

"Good girl."

At that moment an orderly pushed a gurney into the room and up to the bedside. A nurse accompanied him and transferred the IV to a pole on the litter. She talked softly to Tracie while she performed her duties, explaining exactly what she was doing.

"I'm disconnecting the feeding tube that we clamped last night. After the surgery, we'll restart the feedings. We have to keep you nourished so you'll heal faster." She smiled at the girl. "Are you ready?"

Tracie nodded.

The orderly and the nurse lifted Tracie's body as if she were a doll. Emma gave her a kiss and waved good-bye as she began her journey to the operating room.

"That surgeon has a great bedside manner," Nate said. "Did you see the way the girl responded?"

Emma nodded, swallowing the lump in her throat. "She needs someone like that in her life." She sighed, wondering if Maria's family would consent to take the girl. They could give her so much love; the real family that she never had.

The clock ticked slowly; the hands seemed frozen in time. Emma read an entire chapter in her book before closing it. She had no recollection of any of it. She looked at Nate, staring out the window.

"I wonder if they've found Evans yet?" she asked, just to hear the sound of her own voice.

"It's only a matter of time, if the sharks don't find him first."

Emma shuddered at the thought. He certainly deserved to be punished, but the violence of some of these people was unthinkable.

Nate turned to her. "I brought up the problem at the condo association meeting yesterday. The lawyers swore they did a background check on Evans, but I don't believe it. I made it clear that if this sordid story appeared in the media, the property values of our condos might drop."

"How did they take that?" Emma asked.

"That got their attention. I promised to keep it quiet, but insisted that any prospective buyer be thoroughly checked. I don't think we'll have any more trouble with neighbors.

"And," he continued, "I'm getting rid of the gate. I'll have the area bricked in to join with the wall and wrought iron on top to match that along the outside wall."

"Did anybody object?" Emma asked.

"No one said a word. We will have privacy. And if you want to put a row of small evergreens along that wall, so much the better."

She smiled. It did sound like a good plan. She envisioned pots with dwarf Alberta spruce lining the bricks between the two properties, decorated with lights at Christmastime.

Four hours later Tracie returned from surgery. She looked so vulnerable lying there, almost like a young child now that all the rings had been removed. A paper cap covered her multicolored hair. Neat stitching coursed down her lip and her ear; no dressings covered the wounds; but her mouth was swollen from the trauma.

The doctor walked in. "She did fine. Should recover completely. The wires in her jaws will have to remain for about six weeks. She should carry a small pair of wire cutters with her at all times. In case she has to vomit, all she does is snip the wires."

Emma cringed at the thought.

"She'll have a very fine scar on her lip that will fade with time, the same with her ears," the doctor continued. "I think this young lady is almost ready to return to the real world. I want to keep her for another week, just to be sure she's progressing as she should, then she'll be ready for discharge." He shook hands with Emma and Nate and left the room.

They looked at the frail figure dozing on the bed. The nurse readjusted the IV, restarted the feeding, checked her vital signs, nodded to Emma and Nate and left the room.

Ready for discharge, Emma thought, but where?

"I SUPPOSE WE SHOULD talk to the social worker about Tracie," Emma said, putting a pan of muffins in the oven. She felt safe once more baking her favorite recipe.

"Um hum," Nate murmured, turning the page of the investment journal. Hope wound herself around his legs, mewing. He reached down and scratched the animal's ears. "By the way, what do you intend to do with this cat?"

"I don't know. This whole situation is so sad." She looked at him with pleading eyes. "We can't just abandon that girl. She has no one." Emma sat down, shaking her head. *Oh Guardian Angel, tell me what to do.*

Tell him your plan, the voice said. She nodded and looked up at Nate. He seemed to be waiting for the other shoe to drop.

"I've been thinking."

"I thought so. I heard the wheels turning."

"I talked with Maria about taking Tracie, just until she recovers and decides what to do with her life."

His eyebrows raised. "That's really straining a friendship. What did her daughter say?"

"She was going to discuss it with her. You know, since one of her granddaughters got married, they have room. And Connie, the younger granddaughter, would be such a good influence on Tracie. She's outgoing and friendly, just what she needs."

"And?" Nate asked.

"I haven't heard from her yet." Emma felt dejected. What did I expect? That they would jump at the chance to take in a girl who looks like a freak and is loaded with personal baggage? "Oh dear." She heaved a heavy sigh.

Nate shook his head and turned his attention back to the journal. When the phone rang, he motioned Emma to stay put and went to pick it up.

"For you," he said, handing her the instrument.

"Hello."

"Mrs. Winberry, this is Father Michael. How are you?"

Emma winced. She knew the call involved Minnie and wasn't in the mood just now. "I'm fine, Father."

"You have been so supportive of Mrs. Walden that I'm going to take advantage of your generosity one more time."

"What is it, Father?" She felt Nate's eyes watching her and glanced up to see him suppressing a grin. She frowned.

"She has to go for her final fitting today and, hopefully, will be returning with her prosthesis. Could you possibly take her?"

Emma grimaced. "Yes, Father, we'll take her."

After she concluded the call she poured coffee for herself and Nate. "Minnie has to pick up her prosthesis today. It should be the last visit."

"What time?" he asked without looking up.

"Oh Nate, you are a dear. Two o'clock this afternoon."

MINNIE WAS COOPERATIVE for a change. She didn't complain about the rectory or anyone bossing her around. In fact, the entire way to the hospital she talked nonstop about the new program Father Michael planned to implement for the homeless.

"The church is gonna have a big rummage and bake sale to raise money, and I'm gonna help. I'll have my new leg," she said, a note of pride in her voice. She looked at Emma, a sheepish grin on her face. "Was wonderin' if you'd make some of them great muffins, for the sale, ya know."

"Of course I will. I'll make three dozen. How does that sound?"

"Great."

Emma noticed Nate's grin, though he said nothing.

"Father Michael offered me a job," Minnie said.

Emma's eyes widened. "He did? Doing what?"

"Helpin' at the rectory. He said I'm real good in the office, filin' and typin' and stuff like that."

"Typing?"

"Yeah, I used to type real good, in another life. All I need is a little practice." She lowered her eyes to her hands, the nails clean and manicured. "I used to do a lot o' things," she whispered. "Before the drink."

"But you're over that now, aren't you, Minnie?"

"You bet."

"So you can live a meaningful life again. Father Michael is giving you the opportunity. Take it," Emma said forcefully.

"I'm gonna, Goldi. I'm gonna try my darnedest." She gave Emma a smile that lit up a face that had become almost attractive, her hair parted at the side, a slight curl turning the ends under. Her eyes had a soft look, light brown with gold flecks.

Emma took her hand and gave it a squeeze. "I'm proud of you, Minnie."

The woman didn't answer, but Emma noticed a tear slide down her cheek. She turned her head and quickly wiped it away.

Minnie didn't complain about the wait at the hospital. She held a box in her lap with a pair of new shoes Father Michael had given her. She took a book from her pocket and quietly read. Emma and Nate exchanged glances.

When her name was called, she walked in slowly with the aid of her crutches, her head held high, the shoebox under her arm. When she came out an hour later, she was walking on two legs and wearing the new shoes. A broad smile crossed her face. The prosthetist accompanied her.

"The fit is perfect," he said to all three of them. "She has all the instructions in this packet." He pointed to a folder Minnie clutched in her hand. "And here are three extra stump socks to wear under the limb." He turned to Minnie. "You will remember to wash them every night by hand. They will shrink if you put them in a washing machine."

She nodded vigorously. "See Goldi, I look like everybody else." She walked proudly across the waiting room, only a slight limp indicating an abnormality.

"In time she won't limp at all. A physical therapist worked with her today and would like to see her a few more times, but she seems reluctant to come back. It's in her best interests." He handed Emma a card. "Call for an appointment."

Minnie was so pleased with her new limb she almost pranced to the car. Nate carried the crutches. When they were settled on the return trip, Emma asked, "Why don't you want to go back to therapy?"

"Don't wanna bother anybody to take me."

Emma thought for a moment. "Isn't there a bus that, for a nominal fee, picks up the disabled? Why, they can probably pick you up at the rectory and take you directly to the hospital. We'll ask Father Michael about it."

Minnie brightened. "Ya think so?"

"I'll ask Father."

"Thanks, Goldi, yer a real friend."

FORTY-EIGHT

Now that Tracie was on the mend, Emma turned her attention to the more mundane. Baking ingredients filled her kitchen table. She was furiously mashing bananas when Nate walked into the room.

"What's all this?"

"Tomorrow is the rummage and bake sale at St. Andrew's. I promised Minnie I would bake three dozen muffins. Since Tracie's doing so well, I feel I must do my part for the sale."

He grunted. "Can I help?"

She batted her eyelashes at him. "No dear. Just stay out of my way."

As she filled a huge bowl with flour and sugar, Emma heard Nate answer the phone. He walked into the kitchen talking on the instrument.

"She's up to her elbows in flour, Bertie. Can I tell her something?"

His eyes widened. "What? I think you'd better tell her that yourself."

Emma was already wiping her hands on a towel. She grabbed the phone. "What's up, dear?"

"I've located Minnie's daughter."

"Really?"

"She wants to see her mother. She's happily married, lives in Bridgeview and has an eight-year-old daughter. She sounds well-adjusted to me."

"I'm so glad to hear that. You know, tomorrow is the rummage and bake sale at St. Andrew's. Minnie and I will be selling baked goods. What do you think?"

"I'll tell Penny about it and leave it up to her."

"Bertie, you are a jewel. How did you manage to locate her?" Emma marveled at her daughter-in-law's ingenuity.

"Let's just say I have good contacts and I know how to pull a few strings." She laughed, the musical sound so pleasing to hear.

"All right then. We'll see how it plays out."

"How's Tracie?" Bertie asked.

"She's making progress and should be ready for discharge soon."

"Where will she go? Has some decision been made?"

Emma told her about her discussion with Maria.

"She may be just the right person for her," Bertie said. "And her granddaughter sounds like a jewel. I have a feeling all will turn out well for that girl."

"I have the same feeling. Now, back to the muffins."

Emma hummed and sang to the lively music playing on the stereo while she finished her baking.

Later Nate walked in and nodded his approval at the pristine condition of the room, the mounds of cooling muffins on the counter.

"Maybe you should open a bakery," he said.

"Not on your life. I bake only when the spirit moves me and it's moving full force at the moment."

SALES AT ST. ANDREW'S were brisk. The weather cooperated, bright sunshine, a crisp tang to the early-autumn air. People crowded all the colorful booths.

"We need more pies here," Emma called to a girl behind her.

"I'll go to the kitchen and get the rest," she said, scurrying away.

"Are there any more muffins?" Emma asked Minnie.

"Nope. All gone." She gave Emma a guilty look. "All except this one I saved for myself."

Emma laughed. "You go ahead and enjoy it. You've worked hard. Why don't I send you the recipe and you can make some for the rectory?"

"Sure I could. I usta bake, in another life." The woman looked off in the distance, a wistful expression on her face.

"You know, Minnie, you really look nice today."

She wore a pantsuit of midnight blue with white collar and cuffs. Her hair waved around her face in a fresh cut and style.

"I went to the beauty shop," she whispered. "Father Michael sent me. Got my hair done and my face made up, too." She held her arms out to the sides and gave a little twist.

"Oh, you've done so well," Emma said. "I'm proud of you. By the way, I got a call from Jake the other day. He said he was on his way to St. Louis. He has family there, said he was going to try and reconnect with them."

"That's good," Minnie said. "Folks need family," she whispered, a note of sadness in her voice.

"May I have one of those peach pies, please?" a soft voice asked.

Minnie looked up; her eyes widened. She looked at the woman, then at the child at her side and clapped her hand over her mouth.

"Ah, Goldi, take care of this lady. I gotta go in the kitchen and get more pies." She turned and hurried away, her limp more pronounced.

Emma smiled at the attractive woman with red hair and violet eyes, the little girl a replica of her mother.

"You're Penny, aren't you?"

"Yes, Penny Walden Turner and this is my daughter, Alicia. The social worker called me. I've wondered about my mother all these years, whether she was dead or alive. I wanted Alicia to know her grandmother."

The little girl hid behind her mother.

"Be careful, dear," Penny said. "Don't crush the flower."

The child held out a bud vase with a single red rose. "This is for Grandma," she whispered.

"Let me talk to her," Emma said. "I'll be right back."

She found Minnie in the kitchen, sitting in a corner. "That little girl looks just like my Penny when they took her away." She looked up at Emma. "Is that really my daughter?"

"Yes she is," Emma assured her. "Her name is Penelope Walden Turner."

"My Penny, my shiny new Penny," she whispered, then turned tormented eyes to Emma.

"She wants to see you, to get to know you. So does the child. You have a family, go to them."

Minnie sat, twisting her hands. "But I'm a street bum. They'll be ashamed of me."

"No you are not," Emma said sternly. "You are a respectable woman with a job, here at the rectory. And that is the way you must see yourself."

Minnie sat for a while, thinking, her face contorted in indecision.

"So many years have been lost," Emma said softly. "Don't lose another minute."

Minnie stood up, a resolute expression on her face. "I'll wash my face and fix my hair. Wait for me, please, Goldi."

"I will."

When Emma and Minnie returned, the little girl gave her a shy smile and held out the rose in the bud vase. "For you, Grandma."

Tears streamed down Minnie's face as she took the vase and, hesitantly, the child's hand. "Thank you," she whispered.

"You know, there's a lull right now. Why don't you take a break, Minnie? Go off to one of those benches and get acquainted with your family." She handed Alicia a huge chocolate chip cookie. "Go on, the three of you."

Father Michael walked up as Emma watched them. "You have been a godsend to that woman, Mrs. Winberry. You gave her back a respectable life. I think you may have missed your calling."

"I only shared with her what was given to me, Father." Now where did that come from? Emma wondered, then felt that almost imperceptible nudge she knew so well.

By the end of the day, all the baked goods were gone and most of the other donated items. When Nate came to pick up Emma, Father Michael shook his hand. "We've made a great deal of money today."

Nate opened his wallet and took out two crisp one-hundred-dollar bills. "Here, Father, add this to the fund. My donation."

"This is very generous, Mr. Sandler, thank you."

"Are you ready?" he asked Emma.

"Yes. Look over there." She pointed to Minnie and her family, still busy catching up. "Bertie was right. She's a lovely woman and I think Minnie will be accepted into that family."

"It looks like everything turned out for the best," Nate said as they walked to the car.

"Yes it has."

FORTY-NINE

Within the next week Tracie made remarkable progress. She had gained three pounds since the insertion of the feeding tube and appeared to be stronger.

When Emma and Nate walked into the room, they found her sitting in a chair reading a magazine. Her eyes lit up when she saw them.

"Tracie," Emma exclaimed, "you look great!" Her face was filling out, her eyes no longer sunken, and a tinge of color dappled her cheeks. Someone had washed and combed her hair and fastened it to the side with a barrette. Though it was still three different colors, it looked neat.

"You are really a pretty girl," Nate said, smiling, a look of surprise on his face.

She blushed at the compliment. "I'm feeling good," she said in a garbled voice, through clenched teeth. "Doctor's going to take the stitches out of my lip today. He gave me these wire cutters." She held them up to show Emma. "I have to carry them all the time."

"Good," Emma said. "The swelling of your lip is almost gone. You'll probably have no more than a faint scar."

Tracie managed a smile. A dimple appeared at the base of her left cheek that Emma had never noticed before. The girl proudly held out her hands. The skin was smooth and supple and her fingernails had begun growing out. They were filed and adorned with a thin coat of coral-colored polish.

"My nurse did that," Tracie said.

Emma put her arms around the girl, gave her a hug and kiss on the cheek. To her surprise, Tracie hugged her back.

A few minutes later the doctor and a nurse walked into the room. "All right, young lady, it's show time."

Tracie smiled.

He nodded to Emma and Nate then sat beside the bed. "Now listen very carefully. I'm going to take the stitches out of your lip and your ears. Then I'll remove this feeding tube. Your nurse tells me you have been drinking from a straw quite well now that the swelling is down.

"The wires in your jaw won't come out for a number of weeks yet. Do you think you can drink enough liquids and three cans of this feeding a day?"

Tracie nodded. "Yes, I can," she murmured.

"Okay. We don't like to leave a feeding tube in for too long because it irritates the lining of the nose and throat. If you can't take enough nourishment through a straw, the only other thing we can do is put a tube directly into your stomach through a surgical incision." He looked down at her, a serious expression on his face. "I don't think you want that."

"No, no." She shook her head.

"All right then. Let's get started."

Emma and Nate stepped out of the room while he and the nurse worked on Tracie.

"Mrs. Winberry, may I speak with you?"

Emma turned to see the social worker walking toward them.

"Let's come over here," the woman said, leading them to an alcove where they sat facing each other. "I understand Tracie is ready for discharge. Unfortunately there aren't many options as to where she can go."

"Did you contact her parents?" Emma asked.

"I did. Her mother was evasive. She said she's having health problems of her own and can't possibly look after the girl. That would be the worst place for her right now."

Oh Guardian Angel, Emma prayed. *Why haven't I heard from Maria? Tell me what to do.*

Take her home with you, the inner voice said. She looked at Nate and wondered if he would consider it.

"She's too old to put in foster care," the social worker continued, consulting her records. "According to this, she'll be eighteen next week." She heaved a sigh. "These are really difficult cases. She's made remarkable progress. The psychiatrist has seen her a number of times and she seems to be regaining a little self-esteem. If I place her in a halfway house, she's liable to regress completely."

"You'll do no such thing," Nate said, deep furrows appearing between his eyes. "Why don't we take her home with us, Emma? Just temporarily."

"Oh Nate, yes. Just temporarily." Emma sighed with relief.

"That does seem to be the best solution," the social worker said, making a note in her chart. "You two seem to be the only ones who care about her."

When Emma and Nate returned to the room, they found Tracie standing at the window. She turned to face them, her face free of sutures, the feeding tube removed. She looked down at the floor with a dejected expression on her face.

The doctor turned to them, a question on his face. "When I told her she was ready for discharge, she started crying." He raised his eyebrows and looked at them.

"She's coming with us," Nate said. "Come on, Tracie, Hope is waiting for you. Let's go home."

AS THEY WALKED INTO the condo, Tracie immediately looked around for her pet. Hope, who had been hiding under a chair, bounded out and wound her body around the girl's legs. Tracie picked her up and caressed the soft fur as the cat purred in contentment. The girl sat down and for a long time simply stroked the animal and told her how much she loved her. Hope returned the greeting by licking the tears from Tracie's face.

When the girl and her pet were reacquainted, Emma began settling her in the spare room.

"Gladys is on the phone," Nate called. She took the phone and went into the atrium.

"So how is everything going?" Gladys asked. "I haven't talked to you in weeks."

"Oh dear, ever since we moved into this condo, it's been one problem after another. I almost wish I'd stayed in Brookfield." For the next twenty minutes she recounted the recent chain of events.

"This is like a movie script," Gladys said. "So the girl is there with you and Nate?"

"Just temporarily. There was no other choice. The reunion between her and Hope brought tears to my eyes. Even Nate turned away," Emma said with a deep sigh. "I haven't heard from Maria yet, and I don't want to call."

"Why don't you send her here to us? We'll take her," Gladys said.

Emma didn't know how to respond. "That's sweet of you, my friend, but I think it would be too traumatic to move her into a strange place so far away from us. Besides, she has to see the doctor in two weeks."

"Just keep that option open, you hear?"

Emma could hardly speak. Such a dear, generous friend. "Thanks, I will."

The following day Emma received a call from Maria. "I'm sorry I didn't call you," Maria wailed. "My granddaughter lost her baby and Carmela was at her house taking care of her. Everything upside-down."

Emma heard her friend sniffling. "I'm so sorry to hear that. How far along was she?"

"Two or three months, I dunno." More sniffling. "How is the girl?"

"We just brought her home from the hospital yesterday. She's doing very well. Her jaws are wired and will be for a few weeks, so she has to drink everything from a straw."

"Madonna mia, did they find that *bastardo?"*

"Not yet."

"They should cut off his—you know what."

"Maria, I never heard you talk like that."

"It makes me so mad."

"Me, too. Anyway, tomorrow is Tracie's birthday. I'm going to bake a cake." She hesitated for a moment. "Would you and your daughter like to come and meet her?" She held her breath for a moment. In light of what had happened, they might have changed their minds.

"Sure we come. We get to know each other and talk about things. Connie comes, too."

Emma breathed a sigh of relief. "That's great. What time can you make it?"

"I ask my daughter and call you back."

When she told Nate, he simply nodded, his eyes on Tracie and Hope. "She certainly loves that cat," he said. "Does Maria's family know about the animal?"

"I told them, I think." Emma didn't remember if she had or not. So much had happened.

"I'm going to the hardware store," he said. "Be back in a little while."

When Nate returned, he called Tracie. "Here's an alarm that I want you to carry all the time." He pulled a round disk from the paper bag. "All you have to do is press this button."

A shrill sound filled the air when he depressed the button.

The women covered their ears with their hands; the cat fled under the couch.

He pushed a button on the side. "This turns it off." He

looked into the girl's eyes. "You won't be able to call for help as long as your jaws are wired."

She nodded and took the instrument with trembling hands. "Thanks." She slipped it into her pocket and went to find the terrified cat.

Emma threw her arms around him. "You are a dear."

"That girl has been through enough," he said, holding her close.

THAT AFTERNOON an unseasonable warm spell flooded the area. Emma decided to soak up some sunshine. She set up two lounge chairs on the roof for her and Tracie. Nate had gone to another meeting of the Opera Chapter. She felt they were safe, but, unknown to Tracie, she took the gun outside in a carryall bag; a towel obscured the weapon.

Tracie sipped a milkshake, Emma, a cup of tea. Hope chased a ball around the roof. At first Emma was going to ignore the ringing of the phone, let the machine pick it up, but her curiosity wouldn't let her.

"I'll be right back," she said, scurrying into the house.

Tracie got up from the chair and walked over to the wrought-iron fencing along the edge of the roof. She looked down at the cars speeding along on Michigan Avenue then across at the lake. The color was an incredible shade of blue. She smiled as she watched the boats and decided to draw a picture of the scene. As she turned to get her tablet and pencil, she froze. Her uncle was walking toward her, a disarming smile on his face.

"Hello, Teresa, I see you've recovered," he said reaching out to her. Before she could move he grabbed her and pulled her toward the open gate.

Tracie struggled making as loud a sound as she could, as he gripped her arms behind her back. The alarm! She couldn't reach her pocket.

"Now be a nice girl, I don't want to hurt you."

Tracie winced. The cat arched her back and hissed.

Emma came out the door to see Evans dragging Tracie across the roof. For a moment she stood motionless, trying to think. Then she remembered the gun. She stumbled to the bag and reached inside. The weapon felt incredibly heavy as she raised it and pointed it at the man.

"Take your hands off her. I have a gun," she said, realizing how theatrical it sounded.

Evans merely laughed and pulled the girl in front of him. "I don't intend to hurt her, unless she puts up a fuss. I only want her as insurance. Where's my wife?"

"Gone," Emma answered.

"Where?" he demanded.

"I have no idea. She just said she was packing up and leaving."

"Did she take all the money with her?"

"How would I know that? I wasn't looking over her shoulder."

He shook his head and growled, "That bitch found my hiding place and cleaned it out. At least I have this." He held up a passport. "And you, Teresa."

Emma felt her frustration level rising. What could she do? Her hands shook as she tried to hold the gun level. It got heavier and heavier. If she did shoot, she could easily hit Tracie. *Guardian Angel, a little help here!*

Hope continued to hiss and spit.

"Keep that animal away from me or this time I will fling it over the side."

Emma saw the terrified look on Tracie's face. She had no doubt Evans would carry out his threat.

"You must know the police are looking for you, as well as some unsavory characters who've been hanging around," Emma said. "They did not look friendly. And they demanded to know your whereabouts."

A fleeting expression of fear crossed the man's face. "I'm

getting out of here and taking the girl with me. If anyone tries to follow me, I swear I'll kill her."

Tracie began to tremble and cry.

"Haven't you done enough to her? Let her go. I promise I won't call the police if you leave now, alone." Emma didn't think for a minute he would buy that, but it was worth a try.

"You must think I'm a complete idiot. Now put that gun away before you hurt somebody." He dragged the struggling girl into the condo.

Emma ran through her house and out the front door just as the elevator doors closed behind the two. She looked around. No one in sight. She ran toward the stairwell and almost fell down the six flights tripping on the last one. By the time she reached the lobby, she was breathless and shaking. Sweat streamed down her face.

A woman sat on a chair talking on a cell phone. Emma saw her freeze as she ran to the door. Then she realized she was still holding the gun. She saw the car just as it pulled away from the curb.

She called to the woman, "Write down this license number, now." She read off the numbers she was able to see, all except the last two. "A black two-door Lexus," she said. She turned to the shaking woman who was scribbling on a notepad. "Did you get that?"

"Uh huh. Would you please put that gun down?" the woman stammered.

"Oh, I'm sorry." Emma lowered the gun. Her arm ached, her fingers numb. "Give me your phone, now, please."

The woman handed the instrument to Emma with no objection. She quickly punched nine-one-one and, in almost a shout, gave all the information she could. Then she collapsed in a chair, weak-kneed and lightheaded.

At that moment Nate walked in the door. "Emma, for God's

sake, what happened?" He knelt beside her, took the gun out of her hand and cradled her quaking body in his arms.

Through halting sobs she told him the whole story. The other woman hadn't moved during the entire scene.

"Did you see him take the girl out of here?" Nate asked her.

She shook her head. "I was down the hall. Heard some scuffling, but nothing else. Oh my God, he might have taken me, too."

"Very possibly," Nate said. He helped Emma out of the chair. "Come on. Let's go upstairs and call Detective Spaulding."

Emma sat at the kitchen table staring at nothing, the humming of the refrigerator the only sound she heard. She literally jumped when the phone rang. Nate picked it up, walked into the kitchen and handed it to her.

"Maria," he said.

"Oh dear God. I forgot all about her." Emma took the phone with shaking hands and, as calmly as she could, told Maria what had happened.

"Madonna mia, the malocchio!" she screamed, then began muttering in Italian.

Emma simply held the phone and said nothing.

"Emma, this is Carmela. What happened? My mother is hysterical."

Emma repeated the story.

"Que peccato. Keep us informed. Now we all say the rosary for the girl's safe return."

When Emma pushed the OFF button, she looked at the cake pans in readiness and the recipe lying on the counter. She crumpled across the table, her mind a complete blank.

Nate stood in the doorway. No words came. He, too, felt the impact of this senseless violence. He sat in a chair next to Emma and gently stroked her back.

The next few hours seemed endless. Emma made a pot of

coffee; they watched the news; tried to relax, but that was impossible.

"Emma, it's two o'clock. Why don't we go to bed and, at least, get some rest."

I don't think I'll ever sleep again, she thought as she shuffled into the bedroom.

FIFTY

I HAVE TO GET out of this car, some way—on this hard floor. Uncle said if I don't stay down, he'll kill me. I don't want to die…please! Every time he hits a bump, it hurts my face—wire cutters on the kitchen table—hold my face with both hands, that's better, doesn't hurt so much.

Everything getting better—people nice to me—look pretty again. Then he comes back. He's the devil. If I die, who will take care of Hope?

Oh God, can You hear me? I don't know if You listen to people like me. I haven't been so good. I don't go to church like I should, but will You just give me another chance? I can't let Mrs. Window, and Hope down.

The alarm! In my pocket. Maybe I can reach it. There, I got it!

A SHRILL SOUND permeated the vehicle.

"What the hell is that," Evans shouted, "the police?"

DRIVING SO FAST. Going to crash or something. Make him stop! Going faster. Oh! Hit something—Ouch—glass shattering—screaming—hot—fire…

FIFTY-ONE

EMMA AND NATE stared at each other, hearing the ringing of the phone, each reluctant to answer. Finally Nate picked it up.

"Hello."

"This is Detective Spaulding. We have the girl. She's bumped and bruised a little, but she'll be all right."

Nate breathed an audible sigh of relief as he nodded to Emma. "Where is she?"

"At Stroger Hospital. Evans was driving like a madman. A squad car spotted him and followed. Some kind of siren went off, and instead of stopping, he gunned the engine, lost control of the car and crashed into an abutment. The engine burst into flames, but the police pulled the girl and Evans out in time."

Nate shook his head. "And how is Evans?"

"Not in very good shape, burns, fractures and possible spinal cord injury. They have him in Intensive Care."

"Thanks, Detective. We'll go right down and get Tracie."

Emma already had her coat on and an extra wrap for Tracie. Nate grabbed a jacket and they were out the door. As they drove he told Emma what happened.

"I don't feel sorry for that man," she said. "He got just what he deserved."

Emma almost ran into the Emergency Room. She ignored a man with a bloody dressing around his head, dodged a pool of vomit on the floor and made her way to the desk.

"Tracie Adams," she said in a breathless voice.

The woman looked up at her. "The girl with the wired jaw?" Emma nodded.

"Over there, with that policeman."

When Tracie saw Emma, she rushed into her arms. They held each other, weeping. Nate came up behind, wiping his eyes.

"Are you hurt?" Emma asked, scrutinizing the girl.

She shook her head and pointed to a few bruises on her arms. Emma couldn't speak. She simply held her.

"Can we take her home?" Nate looked from the policeman to a doctor who was writing a note on a chart.

"Yes. She's all right. A little shaken up and a few bruises. She's a real trouper." The doctor smiled and Tracie smiled back.

The officer nodded. "I'm finished."

"I set off my alarm," Tracie said.

"Good girl," Nate said, clenching his fists.

They signed the necessary papers and headed for home.

When Emma finally climbed into bed, the sky was just beginning to brighten. She said a prayer of thanks and fell into a dreamless sleep.

LATER THAT MORNING, while Tracie and Nate slept, Emma baked the birthday cake. It turned out light and fluffy, reflecting her mood. She had called Maria and set the time for seven o'clock that evening.

By the time Tracie woke, Emma was just putting the finishing touches on a magnificent cake with strawberry filling and covered in whipped cream.

"It's beautiful," the girl said through her wired jaw. "I never had such a cake." Then she turned sad eyes to Emma. "But I can't eat any."

"But you can drink it. We'll put a piece in the blender, mix it with some milk and call it a birthday shake."

Tracie smiled. They didn't talk about the happenings of the previous day and Emma didn't ask. Tracie never once mentioned her uncle nor what had happened to him. Today was a celebration. Tracie picked up the cat circling her ankles. "Look at my cake, Hope. You can have some, too."

THE EVENING TURNED OUT to be pleasant and comfortable. At first Tracie held herself back when Maria, Carmela, and Connie came in. But Connie immediately took over.

She went up to Tracie and ran her hand through the girl's dry, frizzled hair. "Boy are you gonna be a challenge. Just what I like." She turned Tracie's head from side to side, studying her features and hairline.

"With me in charge, in two months you won't recognize yourself. I guarantee you'll be stunning, turning heads wherever you go."

Tracie smiled. "You really think so?"

"Absolutely."

After a while Emma saw the two girls whispering, their heads together, a half smile on Tracie's face. She knew it would be all right.

Later they lit the candles, sang "Happy Birthday" and ate the cake with sighs of satisfaction. Tracie drank her cake shake and Hope delicately ate her share.

Tracie opened the gifts that piled up around her, eyes wide with wonder: a new sweater, a silver locket, a fuzzy nightgown, and a new cage for Hope. Tears filled her eyes as she opened each package. "Thank you all, so much. This is the happiest birthday I've ever had."

"When are you coming over to our house?" Carmela asked.

Tracie looked at Emma. "It's up to you, dear," Emma said.

"I don't want to stay in this place. Too much has happened. But you've been so good to me."

"No need to apologize," Nate said. "We understand." He gave her an encouraging squeeze on the shoulder.

"How about tomorrow?" Connie said eagerly.

"Well." Emma thought for a moment. "Is there anything you want from next door?" she asked Tracie.

"No, no!" She shook her head.

"Then first thing in the morning we'll go shopping for a wardrobe, then get you to your new home."

Everyone agreed to the plan.

"What about Hope?" Tracie asked.

"She comes, too," Connie said with an air of authority. "She should get along great with Caesar. He's been fixed by the way." She winked at Tracie and was rewarded with a broad smile.

That night Emma slept a deep dreamless sleep for the first time in weeks.

FIFTY-TWO

THE FOLLOWING DAY Emma and Nate took Tracie on a shopping spree. "We'll buy everything loose," Emma said. "If I know Maria, she'll be on a mission to fatten you up."

When they returned home, their arms loaded with purchases, Tracie looked tired, a pensive expression on her face.

"Would you like to lie down for a while?" Emma asked.

Tracie shook her head. "I changed my mind about going next door. There is something I want."

"Do you have a key?"

She nodded and, without another word, headed out onto the roof. Emma followed.

"Do you want me to come with you?"

Tracie nodded again and grabbed Emma's hand. She was trembling and icy cold. After fiddling with the lock on the door, they managed to slide it open. Emma looked at the few plants in the atrium, their leaves dry and curled. It always hurt her to see neglected plants, but these were beyond help.

They walked into the condo. Nothing had been touched since the thug and, later, Evans had searched. Drawers were pulled out, papers strewn everywhere, cabinets stood open.

Tracie headed directly for her room, opened the door and switched on the light. Emma stood in the doorway while the girl opened a dresser drawer.

An aura of sadness permeated the room. A strong smell emanated from the litter box in the corner. The closed blinds kept the world out. Everything looked dark and drab.

Tracie took out the items she wanted and, without looking back, hurried out of the room. Emma noticed she was shivering. Within minutes they were back at Emma and Nate's condo.

"I want to destroy these," she said through her clenched jaw.

"What are they?" Emma asked.

"A journal I kept and my sketch pad."

"There's a shredder in the study."

"Okay."

Emma left her alone. Over the next half hour she heard the sound of Tracie's past being cut into tiny slices.

When she finished, she came out of the room with a look of satisfaction on her face. "I feel like I got rid of the past and I'm ready to start a new life."

Emma smiled and hugged her. "I know you'll make it a good one."

In the late afternoon they loaded the car with their purchases, Hope in her new cage, cat food, and kitty litter and left for Maria's house.

AFTER MUCH FUSSING, arranging and rearranging, Tracie was settled in her temporary home. After promising to call every day, Emma and Nate left, satisfied that she would be safe and protected.

Neither one said a word on the trip home. The condo seemed empty without Tracie and Hope, but Emma knew they would quickly adjust to their former lifestyle. The opera season would soon be underway and they looked forward to performing as supernumeraries in two new productions, one was *The Ghosts of Versailles*.

FIFTY-THREE

As Emma cleared the breakfast dishes, she heard the phone ring. "Detective Spaulding. He wants to see us," Nate said.

"What about? I thought this whole mess was over."

"He said something about a reward."

Emma turned, a shocked expression on her face. She saw the smug look on Nate's.

"You're not telling me something, Nate Sandler. What is it?"

"If you're finished here, we can take a ride to the station and let the detective tell us all about it. There are a few details I'd like cleared up."

The station bustled with activity. Emma averted her eyes from a row of tough-looking, handcuffed young men being hustled inside.

"Hey, skinny mama, how'd ya like to try me?" one of them shouted, pushing his hips back and forth in lewd motions.

Emma felt her face flush and grimaced in disgust. Nate pushed her behind him and scowled.

"This way," an officer said, leading them into Detective Spaulding's office.

His face lit up when he saw them. The smile softened the lines around his eyes and mouth, the grim expression gone. "My two civilian detectives, sit down. Want some coffee?"

They declined and Emma again noticed the stained cup he used, a hairline crack down the side. I'm going to buy him a new one, she promised herself again.

He folded his hands on the desk and smiled. "Evans is in

stable condition. He was able to tell us everything. His confession wraps up this case. It turned out that he borrowed a large sum of money from some loan sharks to keep his business afloat. In return he was supposed to obtain the microchip from the ring Mr. Porter wore."

The detective took a gulp of cold coffee and made a face. "Vile stuff. The two losers Evans hired to get the ring stole the wrong one. They took the ring with the diamond from his right hand instead of the class ring he wore on his left. It was only supposed to be a theft. Murder was not part of the plan. Apparently things got out of hand and Porter ended up dead. It seems he had a weak artery in his brain. When his head hit the pavement, it ruptured and killed him. Minnie was in the shadows watching the whole thing. That's when she grabbed the class ring."

"Can you tell us now if his claims were valid?" Nate asked, leaning forward in his chair.

The detective took a deep breath, leaned back and clasped his hands over his ample abdomen. "Porter was an inventor. And, as I told you, claimed to have designed an engine so unique that any vehicle could run on a cup of fuel for over a hundred miles."

"Yes," Nate said, waiting.

The detective shook his head. "The irony of the situation is that our inventor was in the early stages of dementia. When a group of engineers examined the plans on the chip, they found the blueprints impossible to decipher, much less follow."

"Oh my lord," Emma said, hardly believing what she was hearing. "Then the poor man was killed for nothing and this whole mess could have been avoided."

"Unfortunately, that's true," Spaulding continued. "Since all the perpetrators have confessed, there's no need for a trial."

"You mean I don't have to testify?" Emma said, a tone of relief in her voice.

"That's right. You can put the whole thing behind you."

She heaved a happy sigh.

"How is the girl doing?" the detective asked.

Emma told him about Tracie's new home and hopes for the future.

"I'm glad to hear that. She was a victim of many people's selfishness. And Minnie?"

"You wouldn't recognize her. She's neat and clean, walking confidently with her new prosthesis. Father Michael has offered her a job at the rectory," Emma said.

"That's good to hear. We're not going to charge her with the theft of the ring. She's been through enough, and she did identify the killers. It looks like everything's wrapped up neat and tidy, but there's one more thing," he said, a sly smile crossing his face. "The family offered a ten-thousand-dollar reward for information leading to the killers. There's no one who deserves it more than you two."

Emma sputtered, her eyes widened. Nate grinned.

"Here's a check made out in both your names. Mrs. Porter was in here yesterday and I explained your role in the investigation. She's very grateful."

The detective handed the check to Emma. She pulled back for a moment. Nate reached over and took it with a nod and a thank you.

They shook hands; the detective thanked them for their help and urged Emma to stay out of trouble.

Emma said nothing as they left the station. She couldn't quite believe all this. "What will we do with this money?" she asked, settling herself into the car.

"What do you want to do with it?" Nate countered.

"Well, we could save it, or take a first-class vacation. Hmm." Emma kind of liked that idea. "Or we could give it to Father Michael for his homeless program."

"We could do that, or," he hesitated for a moment. "Didn't

Tracie say something about wanting to go to school? That amount would give her a good start."

"Oh Nate, yes. I like that idea best."

"Let's do it then." He turned the key in the ignition then reached over and gave her knee a squeeze.

EPILOGUE

EMMA PLACED THE LAST ornament on the tree, stood back and admired her handiwork. Nate was busy stringing a fresh garland around the living room, adding its pine scent to the spicy smell lingering from freshly baked pies.

"How's that?" he asked.

"Lovely. Perfect," Emma said with a sigh of satisfaction. She had thought she might miss the old house now that Christmas was here, but no. This was home.

"Are we expecting someone?" Nate asked as the doorbell rang.

"No, I don't think so." Emma wondered if she had forgotten something.

"Yes?" Nate asked, depressing the intercom button.

"Merry Christmas. A couple of elves are down here bearing gifts."

"Come on up." Nate laughed as he buzzed them in.

"That was Connie's voice," Emma said. "I'm sure Tracie is with her." She opened the door and stood at the elevator anxiously waiting.

Finally the doors opened to the two smiling girls bundled against the cold. Emma wrapped Tracie in her arms kissing her cheeks with loud smacks. Then she stood back and looked at her with approval. She appeared to be filling out nicely. The wires had been removed from her healed jaw; her skin glowed a healthy rosy color; and her smile radiated happiness. Gone was the multicolored hair, replaced by a thick mane of wavy saddle brown with gold highlights. She looked stunning in a green velour pantsuit trimmed in white faux fur.

"Are you coming in, or are you going to visit in the hall?" Nate asked, standing in the doorway.

The laughing girls put down their bags and held out their arms giving him hugs and kisses. "Connie, you have been a wonderful influence on Tracie. She's beautiful," Nate said.

Tracie blushed at the compliment.

Connie shrugged. "I just brought out what was hidden all the time."

"I brought you both a present," Tracie said as she handed Emma a package. "Open it."

Emma tore off the wrapping to reveal a delicate pencil drawing of a kitten playing with a ball of yarn, Tracie's signature on the bottom. It was beautifully matted and framed.

"Oh Nate, isn't this lovely?" Emma said.

"It certainly is." He studied the simple lines and nodded his approval.

"Where shall we hang it?" Emma asked.

"Right here, by the entryway so that every time we walk in, we'll think of the artist."

Tracie smiled and licked the scar on her lower lip. "I've decided to study Art Therapy," she said. "It's really becoming popular and I think I can help troubled teens."

"I know you'll be a success," Emma said.

She had enrolled in the local junior college with a full schedule of classes and Nate had put the reward money in a special account earmarked for her education expenses. A part-time job as shampoo girl in the salon where Connie worked provided all the pocket money Tracie needed.

"Okay, Trace, we have a party to go to. And, I heard there are a couple of new hunks coming. Let's be on our way."

The girls left in a flurry of hugs and kisses and well-wishing. Emma gave Tracie her gift to open on Christmas.

All was quiet. Emma and Nate looked at each other. "The young are so full of energy," Nate said. "It wears me out." Emma agreed. She felt content as they sat down to brandied eggnog and the music of the season playing softly on the stereo.

THE FOLLOWING EVENING Emma and Nate strung lights along the roof intertwining them between the wrought-iron rails. The gate between the two properties had been replaced with the same brick and wrought iron that surrounded the rest of the area. They sang carols as they worked.

"Nate, look," Emma said. "I see people next door."

"Uh huh," he muttered without looking up, concentrating on replacing a burned-out light bulb. "I heard a couple put down earnest money and were waiting for the approval of their loan. Looks like it came through."

He looked up as two well-dressed men walked out onto the roof, their hands clasped together.

Emma's eyes widened.

Nate slipped his arm around her. "Our new neighbors," he whispered in her ear. "Does that bother you?"

"Of course not," she said. "I'm just surprised, that's all."

"At least they have no criminal records," Nate said, leading her into the house. "They were thoroughly checked. Come on, we still have a pile of presents to wrap, including that new coffee mug you bought for Detective Spaulding."

Emma took one more look at the men, their arms around one another as they stared out at the lake. She thought for a moment, then shrugged. Hmm, I wonder if they like muffins?